HAVISHAM

HAVISHAM

A NOVEL

RONALD FRAME

PICADOR

NEW YORK

HAVISHAM. Copyright © 2012 by Ronald Frame. All rights reserved. Printed in the United States of America. For information, address Picador, 175 Fifth Avenue, New York, N.Y. 10010.

www.picadorusa.com
www.twitter.com/picadorusa • www.facebook.com/picadorusa
picadorbookroom.tumblr.com

Picador® is a U.S. registered trademark and is used by St. Martin's Press under license from Pan Books Limited.

For book club information, please visit www.facebook.com/picadorbookclub or e-mail marketing@picadorusa.com.

Design by Anna Gorovoy

Library of Congress Cataloging-in-Publication Data

Frame, Ronald.
Havisham / Ronald Frame. — First U.S. edition.
pages ; cm.
ISBN 978-1-250-03727-5 (hardcover)
ISBN 978-1-250-03729-9 (e-book)
1. England—Social conditions—19th century—Fiction. I. Title.
PR6056.R262H38 2013
823'.914—dc23
2013003787

Picador books may be purchased for educational, business, or promotional use. For information on bulk purchases, please contact Macmillan Corporate and Premium Sales Department at 1-800-221-7945, extension 5442, or write specialmarkets@macmillan.com.

Originally published in Great Britain by Faber and Faber Limited

First Picador Edition: November 2013

10 9 8 7 6 5 4 3 2 1

I.M.
Alexander Donaldson Frame
1922–2011

Love is in the one who loves,
not in the one who is loved.

Plato

PROLOGUE

Four loud blows on the front door.

I stood waiting at the foot of the staircase as the door was opened.

The light from the candles fell upon their faces. Mr Jaggers's, large and London-pale and mapped with a blue afternoon beard. A nursemaid's, pink with excitement after listening on the journey down to Mr Jaggers's discreet account of me – my wealth, my eccentric mode of life, my famous pride and prickliness.

And the third face. The child's. She was standing a few paces behind the nursemaid; she was keeping back, but leaned over sharply to see between the two adults. She looked forward, into the house, across the hall's black and white floor tiles.

When she was brought inside, I studied her, from my vantage-point on the second tread. Her complexion was a little tawny, as I had been led to expect. She had raven hair, which was more of the gypsy in her, but her eyes were blue, from the English father.

Blue, silvery-blue, and wide open, staring up at me. At where I stood, wearing the wedding dress I should have been married in.

I lifted my hand from the banister rail and moved to the step beneath.

Immediately the child turned away. She raised her shoulder as if to protect herself, and hid behind the nursemaid's skirts. The woman smiled a nervous apology.

I retreated, one step up, then another.

'Too much light,' I said. 'That's all.'

The child's eyes rested on my bride's slippers. White satin originally, but soiled after these many months of wear.

'The light dazzles her,' I said. 'She will adjust. She only needs to get her bearings.'

I

YOUNG CATHERINE

ONE

I killed my mother.

I had turned round in the womb, and the surgeon needed to cut her open to let me out. He couldn't staunch her, and by the end of that evening she had bled to death.

My father draped the public rooms of Satis House in dust sheets. The chandeliers were left in situ, but wrapped in calico bags. The shutters were closed completely across some windows, and part-drawn at others.

My first days were lived out in a hush of respectfully lowered voices as a procession of folk came to offer their condolences.

My eyes became accustomed to the half-light.

One evening several new candles were set in one of the chandeliers. My mother's clavecin was uncovered, and someone played it again – notwithstanding that it was out of tune – and that was the point at which the house stopped being a sepulchre and was slowly brought back to life.

———

It was the first word I remember *seeing*.

HAVISHAM.

Painted in green letters on the sooty brick of the brewhouse wall.

Fat letters. Each one had its own character.

Comfortable spreading 'H'. Angular, proud 'A'. Welcoming, open 'V'. The unforthcoming sentinel 'I'. 'S', a show-off, not altogether to be trusted. The squat and briefly indecisive, then reassuring 'M'.

The name was up there even in the dark. In the morning it was the first thing I would look for from the house windows, to check that the wind hadn't made off with our identity in the night or the slanting estuary rain washed the brickwork clean.

———

Jehosophat Havisham, otherwise known as Joseph Havisham, son of Matthias.

Havisham's was the largest of several brewers in the town. Over the years we had bought out a number of smaller breweries and their outlets, but my father had preferred to concentrate production in our own (extended) works. He continued *his* father's programme of tying in the vending sites, acquiring ownership outright or making loans to the publicans who stocked our beer.

Everyone in North Kent knew who we were. Approaching the town on the London road, the eye was drawn first to the tower of the cathedral and then, some moments later, to the name HAVISHAM so boldly stated on the old brick.

We were to be found on Crow Lane.

The brewery was on one side of the big cobbled yard, and our home on the other.

Satis House was Elizabethan, and took the shape of an E, with later addings-on. The maids would play a game, counting in their heads the rooms they had to clean, and never agreeing on a total: between twenty-five and thirty.

Once the famous Pepys had strolled by, and ventured into the

Cherry Garden. There he came upon a doltish shopkeeper and his pretty daughter, and the great man 'did kiss her'.

My father slept in the King's Room, which was the chamber provided for Charles II following his sojourn in France, in 1660. The staircase had been made broader to accommodate the Merry Monarch as his manservants manoeuvred him upstairs and down. A second, steeper flight was built behind for the servants.

———

I grew up with the rich aroma of hops and the potent fumes from the fermenting rooms in my nostrils, filling my head until I failed to notice. I must have been in a state of perpetual mild intoxication.

I heard, but came not to hear, the din of the place. Casks being rolled across the cobbles, chaff-cutting, bottle-washing, racking, wood being tossed into the kiln fires. Carts rumbled in and out all day long.

The labourers had Herculean muscles. Unloading the sacks of malt and raising them on creaky pulleys; mashing the ground malt; slopping out the containers and vats; drawing into butts; pounding the extraneous yeast; always rolling those barrels from the brewhouse to the storehouse, and loading them on to the drays.

Heat, flames, steam, the dust clouds from the hops, the heady atmosphere of fermentation and money being made.

———

I was told by my father that the brewery was a parlous place for a little girl, and I should keep my distance. The hoists, the traps, those carts passing in and out; the horses were chosen for their strength, not their sensitivity, but every now and then one would be overcome with equine despair and make a bid for freedom, endangering itself and anyone in its path.

The brewhouse was only silent at night, and even then I heard the watchmen whistling to keep up their spirits in that gaunt and eerily echoing edifice, and the dogs for want of adventure barking at phantom intruders. The first brew-hands were there by five in the morning, sun-up, and the last left seventeen hours later, a couple of hours short of midnight.

I woke, and fell asleep, to the clopping of shod hooves, the whinnying of overworked carthorses.

'It's a dangerous place, miss,' my nursemaids would repeat.

My father insisted. 'Too many hazards for you to go running about.'

But should I ever complain about the noise, or the smell of hops or dropped dung, his response was immediate: this was our livelihood/if it was good enough for my grandfather/you'll simply have to put up with it, won't you, missy. So I learned not to comment, and if I was distracted from my lessons or my handiwork or my day-dreaming, I moved across to the garden side of the house. Out of doors, in the garden, the sounds would follow me, but there were flowers and trees to look at, and the wide Medway sky to traverse with my thoughts.

Sometimes I would see a man or a woman reeling drunk out of a pub, or I'd hear the singing and cursing of regulars deep in their cups.

That, too, was a part of who we Havishams were. But I would be hurried past by whoever was holding my hand, as if they had been issued with orders: the child isn't to linger thereabouts, d'you understand. So we negotiated those obstacles double-quick, taking to side alleys if need be, to remove ourselves to somewhere more salubrious, while the rollicking voices sounded after us – but not their owners, thankfully grounded in a stupor.

TWO

At an upstairs window, in Toad Lane, a bald-headed doll craned forward. One eyelid was closed, so that the doll appeared to be winking. It knew a secret or two.

In Feathers Lane lived a man who pickled and preserved for a trade. In *his* window he displayed some of his wares.

There in one dusty jar a long-dead lizard floated, with its jaws open and the tiny serrations of teeth visible. In another, three frogs had been frozen eternally as they danced, legs trailing elegantly behind them. Next to that was a rolled bluish tongue of something or other.

In the largest jar a two-headed object with one body was suspended, and I somehow realised – before Ruth confirmed it for me – that these were the beginnings of people: two embryos that had grown into one.

The window horrified me, but – just as much – I was fascinated by it. On the occasions when I could persuade Ruth to take me into town or home again that way, I felt a mixture of cold shivers and impatience to reach the grimy bow-fronted window where I had to raise myself on tiptoe to see in.

I thought – was it possible? – that through the slightly bitter citrus fragrance of pomander I could smell further back, I could catch my mother's sweet perfume and powder on the clothes stored flat in the press, years after she had last worn them.

I didn't even know where my mother was buried.

'Far off,' my father said. 'In a village churchyard. Under shade.'

I asked if we might go.

'Your mother doesn't need us now.'

'Don't we need *her*?'

'Some things belong to the past.'

His face carried the pain it always did when I brought up the subject of my mother. His eyes became fixed, pebble-like, as if he were defying tears. I sometimes thought that in the process he was trying to convince himself he didn't like *me* very much.

But those occasions would be followed by shows of kindness, by the purchase of another expensive plaything for me. This, the gift of the toy would be announcing, is how we attempt to put the sad parts of the past out of our minds.

I wondered if he really had recovered from the loss, or wasn't still privately nursing his grief, battening it down inside himself.

———

I would hear the cathedral bells every morning and evening. On Sundays and High Days the air crumpled with the pealing of so many other bells, from our Saints, Gundulph and Margaret and Zachary and Jude. All that eloquent and silver-toned pressure to be devout, or at least to appear so.

On Sunday mornings we worshipped at ten.

We would walk to the cathedral. Across the brewery yard into Crow Lane. Across the open sward of the Vines, into the Precincts, past the end of Minor Canon Row, with the Old Palace on our left.

I would always keep two or three steps behind my father.

Along the approach of worn flagstones to the Great Porch. The archdeacon would bend low, his urgent hand pushing into the gloved palm of mine, because a brewer comes next to county stock, his is the aristocrat of trades. Even the lawyers and doctors stood back, and their eyepainted wives and petticoated daughters too, because they knew their place.

Into the gloom, into the reek of leather-bound hymnals and candlewax and withering tomb-flowers, that dry stale odour of old time oozing out of the stone. Heads would turn while I kept my gaze fixed straight ahead.

My sight adjusted to the little light. On the floor, pools of ruby and indigo from the stained window glass. The furious shimmer of candles stuck on spikes.

The pew creaked, it always creaked, as if the planed wood were sounding a complaint, a lament for the forest where it had grown.

In winter Ruth – or Eliza, who replaced her – provided me with a rug, a wrap, a muff, a coal foot-brazier, a water bottle. I imagined I was in a troika, speeding across a snowfield, the drowned Iven Meadow iced over. The ice sparked beneath the metal runners. Rime stiffened the horse's mane, tail, my eyelashes. My breath streaked past me like thin blue smoke.

The noble families were customarily represented at the services, but individual members came and went, and seemed more often away, up in London or at a watering-place or visiting their circle at their grand homes, worshipping – if they did – in private chapels.

By comparison we Havishams were rooted to the spot. People expected to see us there, and I took their expectation as a kind of right, due acknowledgement of our importance in the local order.

I would sit looking at the painted stone effigies on their tombs. I fixed on this or that figure, kneeling or recumbent: on the ruff or cuffs, on the still folds of a dress or the smooth line of a hosed calf. I stared so hard that I passed into a kind of trance. I forced myself to keep staring, scarcely blinking my eyes, not moving a muscle, as if I was turned to stone myself. After three or four minutes of intense concentration I achieved my purpose, supposing I could catch faint signs of life: the twitch of a slipper, the flutter of an eyelid, the trembling of a finger where the hands were closed in zealous prayer.

The grand figures, dignitaries in their time, might be able to deceive the rest of the congregation, but they couldn't fool *me*.

My father had to cough sometimes, or even reach across and shake my arm, to rouse me. I came back, but not quite willingly. In some ways I preferred my fear, the fright of discovering what I wasn't meant to know, where the truth of a situation was turned inside out.

I breathed in, breathed out. I smelt the melting candlewax, the calf bindings of our hymn books, the stuffy air which was the same uncirculated air as last week's.

When I looked again, the figures on their tombs were utterly still. Petrified. Incontrovertibly dead. Sharp-chinned, razor-nosed, prim-lipped, hands ardently clasped in supplication, that their souls should be received into Heaven.

We returned through the park opposite Satis House, known as The Vines. Originally it was the Monks' Vineyard, when St Andrew's Priory stood close by.

The rooks cawed in their high scrappy nests.

'Come on, Catherine. Keep up.'

My father didn't care for the monkish spirits of the place. We attended the cathedral because he wouldn't have been treated with full seriousness in the town if we hadn't, but his devotion was restricted to eighty minutes once a week. That was quite enough.

I never did get to the bottom of his reluctance, but I sensed that it had something to do with my mother's shockingly sudden end: a death that had made no sense to him, then or now, for which nothing and no one – not even I – could console him.

But he didn't talk about that; and in the house of (opportune, always dependable) silences we shared, neither did I.

THREE

I continued to be taken out for my constitutional every day, a walk lasting an hour or so.

Two hours of lessons in the morning, luncheon, and then some exercise.

Exercise for the body and – once I'd won the confidence of the looser-tongued maids – for my mind also.

———

I heard about the old man who sold death in bottles.

About Nurse Rooley, who took away the little unwanteds before the mother grew too swollen: a premature borning.

Florry Tonkin, who sold her affections by the hour.

Mr Yarker, who would model your enemies in wax, and puncture the spirit out of them.

Captain Breen – not really a captain at all – importer of oblivion from Shanghai, via Rotherhithe.

The Misses Ginger, who communed with the dead departed, and spoke in voices.

The Siamese twins in Love Lane, genies let out of the pickling jar, walking with three shoes and two hats; one happy and laughing, the other downcast and glowering.

Miss Greville, who fasted keenly, and scourged herself with a twig switch, and who walked to the cathedral at Easter in bare feet and at other times with pebbles in her shoes.

Another spinster, Miss Maxfield in dirty canary yellow, who stood on street corners fretting about crossing the road for half an hour at a stretch, stamping on the spot, pointing at imaginary obstacles with the Malacca cane of her yellow parasol.

Canon Arbuthnot, who would tell neighbours that a Frenchman or a German friend would shortly be calling; but those callers were never glimpsed, and it was said they too came out of a bottle, a French visitor from Burgundy country and a German from somewhere about the Rhône or Moselle.

The Ali Baba house, whose owner farmed sugar plantations abroad, where four gigantic vases stood in vaulted niches high on the street facade, exposed to everything the elements could throw at them.

Our venerable town.

Children, hand-picked, continued to come to Satis House.

No more than one or two at a time. And my father arranged to have us continuously supervised.

Thinking ourselves too old for playing, we behaved (as we thought) like young adults. I showed them my sewing, my drawings; we attempted a little rudimentary music-making; we walked in the garden. And, in short, we were thoroughly bored. We didn't say anything that couldn't be overheard.

I wondered what on earth was the point of it, unless my father liked to have reported back to him their envy for how I lived, wanting for nothing.

No one pitied me – or dared to mock me – for not having a mother.

The effect was to isolate me further, and to make me feel prouder still of my position.

I used my mother's silver-backed hand mirror, given to her by my father. On the back was engraved a Gothic 'H'.

It was large and heavy to hold. Its weight conferred solemnity. I would look into the oval of glass long and hard, hoping to find some trace of my mother in my own reflection. But I only ever saw a girl with a brow furrowed in concentration, a too straight line for a mouth, a nose which threatened towards the aquiline, and a look in her eyes which was articulating a fear of solitude.

My father ensured that I should lack for nothing material.

Clothes and shoes. Books, dolls. A wooden barrow for the garden, and a set of nurseryman's tools. A leather horse on which to ride side-saddle. A box dulcimer, a recorder. A brush and comb of tortoiseshell inlaid with mother-of-pearl. Two oriental cats, which I called Silver and Gold.

I forget everything, because there was so much.

My father must have supposed that no other child could have had a happier time of it than I did. He showered me with gifts, which he didn't consider treats but things I had a perfect right to enjoy. But even amplitude and generosity pall. When I was by myself, I had a finite amount of imagination to help me play; when another child was brought along, I became possessive, only because I was afraid of having to reveal my embarrassment at owning so much.

Mrs Bundy was our cook. She had come to us when I was very small. Her repertoire was limited, but my father preferred it to the more rarefied fare my mother had favoured.

To look at, she was striking rather than attractive. Wide eyes, a small tilted nose, and a large mouth that reached up into her cheeks when my father made her smile about something. A mane of thick brown hair which she wore rolled up and pinned behind, and was forever re-pinning. Large breasts, so that her apron usually carried a dusting of flour or whatever her chest came into contact with. She also had the curious habit of stepping out of her shoes when the kitchen grew too hot for her and walking about in bare feet, as if she considered herself mistress of this domain.

Mrs Bundy spoke about me. She told my father things he couldn't have known otherwise: about my talking to the workers' children, about disposing of my lunch vegetables in the fire or out of the window.

It was none of her business. Angry with her, I told my father I knew who was telling him.

'It's *her*.'

'Catherine –'

'Isn't it?'

'I don't want to discuss –'

'She's just our cook.'

'Don't speak of Mrs Bundy so dismissively.'

'But she has no right –'

'D'you *hear* me, Catherine?'

He was taking her side – yet again.

Sometimes on my constitutional I passed where she lived.

She came from the other end of Crow Lane to ourselves, but not from the most deprived part of it as I might have expected. Being a cook in a rich man's house, she must have managed to feed herself at her employer's expense, certainly to look as wholesomely nourished as she did.

There was a boy too, a year or so younger than myself. I had glimpses of him, grown a little taller every time, but just as pale – he lacked his mother's robustness – and just as nosy as I went on my way, accompanied by my maid for that afternoon. On one occasion I made a face at him, and the boy pretended to be affronted; but I realised too late that my mistake was to acknowledge him and to show him what he made me feel, and so I'd handed *him* the advantage of that moment.

I always had lunch on Sunday with my father, following our return from the cathedral.

Mrs Bundy would linger in the dining room, after we'd been served, after my father had been asked if everything was to his satisfaction. It seemed to me that it wasn't her place. Several times I would notice my father's eyes moving off her, and Mrs Bundy's eyes narrowing as she looked at me, as if he was seeking a second opinion from her about me. And just as much as on the other account, it seemed to me that the woman exceeded herself.

Mrs Bundy had the task of supervising my other meals in my mother's old sewing room.

'My food's not to your liking, miss?'

'I'm not hungry.'

The fish stared up at me, its eye glazed with stupidity.

'You will be by suppertime.'

'How d'you know?'

'I'll take it away, shall I? My hard work.'

'Take it away.'

'Magic word, miss?'

'Take it away – *please*.'

Later, when she was having some shut-eye wherever it was she went to take it, I would return to the kitchen and raid the storage jars, making the girls swear to secrecy. But – I see now – she must have known about that too, because how else was it that the jars were always kept topped up with currants, dried fruit, peel, nuts?

Mrs Bundy stands in the steam while pans simmer on the range. Bread is baking in the old oven, chestnuts – placed on the oven floor – are bursting their skins among the cinders.

She wipes perspiration from her jaw with the back of her hand.

Her cuffs are undone and the sleeves rolled back. Her forearms are fleshy and white. Last summer they were fleshy but tanned, from her work in the kitchen garden; another summer on, she is pale, as a proper lady is pale, as her son is pale.

Cooling in a bowl are a rabbit's guts, which she earlier pulled out whole and hot. All in the day's work.

She doesn't see me looking as she rests. Briefly she forgets herself, she stands stroking one arm slowly with the fingers of the other. Moments pass, she is rapt in her fancies.

'How proud you are!'

Why shouldn't I be?

'Little Miss High and Mighty.'

'I'll tell my father. What you've just said.'

'Tell him what? That you're proud?'

Tell him that she'd dared to criticise me. (In that accent which wavers between flat backwoods Kent and something better.) But I felt that if I said what I was thinking, that gave her act of criticism some sort of validity.

Better instead that I should ignore her.

I snatched up my petit point, and attacked the canvas with such violence that I missed my aim. I cried out.

'Thumb for a pincushion?' she said. She had a laugh in her voice that incensed me.

'Not pin! Needle, needle! Don't you even know *that*?'

'Don't take on, it's nothing –'

'There's blood.'

'A very little. Suck it and –'

'How common!'

She came closer, but I snatched my hand away and turned my back on her. I didn't know why I was so vexed and angry.

'It's your temper I'd be bothered about, if I were you.'

'But you're *not* me. How on earth *could* you be?'

I was aware, through my anger, that I was being goaded. I closed my eyes.

Her voice moved in front of me again.

'Close your eyes, that's right, and count to ten.'

I opened them again and ran, screaming inside my head, from the room.

———

For as long as I could remember a woman with an emperor's nose had paid occasional visits to Satis House. She wore layers of black, and spoke English in a strangely accented way.

My grandmother: my mother's mother.

My father had the servants address her as 'Madame', as the French do.

She would sit very straight-backed in her high chair, and imposed her powdery presence on us all. I was required to stand in front of her reciting, or playing a tune on my dulcimer. Invariably something in my performance touched her, because I would be summoned forward to have my hair and cheek stroked; her rings were cold, and hard, but not sharp.

Her visits became more infrequent.

And then she stopped coming at all.

On what was to prove her final visit she was very critical of the food she was served, speaking in front of Mrs Bundy. My father started defending our cook. My grandmother sent the woman from the room, and then – while I sat between them – she berated my father for showing his partiality. She did *not* expect to be shown up in front of some kitchen cook.

'Not just any kitchen cook,' my father said.

'Certainly, I agree. A very poor cook.'

'You have no reason for saying so.'

'I have just tried to eat the food you put before me.'

'You think I can't choose a good cook, Madame?'

'Never mind "good". Simply a decent one would suffice.'

'What gives you the right, I should like to know, to –'

'In my daughter's place I –'

'We don't know what Antoinette would have thought –'

'She would *not* have given her approval to *that* woman's being in this house.'

They both turned and looked at me. My grandmother's face was now as sour as a cut lemon. My father, spinning the stem of his wine glass with his fingers, seemed anxious on my account.

Later, before our visitor left, I heard my father saying that he would appreciate it if she didn't speak to the servants without his approval. She denied knowing what he meant.

'You've not been asking the maids questions?'

'Whatever has put that idea into –'

'I'm cognisant of what goes on in my own house.'

'As the maids are.'

'You *have* been asking them –'

'Antoinette would never have stood for it.'

'Stood for what?'

'You know very well what. Don't taint young Catherine, do you hear me?'

'I should tell you, I do not appreciate being advised how –'

'I am not advising, Mr Havisham. I am *demanding*.'

She didn't ever return to Satis House.

Every now and then I would receive a note from her. I would reply, but my father insisted on seeing what I wrote to her, and having me rewrite – more concisely – if he judged so.

I heard one of the girls say Mrs Bundy was relieved anyhow, to see the back of her, no more fancy French stuff to dish up *there*. And another girl laughing back, Oh Mrs Bundy's got her own ideas what she'll do to this place, what's going to go into folk's bellies.

I knew that my grandmother wouldn't be back, even though I wasn't told so. Mrs Bundy walked about more amply; she had the girls running everywhere on errands – I even saw her passing through our hall with flour on her arms or a whisk in her hand. My father wouldn't have risked offending her with another visit from my imperatorial grandmother, even if he was denying the mother of the woman he'd married and lost, and was depriving *me* of an acquaintanceship with my one surviving female blood relative.

I had chased my cats down to the orchard. I happened to look up and jumped when I saw someone, a boy, crouching splay-legged in the fork of a tree.

'What are *you* doing here?'

Then I recognised him. Mrs Bundy's son, in new finery.

He raised himself nonchalantly on one elbow and considered me.

'I could ask *you* the same,' he replied languidly. He spoke as boys do who have begun to receive an expensive education.

'I asked *you* first.'

He smiled.

'Oh, Catherine Havisham has first say in everything, doesn't she?'

I glared back at him.

'It's not *your* garden,' I said.

'It's not yours either.'

'More mine than yours.'

'*Is* it?'

'It's my father's.'

'"It's my father's",' he repeated, exactly imitating my tone of voice. 'Who else?'

'Indeed.'

'Come down from there.'

He did eventually – taking a long time about it, and making it seem that he only pleased himself.

He was tall, lanky, pallid, not filled-out like his mother. He still had his thin foxy face. I had never cared for the look of him, this craven interloper.

'Well . . . ?' I said. 'What are you waiting for?'

'I just wanted to get a good look at you.'

'What on earth for?'

'So you'll give me sweet dreams. When I dream of this place.'

'The garden? It's private, I told you. It's got nothing to do with you.'

'Says who?'

'*I* say.'

He laughed.

'So, you're the boss, are you?'

I snapped at him. 'Don't be insolent!'

'Or else what – ?'

He reached up his arm, and might have been going to swing from a low branch, but he either didn't trust his strength or didn't care to soil his white hands and clean cuffs.

'I'll call my father.'

'Very well, I'm going. Don't you mention this to him.'

'Why shouldn't I?'

'Tut-tut! Speaking to town lads? In *his* garden? Whatever would the old boy think?'

———

And then, quite suddenly, Mrs Bundy left us.

Oh, joy and jubilation!

She was said to be living now outside the town.

I had a sighting one day. She was dressed like a respectable trades-man's wife, with a fur collar and a fur muff and a hat replete with a quiver of feathers. She had her son in tow, still lanky and still sallow-faced and attired like last time in the garb of a young gentleman. Both mother and son shared something I couldn't account for: an air of self-confidence, eyes not ashamed to meet anyone else's on that busy main street of our town.

I mentioned to my father that I had seen Mrs Bundy.
    'Indeed?'
    How grand she was trying to make herself look, I said.
    'That isn't her way.'
    'She seemed so to me.'
    'To *you*, Catherine. But you never approved of Mrs Bundy.'
    'No.'
    'You too question the wisdom of my having employed her? I can't pick my own staff well, is that it?'
    I had bothered him, I could tell that. A tic was pulling in his cheek, throbbing away.
    'I didn't mean . . .'
    'I don't wish us to discuss Mrs Bundy. Not ever again.'

Whenever I saw her son I would look away quickly. He was always watching me, with an expression I found confusing. He was disap-proving, and superior, but also frankly curious. He had no com-punction about staring at me, which I found presumptuous. Of what concern should I, a Havisham, be to the son of our erstwhile kitchen cook?

FOUR

My father's office was in the house. Next to it, entered either from that room or through an outside door in the yard but otherwise quarantined from the domestic premises, was the Compting House, where two rows of clerks sat at high desks keeping their tallies.

Luckily for Havisham's purposes, our proximity to Chatham ensured a large ready market for our brews. A marines' barracks had been built twenty-five years after the army one, and the town was thronged with sailors and troops and their dependents. The dockyards employed thousands. Their thirst was insatiable, and – as did one or two of our competitors – we obliged . . .

Along the Medway the Havisham net was cast – so to speak – by my father, with clever aim. To Gravesend upstream, and to Sittingbourne, Sheerness and Queensborough in an easterly direction.

I knew in which inns, and where, the Havisham brew and porter were sold. My father would point them out to me one by one as we came upon them on our travels. He'd have me memorise the names, and each time I would recite an ever-lengthening litany, as completely as I could. He would listen to me, nodding with satisfaction, and then supply the names I had missed from the list.

The Tun & Lute, Shovel & Boot; Turkey Slave, Cock & Pye.

(I would proceed by an eccentric system of associated images.)
Leather Bottle, Hundred House, Parson & Clerk.
The Rose of Denmark, Goat & Compasses, Q in a Corner.
Trip to Jerusalem.
'And Good King Lud.'
'Good King Lud,' I would repeat.
'It's the one you always forget. But the only one.'

We didn't own all the inns, but we were suppliers to each of them, several dozen in total. This was the Havisham inheritance, and my father liked to hear it retold over and over by my young voice.

———

I saw them at the cathedral on Sunday mornings, those spinsters who had dried on the vine. Some had cared too long for parents, and now housekept for siblings. Two or three had been in love perhaps, but hadn't been decisive enough, and so they had lost the opportunity.

The carers, worn thin, seemed to have surrendered some of their own personality. Those who had failed in love were left with a kind of purposeless animation: restless hands fidgeting with gloves and prayerbooks, tremulous mouths and little lambs' tongues, eyes that flitted about the congregation – as if vaguely searching out someone who was never present.

I tried not to walk too close to them. They were ubiquitous, though, pervasive presences. I held in my skirts, as if I might be in dread of some contagion. The skinny ones had nimble ankles, the plump ones stood sturdily where they impeded free passage to the porch.

Instead of a governess I now had instructors. They came to Satis House, and – when he was a man – a maid sat in the room with us, about her sewing or penning letters home.

If they'd listened, the girls could have acquired an education as I was doing. Latin, poetry, French, arithmetic, drawing, music on the keyboard, elocution.

I knew that my father listened at the door when he could. He replaced a couple of my tutors (one, Miss Boutflower, favoured poetry of a deep religious hue), and he had suspicions about an athletic-looking young man who tried to kindle in me an enthusiasm for the history of our Dark Ages.

My father took advice where he could, but it wasn't as straightforward as he might have envisaged, educating a daughter above her station.

I wasn't beautiful. My mouth was too straight, while my nose showed increasingly imperial tendencies. My eyes were hooded, and looked heavy. I saw what I owed to my doughty grandmother.

I didn't give an impression, so said one of the tutors (subsequently dismissed), of being a country brewer's daughter.

'That's because you're not,' my father told me. 'Your mother had fine features. And you've been brought up with nothing but the best.'

I had thick fair hair with a natural kink in it, and even though the colour darkened a little with time I didn't lose that air of impractical glamour which fairness gives. My complexion was clear and untroubled. I was reckoned to have 'good bone structure'.

My appearance was picked over by the girls in the house, by my instructors when I overheard them gossiping, by the women who made my clothes, by the effeminate old man who fitted me for shoes.

I had this, I didn't have that. I was more than averagely one thing, less than averagely something else.

It was me they were discussing. But it also wasn't me.

I had a claim on this person, but so did others.

And what went on *inside* me seemed to be a different matter entirely: what the others couldn't see, but which they presumed to comment on. There, I believed, lay all the clues to being myself – a truer and more real Catherine Havisham.

FIVE

I was in the house working at Latin gerunds one afternoon when I heard a crashing sound outside. It was immediately followed by a terrible cry to freeze the blood – and then a clamour of voices, men's and women's, shouting and screaming.

I ran to the side door of the house. A crowd had gathered beneath one of the brewhouse hoists. I looked up and saw a length of rope swinging loose. The rope must have snapped and sent its load hurling to the ground.

I smelt the spilt beer before I hurried across. I saw the pieces of smashed barrel. Someone lay writhing on the wet cobbles, roaring with the pain of his injuries. I was going to try to push my way through when a hand on my shoulder roughly pulled me back.

'Don't look, Catherine!'

My father turned me aside, then himself hastened through.

The barrel, I heard the house-girls say, had dropped straight on to the loader waiting beneath.

I couldn't sleep that night.

On succeeding nights I slept fitfully, never far from waking.

In the daylight my eyes were drawn back, time after time, to the hoist. The ropes had been replaced, and sacks and barrels were being passed up and down as before, as if nothing had happened.

I'd learned that tendons had been severed in the loader's left leg, leaving him lame. I couldn't stop hearing the man's eldritch wail, and the shouting and howling of the others. Over and over, I wasn't able to drive the sounds from my mind.

My father kept the man on, and would always remember to speak to him, stooping a little as if he were harbouring some guilt.

I saw for myself that the injuries were worse than I had been told. The right arm had been crushed, and hung loose. He trailed one leg. He now helped out the ostlers, and did watch duty.

His daughter would bring him something to sup at in winter, a bowl wrapped in cloths. It must have been hard going, through the warren of muddy unlit lanes, seeing her way in the dark, and I felt very distant from her as I watched from one of the house windows, comfortably settled indoors for the night.

She was about my own age, a little taller than I; pretty, with thick copper hair, plaited. I could see her better in the mornings, when her father's watch was over and she stopped by on her way to the Dame's school, where she did housework in return for a little learning. Sally's mother was ambitious for her, and had earned a bad name for it, but the town's talk only toughened her resolve to give Sally a better start than other girls of her kind got. A tidy appearance was one lesson she had learned at home, how to show herself well.

I admired her, from my distance. Her quiet composure, her fearlessness in the face of those comments about her which people didn't bother to disguise. Even her frizzy copper hair. I was intrigued by the way she had of keeping her eyes cast down, as if she must be rather sorrowful, and then in an instant raising them; those eyes would be shining with intelligence, I judged, and a ready sort of humour, even with things as they were.

Seeing her father, she would straighten up and smile a welcome. If she was concerned, she also needed to be hopeful. She knew not to take her father's other, uninjured arm, since he needed to get his balance for himself. Her tactfulness seemed to me precocious, prodigious.

———

I had never been allowed to play with the brewery children, nor had I wanted to.

Sally turned out to be the exception.

My father was unsure. But he was still troubled by his conscience, about his liability for what had happened to his loader. So he raised no objection, although I later realised he had set a string of informers among the servants.

Because Sally wasn't allowed beyond the laundry room, I took what I had to show her down there.

I set up my model theatre, and from either side we pushed the wooden characters on sticks and spoke in pretend grown-up voices. She played the servants and hoi polloi, in a local accent broader than her own, while I took the parts of the better townsfolk and the clergy.

I'd had difficulty talking with the other children who came to Satis House. I had none with Sally. I knew so from what my voice *didn't* sound like – tense and squeaky and dried out.

She was less deferential than I had expected her to be, but never impolite. It was strange to me how often our opinions coincided; how, with our very different backgrounds, we regarded certain people or our town's traditions in the same (sceptical) way – and how it was, for instance, that I could gauge her thoughts so well in advance of her saying them, and she mine, that we might finish off each other's sentences and start the next.

———

I taught her some of what I knew.

Good table manners. How to hold herself. How to tone down the Kent in her vowels.

Simple French grammar, and then Latin declensions, which she didn't get from the Dame. Dates in history, from the Dark Ages on. Some verses of poetry, and some prose passages.

She was a solid learner who forgot nothing. She might even have surpassed me if we had been equals, but thankfully we were not, and so I didn't even have to regard the irony of that.

Once I took Sally into the tack room, so she could admire my father's new saddle. My action was reported back to my father, and he told me quite bluntly that I wasn't to take 'company' – as then and in the future he would refer to Sally – beyond the door at the end of the scullery passage.

She had a quick mind. Memory, I know now, is an asset of intelligence; though I also know that to live an easier life, one should have one's full health and a short memory.

Sally, I felt, would always be like this, wanting to make things just a bit more difficult for herself. Needing to know what was in the next lesson before we got there; asking me how long it had taken me to memorise a poem and then learning it in half that time; asking me, how can they be sure of this, what proof is there of that? – King Harold losing an eye, five colours showing in a rainbow, the earth's having a dark side, there being no final number to count to.

'I'm only telling you what the books say, Sally.'

'Don't you want to know if it's true?'

'It wouldn't be there in the books if it weren't, would it?' I answered in exasperation. Sally stared at me, with a pitying expression. Was I really as naive as that?

I had my arm hooked through Sally's as we walked back along Hound Street. There was the sound of a horse being ridden slowly behind us on the cobbles. I turned round. It was my father: suddenly not looking at us, as if he hadn't seen who we were.

He rode past. I held tighter to Sally's arm.

For the next few days I felt he was paying me closer attention; but silently, furtively, between any remarks he had for me. Whenever I looked up my father would avert his eyes, either to hold on the view outside the window or examine some object in the room behind me. He would place candles where I might be clearer to him. He appeared to have some project in his mind.

For a while I saw a little less of Sally. It wasn't by my choosing, but because her mother had been able to find a position for her, lowly and beneath stairs, but such impressive stairs, in the home of two elderly sisters on Bolley Hill. The ladies endlessly sparred, I'd heard, and fought over everything the other had, or might want, including the respect of each new member of their staff. Sister would struggle with sister to win and keep Sally.

'I used to think you were proud,' Sally told me. 'People said you were proud.'

'I'm not proud to *you*, am I?'

'No. No, you're not.'

'And that surprises you?'

'Just a little, yes.'

'I used to think I was expected to be that way. Partly I was – and partly I became it.'

'Not to disappoint them?'

'I suppose so.'

And later.

'I think you bring out someone better in me, Sally.'

I took her hand. She looked quite astonished. I smiled at that.

'Why shouldn't I take your hand if I want to?'

Sally managed to smile back, but in a puzzled way.

'Give me one good reason why not,' I said.

But she didn't, because she couldn't.

———

One winter's night I had her stay with me in the house, all night, to sleep in my warm bed by my side. I was defying my father, of course, and no one else was allowed in on our secret.

In the morning, though, it couldn't be a secret any longer. Sally's mother had gone looking for her when she didn't return home, accompanied by some of her neighbours. She had come to the brewery yard at dawn, and it chanced to be a day when my father was up early because indigestion was troubling him.

He was furious: but with Sally, not with me. I tried to explain it to him; I told him I was the one responsible.

He instructed our Mrs Venn to strip the sheets from the bed and – why on earth? – boil them. I couldn't understand what all the pudder was about, and why the big vat had to be heated especially for the sake of my sheets. I watched the blankets being beaten and then hung up on a line to air.

We had lain telling each other stories, as if we were five years old instead of ten (me) and eleven (Sally). I didn't even feel sleepy, not at first, because of my excitement at having her there. Later, however, I followed her example and dozed off, with my arm covering her waist. Whatever was the harm in that?

My father told me afterwards that he had ordered Sally not to come back.

Her first exile from Satis House was beginning.

———

I managed to meet her a few times, down by the river and away from prying eyes. We arranged that she should be in this or that location on a Sunday morning, so that we could have a sight of each other on my way to and from the cathedral service.

But it wasn't the same as before: it couldn't be, no matter how much I wished it.

'It's what my father says.'

'What do *you* say, though?'

I stared at her, wrong-footed by her question.

'Catherine Havisham sings her father's song, I think.'

It sounded like a remark she must have overheard adults making.

'I do no such thing,' I told her.

'But you have no time for me now.'

'It's different now.'

'How is it different now?'

Because. Because, because, because.

I turned away.

'Why – ?'

'We're growing up,' I answered. 'That's all.'

'No. That's not it.'

Then I felt impatient with her. Why couldn't she just accept that these things are visited on us? We don't have a choice, we truly don't. I was a Havisham; she was Limping Johnnie's daughter, never mind what airs her mother gave herself.

I felt watching eyes were following me down to the river. My flesh crept on the back of my neck.

It was Sally who said we should stop. *Must* stop.

I reluctantly, very sadly, agreed.

I saw how she grew after that. I saw how the coppery colour of her hair deepened, and the hair itself – with ribbons wound through – lost none of its thickness but was restrained still more tightly.

I saw small but significant things: the bruises on her ankles from the distances she walked every day, a red mark on her arm like a kitchen burn which her other arm tried to cover, a downward turn to her mouth on one side when she thought no one was looking.

But *I* saw.

SIX

There's blood on the rug where I've been standing. It has run down my legs from the place I know to keep hidden.

There's blood on the sheets when I go back to examine the bed. And on my nightdress.

How have I wounded myself? I don't feel *hurt*: just a little light-headed, a little muzzy.

A skivvy brings me what I call for from the scullery.

I get down on my knees, gingerly, and try washing the rug.

With water, cold and hot. Then with vinegar. Then with the juice of a lemon.

The stains won't wash out of the wool; or from the sheets either, or my nightdress.

I rub frantically, but the stains are defiant – they seem to have settled there, where I've bled them.

Afterwards it was explained to me by Mrs Venn.

I didn't doubt my father had been informed, if cryptically. He asked me how I was feeling: as if I should be indisposed, ailing.

'This warm weather,' he said, 'very unseasonal; it's best not to tax yourself.'

He didn't let his eyes rest on me, as he normally did when he lent advice. He was embarrassed, as I was. We weren't talking, he and I, about the same Catherine Havisham of two days ago.

Left in my room by myself I sat in front of the fire, preferring to watch the pictures in the flames to what I could see through my window, that view of the yard and rooftops and the drab riverland beyond.

When the flames died down and the pictures faded, I looked instead at the fireplace tiles – tiles from Delft, blue and white – and my imagination wandered among the scenes there.

By the banks of the canals, over the bridges, past the windmills, stopping as people always do at the locks until the barge has nudged its way through. On horseback, galloping bareback across a plain under high sea clouds. In pattens, picking a path over cobbles to reach a friend's door, while the air of the town fills with pealing bells, and with a commotion of birds like a squall.

Until I remembered where I was – because embers were falling with a little rush into the grate, and rooks circled over the cherry trees outside, and the cathedral bells summoned for vespers, and because the room had grown colder around me.

I had been sent off for a few weeks over Christmastime, to a cousin of my father's, who lived a good way off in Berkshire.

While I was away, and during that one quiet time in the year for the brewery when work almost stopped, my father took ill. Vessels burst in his heart. That same evening he'd eaten and drunk too much at a festive dinner, and it was thought that his untypical indulgence and similarly untypical walk home in the cold air must have caused the attack.

However it came about, he fell down in the frosty street. The first to see was Sally's mother; she had my father taken into a cottage and best positioned to restore his circulation. She'd run off to fetch the doctor herself.

I wasn't to be told, but Sally wrote to me nevertheless. I left Windsor at once, pretending on my return that I'd been on my way back anyway. I found Sally's mother tending to the patient; and Sally running errands for my father, whatever he requested her to do.

Sally's readmission to Satis House came about for all the wrong reasons. But I was glad: firstly that my father was mending, and secondly that I had my good friend to hand, to confide my worries to, and – after my shock and double relief – to let me cry, quite literally, on her steady shoulder.

My father was up on his feet a fortnight later. He was able to walk, if slowly for the moment, and to talk down what had taken place, telling everyone he would be back to work as usual before too long.

———

With Sally, it was like old times; there might not have been that two-year hiatus.

I knew that she forgave my father, merely because she never rose to my bait and offered any criticisms of him.

She had cut that wilful plumery, her copper hair, and she showed fewer of those carefree sun-freckles on her face. Now she was under one of the redoubtable, granite-featured housekeepers who organised domestic life in Minor Canon Row, in this case in the residence of that oily archdeacon and his astringent mother and dry-as-dust wife. Sally was worked hard, because every penny spent in that household was required to offer its full value in time and labour.

But Sally kept cheerful. Her own mother was pleased for her, and so – I claimed – was I.

'But now,' I said, 'you have to be my confidante as well. That's two jobs of work, I reckon.'

'Certainly,' she said. 'Whenever I can.'

'I'll be very disappointed if you're ever not able.'

I wondered if it could be quite the same as it used to be. We each had rules and responsibilities that were becoming clearer to us. We had little say in those; but we could surely try to stake other claims for ourselves, obeying our instincts only, about whom we called our *consœurs* and best friends.

SEVEN

For my thirteenth birthday and those following, my father gave me a painted porcelain Easter egg. Each egg was valuable in itself, but the surprise lay inside. There I would find, cushioned by a velvet lining, an item of jewellery: a fire-opal pendant, a bracelet of amethysts, a pearl halter, a gold rope necklace hung with rubies, white and pink diamond earrings, a rare yellow diamond on a ring.

In addition he passed over to me, item by item, my mother's jewels. Those had older-fashioned settings than my birthday presents. He arranged to have a topaz necklace reset, because I had taken such a fancy to the blue markings of the stones, like tiger stripes. The rest showed good taste, and I was happy to wear them.

My mother had inherited some of the pieces, and I was aware of the quiet dignity of their age. They weighed me to my chair, they slowed me slightly when I walked – not because they were heavy, but because they came to me complicated by their history – and it wasn't at all an oppressive sensation. I felt that I'd been granted an intimate contact with my mother. We were sharing this occasion of my wearing a necklace or a bracelet, and somehow my increased pleasure was being transmitted to her, through time and space. This experience was being recreated in another dimension; by wearing the necklace or bracelet, I was helping to close a circle.

My father grew sad and despondent for a while.

He had only just got back to regular work. His illness might have been to blame, still tiring him these eighteen or twenty months on, but I sensed – I had a premonition – that there was some other reason.

Several times he seemed to be on the point of telling me something.

Whenever he ventured beyond the brewery gates, he wore his darkest and most sombre outdoor clothes.

'I married again, Catherine.'

I thought I had misheard.

'Who married again?'

'Me. *I* married again.'

Pause.

'When?'

'A few years after your mother died.'

'Married whom?'

'The woman I wished to marry.'

'Who?'

'The woman I wished to care for.'

Pause.

'But she died. Just recently.'

'Who – who was she? Do I know her?'

'You know – you *knew* her, yes.'

'One of our friends?'

'It was Mrs Bundy. As she used to be.'

I stared at him. I felt I was falling through a hole in the floor. I was without mass; I'd left the sac of my stomach behind.

'And then of course she became Mrs Havisham.'

'No.' I shook my head at him. 'No, that's *our* name.'

At that my father's face sagged. His mouth hung slack.

'And . . .'

He stopped. He stared at the surface of the table.

'There's – something else?'

My head was still spinning, like a top.

'We had a son.'

'A son?'

'You have a half-brother.'

The boy I used to see her with, about the town, who was sent away to be educated.

As he briefly explained, my father wouldn't look at me, however hard I stared and challenged him to raise his eyes.

'I'm sorry I have to tell you like this –'

The boy's age was close to mine. And yet my father had said he married a few years after my mother's death. I knew what that meant.

'I should like something, Catherine.'

I let a few seconds lapse.

'What – what's that?'

'I should like Arthur – that is his name – I should like Arthur to come and stay here.'

'*Here?*'

'Yes.'

'How long for?'

'Satis House will be his home.'

'What?'

'It will call for one or two adjustments to our routine. But nothing we can't –'

'You want him to come and stay here with *us?*'

'He *will* be coming. To be one of the family.'

I didn't speak.

'I've told him. We've discussed it.'

'It's been decided?' I said.

43

'Yes.'

'Why are you asking me, then?'

I fixed my eyes on that gulch of loose skin on his neck, his throat, which had only appeared since his accident.

'I should appreciate – if you could help to make Arthur feel comfortable. In his new home.'

'"Home"? Satis House?'

'Yes. Home now for all of us.'

Arthur was still thin. The Havishams had always had padding, so he was already marked out as being something less than ourselves.

He had thin wrists, a thin neck, but it wasn't the fine sort of inbred aristocratic leanness. I could see the sharp edge of his shoulder bones under his shirt. When he breathed out, or laughed – which meant rolling about at some small witticism from my father, or sneering at me – his ribs poked out of his chest. He had large thin grasping hands; obliged to shake hands with him, I was anticipating a stronger grip, as narrow wrists often produce – but his greedy fawning mitt was turned inside mine like some cornered, half-dead weasel.

Arthur didn't discuss *then* with me.

'That's my business.'

He wouldn't tell me where he and his mother had lived latterly, or how often they'd seen their provider.

It was information I couldn't ask my father for, because asking – expressing an interest – might appear to condone the marriage. (Why keep it a secret as he had unless he was ashamed?)

'Forthwith your brother will be known as Arthur Havisham.'

'But that's not his real name.'

'It will be now.'

I was shocked. How could he be either my 'brother' or a Havisham?

'In time Arthur will need to learn about the business. Receive a training.'

'He will?'

'Well, of course. That goes without saying, doesn't it?'

He was attending a bona fide establishment for young gentlemen in the West of England, not that you would have deduced it from his conduct.

In the house he was late for meals. He dragged his heels on the floor. He entered rooms without knocking. If he took a book from a shelf he didn't replace it; if he dropped something he waited for a servant to pick it up. When my father wasn't there he spat fruit stones into the fireplace grate. One day some coins fell out of my father's pocket on to his chair, unnoticed by him, and I saw Arthur surreptitiously scoop them up and put them into his own pocket. He received his horse saddled from the stable, and left it sweating in the yard once he had ridden it hard, and showed no interest in the animal's well-being. Behind my father's back (and sometimes only just) he silently mimicked me, or he cocked a snook at my father, or pretended to be hacking up food into his hands. He aimed pebbles at small birds, then (as his confidence grew) bigger stones at my Silver and Gold.

After only months he was cocky enough to let his dislike of me stay expressed on his face, not now bothering to hide it from my father.

Our father, as he would have it.

'That sounds like God,' I reproved him.

'Thinks he *is* God too.'

I gawped.

'No one to tell him he isn't, I s'pose.'

And he talked of Satis House, with a leery smile, as his 'dear old chimney corner'.

'You're away at school,' I said.

'It's still my home.'

'I've always lived here.'

'And now *I* do too. High time I got to fit in with you lot.'

'What makes you think you ever will?'

'Oh, I'm adaptable.'

'Don't *I* have to be adaptable as well?' I asked him.

'You've no choice, have you?'

'No. No, I don't.'

'We're agreed on that, then.'

'That's the only thing we *do* –'

'Worry not, sister –'

'Half-sister.'

'– I'll make sure we're all quite cosy together.'

I was surprised by Sally's continuing reluctance to condemn Arthur.

The son of the former and departed Mrs Bundy had forfeited the right to any sort of respect, I felt. I couldn't understand why she should try to think her way into the spiteful workings of his mind. Why should *he* merit anyone's special consideration?

'It's because I stand a little way back,' she said.

No. No, I didn't believe that.

And it wasn't because I hadn't strongly presented my case against Arthur. It might have been that she felt I argued *too* powerfully, but wasn't that a true Havisham's privilege?

—

Arthur had no genuine interest in the brewery.

Between school terms he pretended that he wanted to learn, since he thought saying so would please my father: and he needed to be in my father's good books, to have a chance of his allowance being increased.

My father must have seen how things were; and heard, too. Whenever my father was absent, Arthur was curt and off-hand with the workers, thinking he was above having to deal with them directly; perhaps (I calculated for myself) because he understood that they were very suspicious of him, for having appeared from nowhere and displaying so little acumen for business.

It struck me that my father's brow was more deeply rivelled than it used to be. I could appreciate better now that he had only meant to be open and above board by owning to Arthur as his blood son. He believed he had finally done the right thing: while circumstances seemed intent, rather, on loosening and undermining the soft ground beneath his feet.

—

Arthur, I thought, must have taught himself to be this person from books, or – more probably – from watching plays in the theatre.

He ought to have been seen in the light from candles along the front of a stage. His entrances and exits should have been accompanied by the din of shaken tin for thunder rolls. Why wasn't he wearing make-up? (Or just conceivably he was?)

And I still thought that Sally too often failed to recognise what damned Arthur in my eyes.

He was uncouth, inconsiderate, a bully. Ignorant, and very smug about being so. Bitter, and possibly vengeful.

I read him like a book.

But Sally wouldn't condemn him outright. She told me, hadn't his position always been awkward, knowing he'd been born a Havisham ('half a Havisham', I corrected her), but unable to acknowledge his birth (his bastard birth, as I knew for myself)? Could we either of us, she asked, imagine how uncertain his future life must have seemed to him?

I nearly lost patience with her. I told her, we must agree to disagree; I was *not* to be converted to his cause.

'I don't mean to plead for him. I only tell you what I think.'

Sally was quite composed, and not fired or indignant. Perhaps one reason for my own discomposure was feeling that she could take a clearer and less partisan view, whereas I had the onus – the millstone – of Havisham dignity to defend.

II

DURLEY CHASE

EIGHT

The dining room one evening, suppertime.

My father on one side of the table, I on the other, and Arthur mercifully off at school.

'I've arranged for you to have an education, Catherine.'

I thought he was referring to my lessons in the house. I nodded.

'I mean, to share your studies. And to live with some grander types than you're used to here.'

'Who?'

'The Chadwycks. Spelt with a "y".'

'"Live with" them?'

'An acquaintance – Lady Charlotte and her children.'

Acquaintance? I had never heard of the person, or her children.

'In Surrey.'

Surrey?

'Not so far from Redhill.'

Should the name 'Redhill' mean something to me? It didn't.

'I think it would be the best thing. You'll see how that sort live. You'll become one of them.'

'Why, though?'

'I've told you.'

'Why me? Why the Chadwycks?'

'Because I was talking to Lady Chadwyck about you. And we decided.'

'When am I to go?'

'Just as soon as you can get yourself ready and packed.'

'I've really got to stay with them?'

'Yes.'

'What about my lessons here?'

'Your tutors will find other employment. Tradesmen's daughters round about.'

Already I had been elected to a different league.

I wanted to take Sally with me.

But how? As my maid?

I felt the matter most delicate. She had always treated me as the master's daughter, but I had never – even at my most heedless – treated her as a servant.

I waited for my father to ask if I had anyone in mind, but he settled the matter without our discussing it. He selected one of the girls in the house.

'I shall tell you all about it, Sally. I'll write.'

'You'll have too much else on your mind.'

'Not be able to find time for *you*?'

I knew my own resolve.

'Never,' I said. 'Never.'

———

I twitch my mantle blue: *Tomorrow to fresh woods, and pastures new.*

———

A dome showed over the tops of the trees.

The view cleared along the driveway.

The house appeared. Slab-sided, octagonal. Raised on a knoll. Red creeper on the walls. French doors stood open.

———

They were waiting for me. Lady Chadwyck, well preserved and dressed at least fifteen years younger than the age I guessed her to be, and smiling sweetly.

She had two daughters and a son, lined up in the portico to meet me.

Isabella, the eldest at nineteen, was the more attractive girl, with a commanding manner. Her brother William, home from Cambridge, had heroic good looks. Marianna was darker, and smaller, and more reticent. A plain-featured and soberly dressed cousin from Northumberland, Frederick, was at the same Cambridge college as William, and lived with them at Durley Chase in the vacations.

The memory of Arthur that had accompanied me on the journey fell away as I succumbed to the warm words of welcome, their easy smiles and their fine manners. After only a few minutes I felt I was giving myself to them: like some flower that's had a dark time growing, opening at last to the sun.

They had retained their childhood nicknames. Isabella was Sheba, as in 'Arrival of the Queen of', with a talent for making dramatic entrances. Marianna was Mouse, because that was her way. William was contracted to an amiable mumble, W'm (I was less sure why; he spoke quite clearly, and had an open, confident manner).

Frederick wasn't called that, but instead Moses, after Moses Primrose in *The Vicar of Wakefield*. Goldsmith's Moses was the second son, not very bright, and yet a pedant; sent to the fair to buy a horse, he was talked into spending the money on a gross of green spectacles. Cousin Frederick (a third son) was the cleverest of our group, by their say-so, and even if he was inclined to be pedantic, the name didn't seem to fit at all.

'That's the point,' Isabella said. 'Moses Primrose wouldn't have complained. And neither does Frederick, ever. So, that's the connection, you see.'

Quite frankly, I didn't see. I could tell why modest, restrained Marianna was Mouse; Moses in the Bible was a figure of some passion and vehemence, while *this* Moses in clerical black seemed forbiddingly introverted, certainly compared to either Sheba or W'm.

But I felt I wasn't entitled yet to question the Chadwyck family lore.

———

I would wake in a golden glow, early sunshine through the new yellow damask of my bedroom curtains. I felt the soft dense mass of duck feathers in the pillow beneath my head and inside the new coverlet.

Comfort and refinement. (This one room had been refurbished for my coming, Sheba told me. I couldn't fail to notice the signs of hard usage elsewhere in the house, but that was as charming to me as the freshness of my bedroom.)

A housemaid came in to stir the fire and bank it up, and then – when I'd given my consent – to open the curtains. She returned with bubbling hot water for my ablutions, and a service of tea presented on a tray.

Might she lay out my clothes?

Yes, of course.

She worked very quietly, but it wasn't a petulant silence as Biddy's sometimes was at home. It was as if she were trying to shade into my surroundings, and often I did forget she was there, and was startled when she took her leave of me, as if one of the pieces of furniture had mysteriously come to life.

Once she'd gone I sat for a while by the window.

There was dew on the grass, and fox trails. Swifts swooped low, criss-crossing. The trees gathered serenity into themselves.

At home I would already have been hearing the first bustle out in the yard. There I could never be quite alone with my thoughts.

Here stillness reigned, with only the rustle of coals in the grate and the tiny scrabbling of a mouse behind the wainscot to momentarily interfere, and hardly even that.

———

Out of term time Moses helped me with my Virgil translation.

We were tackling Book IV. Dido, Queen of Carthage, is consumed with love for the adventurer Aeneas, but he rejects her.

I didn't look for assistance, but Moses was always ready with it. How simple *he* could make it seem.

> 'Dido, fetter'd in the chains of love,
> Hot with the venom which her veins inflam'd,
> And by no sense of shame to be restrain'd . . .'

He had me read aloud the original first, before I construed. Then he would demonstrate how.

> 'Dido shall come in a black sulph'ry flame,
> When death has once dissolv'd her mortal frame.'

He put me right about my pronunciation, and the stress I placed on words, and helped me correct my errors; then we moved on.

I didn't know why he gave up his time to me. Sometimes I thought I caught a smile on his lips, especially when the back of his hand was raised to his mouth, as if to conceal it.

'Are you mocking me?'

His face was all shock.

'Well,' I said, 'weren't you smiling?'

'Was I?'

'I'm amusing to you? Or my inability is?'

'Not at all. If I was smiling, then it was involuntary.'

'So you may have been smiling after all?'

'At your achievement,' he said. 'To hear you conquer the text.'

'Oh, Dido! I wish we could be done with her.'

'She fascinates me, though.'

His craggy face, which put me in mind of his Northumberland provenance, lightened. His I found a stilted, rather saturnine kind of levity – as if the features of his face were a little too stiff for ready smiles, even at *my* expense.

'Because she's weak?' I said.

'Not at all. Quite the reverse. All that guilt she has.'

'Doesn't a clergyman-to-be regard guilt as a failing?'

'It can be an inspiration too.'

'Isn't Dido mad? "*I rave, I rave!*"'

'She sees that everything will be a falling away, inevitably. So she consecrates herself to a greater cause – the happiness she knew with Aeneas – she refuses to let *that* die.'

'But she has to die herself.'

'A minor detail.'

'Throwing herself on to a pyre?'

He was smiling again.

'You care for empresses and queens?' I asked him.

'No. For tragic heroines.'

'Why them?'

'Suffering and courageous women who deserve their own immortality.'

We were all talking about the beauty of music. Mozart, Bach. And Purcell, who was their favourite.

Moses said, 'It's *almost* perfect.'

'You could write better?' W'm ribbed him.

'I mean . . . It intimates the perfect, the ideal. It takes us to just a hair's breadth away.'

At that Sheba groaned and W'm winked at Mouse. But I found myself listening more attentively.

'It's never absolutely perfect,' Moses continued. 'Because then we would have heard everything. The apotheosis.'

'Heaven on earth?' Sheba said.

'That's impossible.'

'"*The music of the morning stars* –"' Mouse sang the words softly. '"– *Here in their hearts did sound.*"'

'The utterly sublime is impossible,' Moses said. 'Until we reach the Godhead. Only God, and our absorption, is immaculately perfect.'

General hilarity. Moses caught me sober-faced, and because I didn't want him beholden to me I smiled quickly, then widened the smile unapologetically.

———

I had a way with the reels, particularly when I was dancing with W'm.

He would often choose me in preference to the other candidates in a crowded room. I guessed they were just as worthy, and I sensed his mother's impatience sometimes, that he ignored the choice she was making with a discreetly indicating closed fan.

Handsome, lively W'm – how could he not inspire me to my best?

My feet would turn the nimblest little skip-step of them all.

In the dance I felt impossibly light. Cotillion or quadrille or double-time galop. I had air beneath my feet.

The Chadwycks had friends who had ballrooms in their homes. And public spaces that linked together, a succession of galleries allowing you to admire the company and price it. Outside, there might be a knot-garden or a temple.

Those friends would have a farm to supply them with milk and whey and cheese; they reared and killed and cured their own meat. Provisions would be sent up to London, to their residence there.

Those friends had friends who had a ballroom in each or all of their homes, who could make a party last across several counties, when a moon was clear to journey by. Their farms vied with one another to supply the best foods; every farm was separated from the next by a forest. So vast were the estates, I heard, that they contained space to erect alternative fantasy worlds: a jousting field, a galleon (or two) on a lake, a private version of old Rome, or St Petersburg, or Nile Egypt, to whatever scale the owners' ingenuity and means could take it.

The thoughtless day, the easy night,
The spirits pure, the slumbers light,
That fly th' approach of morn.

I accompany them across the fields to the chapel. The mist is still lifting. Further off it hangs like tattered banners, like dreams of glory fading. The cattle are like the ghosts of cattle. The grass is silvered with dew.

We follow a path of dried, hard mud. Sheba walks, as always, with an exquisite grace I cannot match; she is an example to us all.

The church bells carry, a soft peal. I hear them inviting us, not admonishing us.

'I think', Moses said one Sunday, walking closer beside me on our return, 'everyone is two individuals.'

'Ah.'

'There's the person here and now, the local person. And there's the self that watches, from outside, looking down. The transcendental person.'

Why was he telling me this? Was Moses quite right in the head?

'The local person works towards the other.'

'"The other"?'

'Towards conscience, I believe.'

I smiled, vaguely. Was there anything else I could do?

'We're lagging behind,' I said, nodding to the others ahead.

'Are we?'

I moved away from him, and without looking round I started running to catch up.

I realised it had been a ruse of sorts. The beasts of the field – *that* field – didn't appreciate it was a Sunday, and Moses had wanted me not to notice they were at their rutting. A transcendental topic, and all to preserve my maidenly modesty.

NINE

Five miles away from home, I could start to smell the marshes. Mud, weed, iodine, salt. Sour and nippy. Watery, then vegetal. I was being sucked back to the place.

The mudbanks. The drowned fields of spargrass. The fast secret tides running beneath the old slow river-water on top. The calls of the godwits and plovers, 'tu-li', 'wicka-wicka', the different cries, of the birds flying free and those caught in snares.

Chimes blown from church towers further down the estuary. The hellish shudder of a frigate being unmasted at the dockyards. The sombre boom of cannon fire from the hulks sited downstream.

Was I returning to the spot? Or was it reaching out its tentacles on the salty breezes to envelop me?

'So, the reek of hops is not to your fancy, Miss Havisham?'

My father said it with a smile. But the smile, lopsided, was pulled back over a top incisor, so I knew to be careful.

'It is a strong odour,' I told him.

'Hops are a serious business.'

'But the smell gets everywhere.'

'Surely that is a small inconvenience to you. Given the benefits they bring this residence of ours.'

He waved his hand to indicate the many silent rooms of Satis

House. The volume and shadowy grandeur of our surroundings, as he believed.

Even with the temporary absence of Arthur, Satis House wasn't Durley Chase, though. My father seemed to see what I was thinking.

'Hops have fed and clothed you these seventeen years.'

I turned my head, glanced away into a corner, fixed on a little framed view of a people-less street in some trim unvisited town.

I could hear my father catch his breath.

'The Havisham name isn't good enough for you, is that it?'

Why was he so irritable, unless he was also trying to justify his life to himself? Had I touched a bared nerve?

'What would you be known as?'

'The Havisham name suits me very well,' I heard myself telling him.

I was acquiring the honed vowels and clipped delivery which he did not have; I could be brittle and sharp and speak as if the remark was only an aside. It kept the colour from rising to my face. I was a little in awe of my own composure.

And so, I realised, was my father. But he had cause for satisfaction too, of an ambivalent sort, because this was what he was paying good money for, to raise me from hops, in elegant company.

———

The carriage bowled out of Durley village, and when we'd swung round the last corner the water-meads came into view. The purple haze of the wych elms; the blue flash of a kingfisher's wings; the statuesque *rightness* of the milch cows in that green place chomping on the rich flood-grass.

'*Un gentilhomme*,' Lady Chadwyck said of my father, after enquiring of his health.

She fluttered some pastry crumbs from her fingers. The tea party was in my honour, to welcome me back.

I smiled politely, but sat straighter in my chair, bearing my grandmother in mind, not wanting to let any of them suppose I was a complete ingenue.

Lady Chadwyck had had me sit beside her. She had invited neighbours, in the men's absence, and was in a mood for gaiety. Her face shone. She had that girlish, slightly simpering sort of prettiness which has a degree of pathos to it, because it comes dangerously close to being comic.

I had previously observed a girlish enthusiasm also; she would decide on a course of action in a moment, rising quite suddenly from her chair, dragooning us into a party to go off to . . . The obverse was – something she preferred us not to see – an equally impromptu retreat from high spirits, which her children were used to; this torpor confined her to her own quarters and left her merely watching us from a window.

All was well today, however.

'And now we have you back with us, Catherine!'

There was a new mint silver service, reflecting us where we sat in our chairs. The silver gleamed, and all the more so against the fine but sun-faded furniture, the once expensive but threadbare rugs.

'I am very glad to *be* back,' I told her, in all honesty.

Glad and relieved.

———

I had brought my box of books back with me, and my sketching pads which I'd been working on in the Cherry Garden at home, and my dancing pumps, in which I'd been practising in my bedroom above my father's office, and half a dozen new dresses. And two hatboxes.

They were the tools, the *emblems*, of an education, although

I couldn't yet judge for what end – other than a veneer of accomplishment – I was being prepared.

———

We dressed three times a day. For morning; for riding; and for dinner.

In the mornings, where I used to have cotton or linen for my gowns, my negligees now were tabby, dimity, Canterbury muslin. Away from Durley, our promenades called for pattens and parasols, a new Camperdown bonnet.

For riding, to match the others, a habit of pompadour broadcloth (a shameless guinea per yard); white dimity waistcoat (with lapels, like the habit); a habit skirt of long lawn; habit gloves; a hat with a trailing feather. I acquired a vast greatcoat, and knotted a white handkerchief round my throat. We resembled strolling Gypsies.

In the evenings, after most of an hour's dishbill (Sheba's favourite neologism from *Fanny Burney*), we emerged like butterflies from our chrysalides. A clouded French satin gown, or rich-toned taffety. An otter-fur tippet for walking out, and a brown silk pelisse, which was the newest thing in greatcoats.

Is it me, that person?

My father dutifully settled all accounts. (£7 4s 0d for a riding habit? Very well.) He didn't demur whenever I felt I had to be in a smarter fashion, because we would be bound to meet even more exalted types soon: that black beaver hat with purple cockade and band. And I had been given the name of a simply divine mantuamaker, a Miss Williams of Tonbridge; everyone – absolutely everyone – swore by her.

———

I'm not beautiful, not by a long chalk.

I'm not plain either.

My appearance is . . . distinctive. People suppose they can read my character from it.

My eyelids are the heavy Arab sort, and that makes my hazel eyes seem secretive, and possibly supercilious.

My mouth is straight, and is judged to indicate personal severity.

My nose is Roman, but that is *not* a hook.

I have clear facial bones, and a tidy oval chin.

My face is narrow; so is my forehead, but I also have a high brow, so I'm said to have more intelligence than I care to admit to. (I don't quibble with that, although I wish it were true.)

But I'm not just a face, or a body. I'm a Havisham. My appearance is wrapped around with an aura of wealth (provincial, not metropolitan; but money is money) and high living (vulgar rather than sophisticated; but time, between one generation and the next, is the best civiliser).

I don't *need* to be a beauty. Yet no one, except some person ignorant of my name, would consider me less than handsome.

———

W'm and Moses returned at the term's end.

Other than my father, I had never been as close physically to a man as I found I now was to W'm.

At his own instigation, I felt sure.

Sharing the table in the small study where I did my preparations and he his. Seated next to him at the dining table. Passing him in the corridors. Having my hand taken by him on the inclines of lawn, or at a stile. Letting him place my walking cloak around my shoulders.

Whenever Moses stepped in to do any of these things, it wasn't the same. He was self-conscious where W'm seemed natural and unaffected. I felt that Moses was looking at me every time so that I would register my approval of the deed; which was the reason for my feigning inadvertence.

I asked W'm questions about my schoolroom work. I asked him to explain, several times, Plato's theory of the 'idea' of things: a reality that doesn't alter despite the changing appearance, which – beyond mere sensations' reach – reason alone proves.

All the while I feasted my eyes on him: his sweep of fair hair, and white teeth, and golden eyes, and Greek profile.

I remembered to nod my head, as if I were really capable of understanding.

Moses would tell W'm to slow down a bit, to explain more clearly, and I was irritated. It was as if he assumed I was too stupid. But he had also seen that I truly made very little sense of it all. What right did he think he had to expose me like this?

I ignored Moses as much as I could, and gave my attention – I made a show of giving my attention – to W'm. But W'm wasn't always aware of it, and that was my true vexation.

They had two passions: performing *tableaux vivants* and attending masquerades. They read up about masques in the newspapers. Sheba kept illustrations: the Duchess of Bolton in a man's domino, and then wearing the costume she'd had on underneath, 'the most brilliant Sultana that ever was seen, covered with pearls and diamonds'.

Lady Chadwyck had opened an account at Jackson's Habit-Warehouse in Covent Garden, so I knew that it was a serious pursuit. For the first masque we went as 'Bohemians & Tziganes', in brown stuff jackets and blue stuff petticoats, with straw hats fastened beneath the chin; and red cloaks, in silk instead of rustic wool. Sheba had equipped herself with a crook and live lambs. Our hostess was in peasant wear, as she understood it; a fine pink-and-white dress in her wardrobe had been cut down, but it was judged a sacrifice worth making.

The theme of the second *bal masqué* was 'Van Dyck'. We didn't have time to seek novel inspiration in the paintings, but had to take what was left in stock that was ruffed and lacy. Once we were decked out, as Charles I or Henrietta Maria or Stuart notables, we had to try to appear – aided or hindered by a hired monkey or spaniel or greyhound – as if we had just walked out of our frames.

Dressing up and acting out was one aspect of my Durley life – the theatrical one. The other was the academic: studying my text books, completing exercises, memorising high-minded and high-flown verse. Somewhere between was the business of singing, playing the keyboard, and drawing and painting: all of which, it seemed to me, involved not just *doing* the task in hand but taking up such a pose and attitude that it was incontrovertibly clear that that was what you were about – delivering a Purcell song with an Amazonian bearing, using the arms like pistons while playing my keyboard preludes and sonatas, musing with crayon or camelhair brush held hovering over the drawing pad or easel.

We learned to be nymphs and goddesses, Gothic abbesses and devout pilgrims, Persian empresses and desert potentates. We plundered the legends of Greece and Rome.

When we went to *bals masqués*, we also had to unmask, at one certain point in the proceedings. Then we were ourselves again: but not entirely so. It was stranger than the masks, seeing familiar faces in unfamiliar guises, aspiring to be somehow larger than life, with grander emotions to dispose of.

I was still being paired with W'm: on walks or at meals, over cards or playing music or at the dance. I wasn't sure how to deal with him.

There was the matter of our proximity; he was taller than my father or Arthur, taller than Moses, with an actor's archetypal good looks, and an actor's way of both positioning himself in profile and – in company – declaiming rather than speaking, yet doing neither with any hint of awkwardness.

More than this physical closeness, though, I felt uncertain about his way of thinking. He didn't seem aware of things like the weather, or atmospherics, as I and his sisters were, which made me think *our* concerns must be trivial in comparison. His had a broader sweep – classical history, his colleagues' reputations (or lack thereof), politics, the cost of property, philosophy, ketching, the price of a Smollett translation of *Don Quixote* he'd seen for sale in Cambridge market.

He never put me down. He assumed that my learning would cease once I was married, but in the meantime he knew not to discourage me. He wasn't adversely critical, as I felt Moses was, and he left me to get on with my own studies; it didn't occur to him that I might need the sort of help which Moses, in his clumsy way, offered me.

The trick was to shift my eyes away before he could catch me looking at him, which was difficult.

If we danced together, I held a fan or handkerchief to my chest, so that he shouldn't see the colour he brought to the surface.

I hadn't come across anyone who comported himself *de profil* like that, and who simultaneously scanned a room so exhaustively. I thought that it must be done for effect – until I discovered, firstly that he was quite short-sighted but wouldn't consider spectacles or a lens, and subsequently that it galled him if he failed to acknowledge someone whom his mother had warned him deserved to be recognised.

———

If we were ever *alone* together, I immediately sensed his unease.

It was a simple matter of etiquette, of course. But without others around us, it was as if he started to lose his nerve.

At breakfast. In the book-lined passageway that constituted the house's library. Or in the summerhouse.

'Oh, Miss Havisham . . .' (No conversable, free-and-easy 'Catherine' now.) '. . . have I disturbed you? If I'm disturbing you . . .'

'Not at all,' I would say.

In extremis he made an immediate getaway. 'Actually, I've just remembered . . . you must excuse me if I . . .'

And then he was gone.

Sheba and Mouse were loyal admirers. 'You *do* like him, Catherine?' they were eager to know.

'Oh yes.'

'Not as much as *we* do, of course!'

'But almost,' I said.

'Really?'

'Really.'

'We've noticed, naturally. We've been watching.'

'Oh.'

'And he likes *you*.'

'Yes?'

'Very much. We're both quite sure of that.'

———

I could tell my father was impressed by my progress. I had snatches of Italian and (less confidently) German to complement my French. I could quote lines from Horace and Sallust. Even when he couldn't understand, he was very taken by the sounds, by the false conviction of my delivery. He could already put a value on returns from his investment.

'Another six months and you'll be up to the best hereabouts. The best, and no mistaking.'

Satis House smelt old and stale to me, as if history had been stacked up in the rooms behind the closed doors. At Durley Chase sunlight swilled about the rooms, and they sweetly smelt of beeswax polish and the scented bulbs and flowers distributed in bowls. My home oppressed me with its sombre fumed-oak panelling and the shadows of the glass-leading on the windows which barred and squared the dark uneven floors.

Arthur would brush against me, shoulder against shoulder, and push ahead of me leaving a room. It exasperated me.

'What do they teach you at that school of yours?'

'Not to go about with our noses stuck up in the air.'

'Not good manners, anyhow.'

'*You* know all about those, do you? Living with that rout.'

'Don't call them that.'

'I don't know why you bother yourself with them.'

Because I have a brother like you. Because he says things like that. Because he's not able to work it out for himself.

'Well . . . ?'

'It doesn't matter.'

'It matters, or you wouldn't go chasing after them like you do.'

'It doesn't matter, about having to explain anything to *you*.'

'Because you can't.'

'Because I'm tired of listening to you.'

'Can't you move all your stuff there?'

'And leave you with the run of this place? That's what you want, of course.'

'What do *you* know about what I want?'

'Precious little. Or care to.'

———

I gave Sally some of the clothes I no longer wore. They had to be lengthened a little; but since she was thinner in proportion to her height than I was, they didn't need taking out. The fashions had dated slightly, but Sally wore them with such panache that it didn't matter.

'They might have been made for you.'

'I suppose they were. Now that I'm wearing them!'

She had a natural grace, which I envied, because I'd had to concentrate on choreographing my movements with the Chadwycks'; I worked hard to look so languorous. Sally was unaffected and simple, and never gauche. How was it done? I could have taken her into, say, an Assembly Room and passed her off as my cousin – my red-haired cousin – and no one would have suspected. I suggested it once or twice, but Sally declined, politely but quite firmly.

'Then what use will the dresses be?' I asked her.

'I do wear them. I promise you.'

'*When?* Tell me.'

She didn't say.

'You *don't* wear them,' I teased her.

'I do.'

'Promise me.'

'I promise.'

'When, then?'

'When I wish to do my passable imitation of Miss Catherine Havisham.'

'I haven't seen that.'

'No, of course not. We never recognise ourselves.'

We ended up laughing.

'This is silliness, Sally.'

'*You* started it.'

I reached out for her wrists. As I held them, her arms stiffened.

'But you'll take more dresses?'

'Any dress you want to give me.'

'Let me think.'

I continued to hold her wrists. She smiled again, but over her shoulder at the window, out into the yard. My captive.

TEN

The Cam River had frozen over.

The life beneath was trapped under frosted glass: a wintry half-life. Slow-motion fish and the solidified tendrils of riverweed. A pike, caught by its iced tail, fitfully thrashing; other pike gnawing at it.

A punt was boxed in beside a wall. The funnel of a green bottle stood upright, in magical suspension.

———

We sat on by the fire. The men talked. Or rather, they *debated*, symposium fashion.

On one side, by the fire-irons, W'm was arguing for rational, scientific thought: pure reason, the Greeks' crystalline *dianoia*. Everything in the universe could be explained.

'Except people's behaviour,' another student said.

'That too. Cause and effect.'

Moses, perched on the fender, was warming to the subject. He took the opposite tack, claiming that the world was quite unreasonable. Think of what lies beyond where the stars end; *do* they end? (I felt light-headed suddenly, just trying to imagine.) Life is an enigma. We have to approach it not scientifically but poetically.

'Piffle!' W'm said.

'Why have we been given souls? To elevate us above substance.'

I sat between the two of them. I inclined first one way and then the other, and back again. To and fro.

Outside, dusk drew on. A red blush rose in the sky, outlining towers and spires and cupolas. A red glow fell on to one wall of the room, and we all seemed to turn instinctively towards it.

'There's a perfectly cogent explanation', W'm said, 'for what we see.'

'We're not looking to understand *why*,' Moses responded. 'We're thinking of God. Or of a memory of some other time, a place. Or it's like life before we were born; swimming in the womb.'

W'm shook his head.

'Light and how it falls is a sequence of connected circumstances. Nothing more.'

'There's always something behind what we see,' retorted Moses. 'An image. A renaissance, or an ideal. Reality has a fourth dimension.'

W'm tapped his head. Sheba, who had said little, gave vent to some good-humoured laughter. Mouse sighed at the conundrum.

And for myself, I jumped when a coal in the hearth split, and sparks went whistling up the chimney into the dark.

Wine, heated and honeyed, was served to us from a silver chafing-dish embossed with the college's coat of arms.

Sitting there I had a sense of completeness, even though the argument hadn't been won by either party. There was a fitness, an appropriateness, about everything: whether conspiring to this end, or accidentally achieved. I felt I belonged here, in this set of rooms at the top of a flight of old worn wooden stairs, with these people, on this particular evening with the redness in the sky flaring to indigo and the sweet marsala wine in my old fluted glass sparkling against the firelight.

A door was unlocked, a bolt drawn back, and then we were admitted to a long colonnaded gallery furnished with stone heads, torsos, dislodged limbs. There were several dozen fragments of Greek and Roman statues, each of them many times larger than life. Our footsteps echoed in the skylit gloom – as did our exclamations of astonishment.

Muscular shoulders. The spine's runnel on a goddess's back. Smooth buttocks, inviting a hand's touch. Assorted *parties intimes*, with or without sculpted vegetation for cover.

I didn't want to catch anyone's eye, so I stood behind the others to glean their reactions. Mouse contriving to be studious; Sheba, slowing by the goddesses and naiads to take note of the classical dimensions of beauty; W'm, with a reminiscent air, fascinated by first a hand and then a foot; and Moses, poor Moses, so horribly embarrassed, and making one believe – because he looked the opposite way – that the intimate parts on display were far below his high-minded regard.

It was Moses who later rounded up the other four of us and our two companions, older women friends of Sheba, and urged us to leave.

'Aren't you cold? I feel I'm turning to marble myself –'

I waited a while longer, to prove that I wouldn't be rushed, but I felt my eyes were out of my control, either swivelling about or waterily staring.

It *was* cold in here. More than that, though, it was airless, quite airless. I fanned myself with a pamphlet, as I might have done in the heat of high summer, and when I became a little dizzy I had to lean against a pillar. I closed my eyes. I felt a strong grip on my arm, my elbow, someone was holding me up. My eyes, still closed, saw W'm's face, but when I opened them he was at the door, and protecting me was Moses. I took back my arm.

'Thank you. I – I'll be fine.'

That long face of angles, with all its sensibleness intact, the redoubtable decency.

I hurried away. I didn't know why he had this effect on me, or why I was making so light of his kindness, even punishing him for it.

ELEVEN

Lady Elizabeth Gray was a favourite subject for tableaux. We took our inspiration from a couple of engravings. Valentine Green's for 'Lady Elizabeth Gray at the Feet of Edward the Fourth, Soliciting the Restoration of her late Husband's forfeited lands, 1465'. John Downman's later work caused us to enact 'Edward the Fourth on a visit to the Duchess of Bedford is Enamoured of Lady Elizabeth Gray'.

We portrayed the death of Lady Jane Grey, as Green devised it in our essential text, *Acta Historica Reginarum Anglia*. There was the Marriage of King Henry VIII with Ann Bullen. And – marking my preferment to the centre of stage, where I had expected to be a grieving lady-in-waiting – Mary Queen of Scots, about to be executed.

Look at me!

I'm dressed in black satin and velvet, with a high white ruff. I wear two crucifixes and a rosary. I have walked, quite composed, into the great hall of Fotheringhay Castle. I have instructed my trusty servant, Melville, to take word to my son James, the King of Scotland, that I have always sought the unification of the two kingdoms, Scotland and England. I have listened as the execution warrant was read aloud to me, telling me I am about to be put to death like some ordinary felon. I have prayed in a voice that might carry to the nearly two hundred spectators gathered here, for blessings on the English Church, for my son James and for the agent of my

75

doom, Elizabeth of England. I have given solace to my sorrowing attendants, I have – strangely – spoken with no little wit to the men who will put me to death, my killers. I have stretched out on the floor and laid my neck on the block, placing myself in the hands of God. My ladies weep. The axe is raised. I am on the point of speaking those words which will be my last. 'Sweet Jesus.' Secreted beneath my gown but visible is the little Skye terrier, true now as ever to his mistress, offering me my final comfort.

The tableau has been given the motto Mary embroidered herself on her cloth of state, which is placed beside the block. 'In my end is my beginning.'

Look at me!

Awaiting the death blow.

I have laid my head sideways, so that the audience can see my face and I can see theirs. Just out of my sight – I'm thankful about it – is the executioner's blade, which has to be held quite still for the two minutes it takes as the commentary is delivered from the side of the stage.

Only the wee terrier moves, but even he might be conscious of the solemnity of the grand event being depicted.

Some in the audience take handkerchiefs to their eyes. There's a good deal of troubled wriggling in chairs. I feel chastened myself, and sad.

But this is Catherine Havisham's dignification, even though I'm wearing a red wig – hair as red as Sally's – and have my face heavily powdered. (There's a little drift of the stuff on the block, on the black velvet of my gown.)

I feel I'm at the centre of everyone's attention: or at any rate, the figure I represent is the focus of every pair of eyes in the room (the dog's apart). I shall never feel more essential to the Chadwycks and their friends and their friends' friends than I do at this supreme moment – actually two, extending to nearly three minutes – until the blade starts to wobble, and the dog (snuffling) wanders off, and the most pious in the audience need to excuse themselves for air, and one of my genteel ladies threatens to faint, and the dog barks.

Curtains are drawn across our stage. The actors all relax, and make for the side tormentors. For some reason no one thinks of assisting me to my feet. But what of it, I am only a pretend queen, and a queen done to death, as if the ritual of human sacrifice was still being practised in the year of grace, *anno domini* 1587.

———

We were also attending Assemblies, in the towns of fashion in the South. We accompanied Lady Charlotte to Cheltenham. And thence to Bath, where we bathed with her in our caps and shifts. There too we were drawn to the lights and music, like moths.

A personable stranger's face meeting mine. The same pair of hands crossing with mine several dances apart, then for a couple in succession.

'You don't recall?'

'"Recall" . . . Should I?'

'The theatricals. At Chartridge. I saw your Mary Stuart. Splendid. I shed a tear or two.'

I was carrying my fan and a woollen shawl Mouse had lent me, since she knew about the Bath draughts.

In my embarrassment I let go of the fan. My interlocutor picked it up for me.

'A famous trick, that one.'

'I beg your pardon?'

'A lady dropping her fan.'

He laughed. I was puzzling how to respond when I felt a hand on the small of my back and I was very swiftly propelled from the spot. I hadn't time to do more than look over my shoulder, not even apologetically.

'It was someone who . . .'

'What, Catherine? Did I interrupt you?'

Sheba turned and looked back, in the wrong direction.

'No,' I said. 'Over there.'

But he had gone: and perhaps – quite possibly – Sheba hadn't even meant to look towards where he had been standing.

———

We repeated our success with the Queen of Scots. As I lay with my head on the block, I could see him. My fan-recoverer. I hadn't meant to notice anyone, but . . .

He was in one of the front seats, not at all secretive about his presence. I tried not to notice him after that. I concentrated on Mary instead, on her struggle to see nothing of what was happening to her, not to feel, not to think back or to think forward either, in case she screamed out with terror, but to give up her Catholic soul gladly to her Maker.

He found me.

He left the people he was talking to. Someone called after him, 'Mr Compeyson!', but he ignored the request. He congratulated me. The voices were so loud, he had to lean closer.

'Didn't they let you go on wearing your show-clothes, your friends?'

'Our costumes?'

'Not that I'm objecting to what you've got on, you understand. You could teach most of them here a thing or two.'

'I think not.'

'I beg to differ. Why so little confidence, Miss Havisham?'

'You know my name?'

He held out his programme. He had marked a red cross against my name.

Lady Charlotte was approaching, and I backed away from him. She was raising her glass to her eye. I swept past him, muttering an apology. I fixed my gaze on Lady Charlotte, and smiled boldly, feeling . . . feeling that an aviary of tiny panicking birds was suddenly let loose inside my head.

———

'It's always been understood,' Mouse said, 'that's all. We've always known.'

'And W'm knows too?'

'Yes. He will make a good match, and assure the future of Durley.'

Why was I being told this?

'When?' I asked.

'When he finds whoever she is.'

Mouse smiled, looking out the window, across the small park to where our neighbours' began.

Why did she smile?

'"She"?'

'The one who's destined to be the mistress of the Chase one day.'

I waited.

What else was I supposed to think? W'm was honour bound to act, wasn't he? But I was aware that now there often wasn't a vacant seat next to mine which he could fill. Or a fourth was required for cards at the next table, and would I *or* W'm care to oblige?

He had caught a cold somewhere, and wasn't able to sing, although I didn't see why that should prevent him from turning my pages as I played the Broadwood. He was lent some gun dogs, and when we all went walking it was necessary for him to keep them in order, going off to whistle after them. Even in the dining room: Lady Chadwyck had had draughts on the brain since Bath, and her son exchanged places with her, while experiments continued with rolled sausages of felt under the doors and putty in the window frames. All, so far as I could tell, quite legitimate, but no less frustrating, because no apology was ever offered to me.

My mind wandered off. I found myself thinking of someone else: the stranger. The mysterious Mr Compeyson. (Christian name unknown.)

His ready attention. His unsubscribing spirit as he'd mocked our dancing partners with his eyes. His amusing contrariness as he exchanged politesse with people he knew no better than I but pretended he did.

The sense that we were engaged, just briefly, in some mutual conspiracy.

The way his voice had dropped, warmly, into my ear.

The aviary birds inside my head, and the muffled commotion he'd set up in the pit of my stomach, another little whorl of excitation.

———

I had to lay the canvas on my lap, set out my colours on the little folding table, and paint the view.

'Paint what is *there*,' Signor Scarpelli had instructed me. 'Only what you see.'

What I saw, was that what was present? How similar was it to what Sheba saw, or Mouse?

Signor Scarpelli had demonstrated the grid; the boxes; he had told us about meet proportions, about 'pair-spect-eev'. But it didn't make the job of representing, of turning a presence into its image, any easier.

TWELVE

I pulled my skirts in as I passed Arthur. I could smell the drink on his breath again.

'What? I offend you, do I?'

I didn't reply.

'You're too grand now to speak? And I'm not worth an answer?'

He grabbed my arm.

'Sister Catherine –'

'Let go of me!'

He was tall, nearly six feet already, but he didn't have the strength of mind to resist me. I shook him off.

A sum of money was missing from my father's quarters. He summoned the staff, one by one. They left the room looking more shocked by the questioning than indignant, as I felt they had a right to be.

'It was bound to happen,' I told my father.

'Why so?'

'It's not something that's ever happened before.'

'Exactly. What's changed, then?'

Then we didn't have Arthur living under the same roof as ourselves. I didn't need to say it. My father's eyelids dropped with the realisation, he made a little funnel for air with his mouth.

Arthur seemed to have no compunction about helping himself. He ordered clothes without telling my father, but expected him to pay for them. He took my father's horse one evening when we had guests to dine in the house. At three o'clock one morning he was found feeding his friends from the larder. He was revenging himself for the obscurity he'd had to suffer while living with his mother.

Other thefts were taking place, from coffers and sideboard drawers and the backs of presses, and we only discovered because a colleague of my father came across for sale in Canterbury a small silver dish engraved with a style of 'H' he recognised. I didn't know how many addictions he was having to finance: tobacco (his fingers were yellowing at the tips), snuff (his nostrils had a raw red look), wine (he only drank vintage Bordeaux). A pokerwork box containing ivory dice and several decks of playing cards was missing, a minor loss, but I thought it significant. He goaded the guard dogs, and I wondered if that was because he watched dogs turned against each other for amusement.

A curfew was set.

'In my own home?' Arthur objected. 'That's ridiculous.'

'You've got an answer for everything,' my father said.

'And if I forget?'

'I shall regard forgetfulness as disobedience.'

Arthur's response was to emit through his teeth a long, dying whistle.

Bolts were attached to the doors, to enforce the rules. Arthur tried climbing in through the windows, until the shutters were fastened by bars. He attempted to bribe the more gullible of the housemaids to let him in, but on the second occasion he was sick in the hall before falling heavily on the staircase; he was too drunk to get up, and my father found him there in the morning, in a sot's thick sleep.

'Say something to him, sister.'

'Say what to whom?'

'"Oh father of ours, forgive Arthur. It's just high spirits. Don't keep him short."'

'I'll do no such thing.'

'No, I didn't think you would. Selfish bitch.'

'You disgust me.'

'Always taking his side. What else should I expect?'

'Don't blame *me*.'

'Dead against me, aren't you?'

'You're an enemy to yourself. No one could do it better.'

'*You* told him. "No more cash." It was *you*.'

'My father can make his own mind up.'

'Whisper-whisper in his ear.'

'You're revolting.'

'You've put him up to this.'

'I don't know what you're –'

'"Make Arthur a pauper." As if I don't deserve the ready. Every bloody farthing.'

'You're a savage.'

'And you're a liar. A creeping Judas.'

'I'm a Havisham.'

'But so am I.'

'How do I know that?'

His face darkened. His features set to the hardness of mica.

'Well, I don't, do I?' I looked away. 'Your father could be any Tom, Dick or –'

I didn't see until it was too late, his hand taking aim, then swinging out at me.

Where did that strength come from?

He caught me full across the face. I felt – I distinctly felt – the sharp edge of his signet ring, tearing my skin. The stinging pain.

I doubled over with the hurt. A gash on my cheek was oozing sticky blood.

White flares dropped in front of my eyes; the floor ran away from me. I thought I was on the point of passing out. I closed my eyes and concentrated on not fainting, not fainting.

I was left slumped over the banister. I had a presentiment he was gone, and wouldn't be back for a while.

When I'd found a mirror I saw my face burning red, I had a cut on my cheek, and the first bruises were already spreading.

———

My father had the brutal evidence in front of him.

'This is your brother's doing?'

'Not my brother,' I told him.

My mouth was swollen. I had to slowly shape words to come out, woolly approximations to words.

But I didn't need to tell him, anyway, that a real brother would not have done such a thing.

I had to wait until my face started to heal before I could leave.

My father had collected an inventory of complaints. I anticipated the trouble there would be once I was safely away.

Sally comforted me. She listened to my tales about Arthur, and didn't defend him; she was careful about criticising him directly, out of her own mouth, as if she felt she might be speaking out of turn. She sat with me in the garden. I described goings-on at Durley Chase, and I regaled her with it all. The tableaux, the masques. The sights of Bath and Cheltenham. W'm's mysterious preoccupations. My encounters with the stranger, Mr Compeyson.

'He sounds quite a familiar stranger.'

'It's a small world,' I said.

'Of course it is!'

I laughed with her, and even though it hurt my face, I couldn't stop laughing.

———

My carriage bowled out of Durley Tye. When we'd swung round the last corner, the water-meads came into view. I was never so relieved to see them.

The thirsty willows, the cattle wading to their knees in the flood-grass, the sheep idly grazing on the drier pasture beyond.

And drowsy tinklings lull the distant folds.

Another theatrical evening.

We were rehearsing our contribution, a *tableau vivant* of 'The Flight of the Duke of Northumberland, on the Entrance in Triumph of Queen Mary to London'.

The house was called Wix Grange. The owners were called Merriweather.

In an interlude I walked off to clear my head. I found myself in a walled garden, then in a second.

Suddenly – urgent footsteps, scattering gravel. Rounding a corner, W'm appeared. His face lit up when he saw me.

'The very person!'

He accompanied me, at a more seemly pace, to a temple standing by a pool. Or so I thought it was, until we came closer, and I realised it was only a windowless facade. On a pediment, in freshly gilded lettering, the name THESPIS. Twilight was falling on us.

We seated ourselves in the little temple, on a scroll-ended stone bench. As we sat there, bats we had disturbed flitted in and out above our heads, scratching about in the rafters. Swifts came darting low to drink at the pool, taking up water as they dipped, setting off tiny ripples on the dark surface of water, a hypnotic pattern of circles.

And all the air a solemn stillness holds.

The air itself smelt of lilac and magnolia, thickly sweet, and of sharper-tanged rosemary from the walkways where an occasional rabbit frisked along the brickwork. Rosemary for rue.

The temple was a folly. Somehow I forgot that it wasn't genuine, and it was a fact easily overlooked in the welter of other sensations.

> We are led to Believe a Lie
> When we see not Thro' the Eye,
> Which was Born in a Night to perish in a Night.

What did we talk about, sitting there? Trivia maybe. I only remember that I was trying to read a different meaning into everything W'm said, which became the primary meaning.

How long did we talk for? A quarter-hour? Or was it half an hour?

I recall a man's figure twice, three times appearing in the outer garden, visible through an archway. He stopped to watch us. The third time he was there W'm drew closer to me, pointed to the closing eyes of the water lilies in the pool, and I thought it must be to distract me from the silver-haired observer in the dusk, to exclude him from this intimate ambience – scented by the shrubs, with its inaudible serenading of bats, written to the frantic crotchet runs of the swifts flashing past in the inky air.

I was chattering. I asked him, did he agree with Aaron Hill? In his book.

Agree about what?

Well, about there being – how many was it? – ten emotions to play out on the stage. Ten humours. I tried to remember what they were.

Joy. Sorrow. Anger. Envy. Love. Hate.

W'm didn't make any suggestions for the list. Four remained. I thought at first that he couldn't have been listening. But surely not. He came close enough for me to feel the heat of his breath. And then to catch traces of his perspiration: a dark musky fragrance, which had the effect of deliciously knotting my stomach.

We were still being watched. The man was dressed as David Garrick, after Gainsborough. I had seen him earlier, with a young woman in the guise of one of the painter's feathered and pearl-draped sitters; they had been laughing together in the comfortable way of people who haven't just newly met, who weren't aware that W'm was anxiously scrutinising them. (Could it have been to her that W'm had directed his letter, at the afternoon's end? I'd noticed him slip a sealed item of correspondence to a footman and tip the fellow a generous minding.)

I watched our watcher walking off. Diverted for those moments, I failed to register that W'm had lost whatever interest he'd had in talking to me. He jumped to his feet and told me, he must be off now. He didn't offer to walk me back to the house.

'Remember, half past eight.'

'Yes,' I said. 'I'm remembering.'

He didn't go out by the archway, which I supposed was the only egress. I heard a crackle of undergrowth, disappearing footsteps.

Making my own way back to the house, I felt a chill through my costume. From nowhere I had gained a companion. Moses. That absurd, juvenile name.

'Frederick –'

'Nobody calls me that, you know.'

'You frightened me. Why won't you announce yourself?'

I hadn't asked any such thing of W'm, but I wasn't comparing like with like.

'Are you feeling quite well?'

'Of course I am,' I said. 'Why shouldn't I be?'

'You look . . . downcast.'

'What?'

'Melancholic.'

'Why on earth –'

'A little pale. Don't be nervous.'

'What about?'

'The tableau.'

He offered me his arm, crooking it so that I might insert my own. I drew back.

His long face and outsized jaw. The large eyes, the bulbous nose. The hesitant and eternally patient smile.

'I can walk, thank you. I'm not as weak and vapid as you like to think I am.'

'I would never presume such a thing.'

'Someone else might require your propping up instead of me.'

He was mumbling, and I didn't catch all that he said. 'Moral support,' I heard. And '. . . no more than . . .'

He followed a few steps behind me, trailing me, a shadow to my shadow. The faster I walked, the faster he did. I dashed up the side steps, but somehow he reached the door before me, and was able to hold it open. I walked indoors, and felt the searing reprimand of my conscience – a necklace of hot coals round my neck – as I declined to offer him any thanks. I had tears in my eyes, and I didn't want him to see. Tears of frustration and disappointment, which blurred the interior of the green marble hall and transformed the staircase to a water cascade.

In the carriage at our departure Sheba was on the look-out for someone among the throng on the main steps of the house. She spotted the young woman who had earlier been the Gainsborough imitation, and she clasped Mouse's arm to have her look too. The sisters exchanged words out of the corners of their mouths.

Suddenly the woman turned to observe our carriage, as if she had known all along we were there, in the queue of transport waiting to leave. Her eyes had drawn me earlier as we passed in a corridor. They were half-closed, and yet I could have believed they were more alert than all the others, so wide and shiny and artificially sparkling, in the throng around us.

W'm was mounted immediately behind us. I couldn't see him, but I did notice a smile pass for the briefest instant across the woman's face as she turned away. The silver-haired man from the garden was descending the steps; clearly he considered himself the woman's proprietor as he alighted on her – as keenly, I felt sure, as any bird of prey on its quarry.

———

The look of love alarms
Because 'tis fill'd with fire;
But the look of soft deceit
Shall win the lover's hire.

———

I mentioned to W'm the Temple of Thespis three or four days later.

'Eh?' He gave me a charming, unremembering smile.

'By the pool,' I said. 'With the swifts.'

'Oh yes. Of course. The Temple. Of Thespis. Very good!' He laughed.

I couldn't break his spell, even if I were to try. His fall of fine hair. The firm, straight nose. The high cheekbones. The elegant, baroque mouth. Golden eyes. Couldn't those eyes see the truth in front of him – that I had been smitten from the moment of first seeing him? Nothing had changed. Yes, W'm played his little games, and he would carry on playing them. But I forgave him, as we all did. He allowed us no choice about that. Charmed by him, we could do nothing else.

THIRTEEN

Thereafter, we proceeded – advanced – to the Discourses.

W'm expressed his purpose: to unify Grecian grace and Etruscan simplicity.

Sheba stood on steps, right arm on her hip, to resemble a statue we knew from engravings, the Mattei Ceres in Rome; she wore a sea-green mantle, and in her left hand she held a blood-red rose.

I was Hebe, and a different challenge. I wasn't called upon to dance, but to stand – my torso slightly twisted – beside a plinth, one arm wrapped round a jar. A gold strophion plaited about my pink dress held my breasts high, in the antique way. My hair was piled and knotted, as the ancients would have appreciated.

I was the handmaiden of the gods, a creature of heavenly favour. I was about to pour out nectar from the vessel. I represented perpetual youth.

I tried to convey, as Milton had described, 'the Nods and Becks and wreath'd Smiles, such as hang on Hebe's cheek'.

Above me, supported from the side of the stage, was one vast, cleverly painted, outstretched wing of golden feathers: the wing of the mighty eagle which Jupiter had taken as his disguise. It overarched me, threatening to overwhelm and devour me – a menace every bit as much as a guard. But I continued to smile, not too broadly, to convey (so W'm had directed me) something of the unsuspecting, trustful joy of youth.

—

The others were with various of their friends, who had descended on them at the same juncture, which meant he could find me quite straightforwardly. I was aware of his approach. I busied myself with a pot of black and yellow tulips.

'Miss Havisham –'

'Mr Compeyson –'

He drew me into conversation. He was unsure about the legends; he confused them – or pretended to – and told me he'd had a misspent youth. But he spoke so well, so eloquently, and was so much the picture of a gentleman, and wouldn't say how he'd misspent his time, that I happily gave *that* admission – his purported admission – no credence at all.

He was good-looking, if in a more predictable way than W'm. Summer-blue eyes. A straight but short nose. Brown hair that curled. Top lip a little thinner than the lower one, which had a sensual amplitude, as if, I fancied whenever I took advantage of his distracted eyes to look at his mouth, head had been set against heart.

He set out to persuade me I should tell him about myself. He wanted to hear.

'What about?'

'Anything you like.'

'You're so eager to hear for some reason – I could tell you anything, and you'd believe me?'

'I'd believe Catherine Havisham.'

I fussed with the petals of some of the black tulips in the jardinière. He stroked the stem of a yellow.

'You wouldn't *know* if it was about me or not.'

'Who else *could* it be about?'

'Sally,' I said, and laughed.

'Who on earth's Sally?'

'She might be more interesting to hear about than me.'

'I think not.'

'You can't say most definitely. You'd need to contrast and compare.'

'Well, about this Sally first. And then, please, all about *you*.'

———

Sally. In my old loose chintz sack. In my blue satin pumps with the yellow bows. With my copy of *The Sorrows of Young Werther*, and a list of quotations from the text which she has copied out in the neat script which I taught her.

'I tell him about you, Sally.'

'About *me*? Gracious, what for?'

'He likes to hear.'

'But what d'you say to him? There's nothing *to* tell.'

It was an innocent enough pastime. I tried to draw him out, on the sort of looks he preferred.

'Sally has green eyes.'

'Nothing so nice as tawny.'

'Thick hair.'

'What colour?'

'Copper.'

'Fair for *me*. Like yours.'

'A long neck.'

'That's fine for swans.'

'Quite dainty feet, considering.'

'Tire too easily.'

'Well, you won't believe me. But she's a very attractive girl, I assure you.'

'Good for her, then.'

'She's wasted. She should be set up as – some merchandiser's wife. At least.'

'Maybe she will be.'

'She doesn't rate herself highly enough for that. She needs some-one to tell her.'

'And do *you?*'

'Oh no! I don't want her to go and desert me, do I now?'

I was avoiding Arthur, but he followed me into the garden one eve-ning. I didn't look at him.

'He used to play with me. Gave me things.'

'Who did?'

'My father. He told me I'd be rich one day. And my mother would be proud of me.'

'I know nothing about that.'

'He's setting *you* up very nicely, isn't he?'

'And he's sent *you* to school. You don't look poor to me. Those clothes and boots −'

'What are you saying to him?'

'It's none of your business what happens at Satis House.'

'I should have an equal share of it with you. When he croaks.'

'I'll tell him *that*, shall I?'

'Go rot in hell.'

I couldn't forget the strain of work on my father's heart, and I longed to ease the burden, however I could. Enlightening him as to the truth of Arthur's character wasn't the way.

I showed Sally what had been delivered to the house. A small pot containing miniature black and yellow tulips.

'Don't you wish you were me, Sally? But you'll share the pleasure of looking at them with me.'

She admired them, but guardedly.

'Can you guess who they're from? Of course you can.' Of course she could.

Mrs Venn informed me later that it was Sally who had brought them to the house.

'*You* did, Sally?'

'Well, I was walking by. A horse with a pannier drew up and the rider asked me where I might find Satis House.'

'Was it him?'

'I hardly saw.'

I had her describe him to me.

'Brown hair? And curly?'

'Yes.'

'His face?'

'The details have gone.'

'Why didn't you say?'

'All I had to do was take the pot from him.'

'So, it wasn't a surprise? When I showed you?'

'I'd only glanced at them.'

'You sly-boots!'

Not that I minded at all. It brought Sally closer in to the delightful confusion of my afternoon.

'How shall I acknowledge it?'

'He'll know you've received it.'

'But I must thank him,' I said.

'D'you have an address for him?'

'No.'

'Then he can't mean you to thank him.'

'Until I see him again. Oh, what if I *don't* see him again?'

'I don't doubt you will.'

'Here, in the town. Whatever was he doing here? Did he come especially?'

'He meant you to have a souvenir. The tulips.'

'Yes,' I said. 'He must have.'

A few moments later it occurred to me: I hadn't supplied that particular – the arrangement of tulips – when I'd described the evening of the Discourses to her.

She had divined it somehow, that the choice of flower and colours wasn't accidental. I put my arm round Sally's waist.

'How lucky I am,' I said.

'To have met your Mr Compeyson?'

'No!' I laughed. 'To have met you first.'

FOURTEEN

I wrote to my father from Durley Chase. And then, when he'd granted his permission, I wrote to Sally. I had been invited to a Carnaval Masque (spelling thus). It promised to be one of the highlights of the season. Would she like to see it for herself? She wouldn't, needless to say, be my *maid*, not as such, but for purposes of form and protocol, we would have to agree she be called that for the evening.

Sally didn't reply immediately, and I thought I might have to write again. When I did hear from her, she sounded less effusive than I'd been expecting. Nevertheless, 'if my situation permits', she was willing to accept my proposal. She didn't mention anything about her duties, having to attend on me, and I was grateful that she spared us both that embarrassment.

At Durley Mouse explained to Lady Chadwyck, and the housekeeper was instructed to treat Sally more favourably than was usual for the two nights she would be under their roof.

Sally carried herself with a suitable dignity, and the housekeeper was impressed, supposing this was the calibre of staff we insisted on in Kent. To me, though, she seemed to be abstracted about something.

'You're not going to be in any trouble with the archdeacon, are you, coming away like this?'

She said, no, it had all been attended to quite amicably.

I asked after her widowed mother, was she well?

'Oh yes. She'll live to be a hundred.'

'Nothing else is bothering you?'

'No.'

'Nothing about the Carnaval? What you have to –'

'No.'

She smiled and put some cheer back into her face, but I wished I could feel more convinced. I hoped *I* wasn't responsible, guilty – inadvertently, through decent intentions gone awry – of compromising her good nature.

Even the Chadwycks, I sensed, were taken aback by the extravagance of the occasion.

The rooms had been hung with panels painted with scenes of Venice. Even though I had never been, I recognised the locations at once, the palazzi and bridges and receding canals, the grand salons – even grander than ours this evening – glimpsed through arched windows.

The footmen were dressed as they might have been in the Doge's Palace, while the waiters were imitation gondoliers. The food was prepared as spectacularly as if for a Venetian feast-day, piled high on stepped salvers. The goblets were of blue Venetian glass.

The company moved about in their masks – gold, silver, scarlet, multi-coloured, or stark black or white – and sweeping their trains and long cloaks. I could recognise almost no one.

Our hosts were in elaborate disguise. Lord Villiers carried a long staff surmounted by a large circular medallion trailing gold tassels. Lady Villiers's dress was in several sculpted sections, like the queen on a suit of playing cards.

We glided about the rooms obscured by our masks, the ladies further protected by our spread fans. We were serenaded with the music of Vivaldi and Uccellini, played on flutes, theorbos, violas da gamba. The musicians wore lace jabots and two-foot-high white wigs.

Red and silver roses were growing from Sheba's head. Her face was striped like a cheetah's. Her mouth was barely open at all, and she seemed to be taking her last earthly breaths of air. The mask-maker had provided me with a harlequin style, with lozenges of blue and yellow. The high, exaggerated lines of the cheekbones and the sharpness of the nose allowed a little vital air to circulate under the close-fitting shell.

Moses had excused himself from the evening, denying it was because he disapproved of the theme. Mouse might have taken him at his word, but W'm told her that Moses wouldn't have said it if he hadn't been feeling morally superior. Anyway, W'm added, Moses had another, very good reason for not joining in: leaving his preparations too late, in the little time left he'd failed to find a costume that would fit him. (Prosaic, I thought, but quite probable.)

At either end of one of the reception rooms two figures were suspended from the ceiling on platforms. On one, surrounded by aureate rays, the sun – androgynously dressed in gold-coloured material and skin painted in gold. On the other, a silver figure – similarly sexless, astride a crescent moon.

A plague doctor. Black-faced, with a fall of scarlet ribbons on his chest; a long beaked nose, cruel and pointed like a razorbill. A three-cornered hat, as black as the cape, with a plumage of black ostrich feathers. A white cane, tap-tapping on the polished floors.

But who was this?

A silver mask floating past mine. Or, when I turned my head, it would be only a couple of feet away over my shoulder.

'You really don't recognise me?'

I stared into the almond-shaped eyeholes. I couldn't tell the colour of those irises, even by the shine from the chandeliers in the atrium. His voice, it was only affecting the aristocratic drawl –

His hand reached out and lifted mine by the fingers, gently holding it in mid-air.

'Signorina –'

It was the rush of heat to my neck which told me. I pulled back my hand, even though it wasn't my true choice.

'Mr Compeyson? *You* were invited?'

'No, no. Certainly not.'

'What did you do – ?'

'Filched an invitation.'

'How?'

'There are ways.'

'But the Villierses . . .'

'. . . wouldn't be bothered with the likes of me?'

'No. I didn't mean . . . Why – why have you come?'

'Can't you guess?'

At least he couldn't see my full discomposure.

'What if they ask you to leave?'

'They won't.'

I noticed Mouse watching me through her eyeholes. From another direction I saw Sheba's rose garden moving towards us.

'We'll meet here again,' I said, 'in half an hour's time.'

He didn't ask, where's 'here'; like me, his instincts would lead him back to the spot.

There was always someone to interrupt us. I felt that the lagoon tides themselves were at work, allowing us to approach and collide and then, just as inevitably, sweeping each of us away again, on the night's irresistible flow. Because we had to speak in snatches, we let ourselves be more outspoken about our surroundings and the company, and I didn't interrupt, and by not stopping him I felt I was colluding with him, right at the hub, and I didn't care; it was a release to me, a brewer's daughter who found herself here by some nonsensical but (so far) undetected accident.

Some costumes were fabulously coloured, trimmed with stones and pearls that might be precious or not, they glittered in front of your eyes for an instant and then they were gone. All the unknown colours of Africa and India. Voluptuous silks, the softest furs. Immaculately impassive faces, perhaps studded with jewels, or glass. A movement of an eye inside a hollow socket, a glimpse of teeth in the shadow behind the parted lips, and that was all to serve as a clue to identity.

'The jungle cat's face –'

'That's Sheba.'

'Who?'

'Isabella.'

'I wondered why she was always prowling about.'

'She means well, I expect.'

'Yes?'

'She's protecting me.'

'From what? Or from whom?'

'I – don't know. I didn't ask her to –'

'Better to be safe.'

'I don't feel I'm in danger.'

'Big cats could do you more harm than anything.'

'Not Sheba.'

'You could trust your life to her?'

'I think I'm wanted. You'll have to excuse –'

'Fifteen minutes?'

'Let's say twenty.'

'The lady decides. Twenty it is.'

The rooms echoed with laughter, with shrieks and exclamations, with the sounds of frivolity. Yet eyes looking out from behind the gouged sockets might seem strangely old and tired, while the faces bore no blemishes and were infallible symbols of youth.

And always there was the plague doctor, with his long snout hanging down in front. He had the knack of materialising a few feet away from me, even fleeter than Sheba, and brazenly coasting past. He left a chill behind him; stirred in with the funereal perfume of the luxuriant white lilies forced for months under hothouse glass to offer just moments of diversion during the hours of this long night.

By the time the masks came off – there would unfailingly be an unmasking at some point in any evening – I couldn't find him. My eyes roamed around the rooms. I slipped away from the others, having shed my own disguise, but feeling that somehow the music that continued to serenade us would be a discreet cover.

Was he hiding from me? I was quite determined to find him. I knew that he couldn't escape me if he was still here.

Why leave without telling me?

Was it to save me embarrassment?

Or – or because he knew better the hold he had over me, and he meant to keep me in thrall? I went looking for Sally. Our maids and servants, milling about the back quarters, spoilt the illusion for us, not being in Venetian dress.

I discovered Sally by herself in a requisitioned laundry room, head down, sewing the hem of her dress. She jumped when she saw me.

'Oh, it's *you!*'

'Don't tell me you forgot about me?'

She forced a smile.

'I had a mishap, I caught my foot in the hem –'

I wanted to tell her who was here, but I didn't dare risk a disclosure at the moment, not even to Sally. She looked tired. Her eyes were a little puffy. Venice had had its back rooms of servants too, serving the formal ceremony – the pomp and circumstance – of the salons.

'Have you seen it, Sally?'

'A little.'

'You've been outside, at the fireworks? You have mud on your shoes.'

She looked down at her feet.

'Aren't you glad you came?' I asked her. 'Imagine having missed this!'

We left the house at three in the morning, in a drizzle. The candles in the outdoor lanterns fizzed and sputtered. Sally had my cape ready. I sat in the Chadwycks' carriage watching the departing guests. One with his silver face back in place proffered his three-cornered hat and bowed deep as we rolled past. My heart thumped in my chest.

He remained bowed, and I hoped Sally would see from the carriage behind.

I forgot all the other masks of the evening, remembered that peerless silver one, the smooth and featureless visage. Later, starting to doze a little, I opened my eyes and saw, here and there on the burgundy wool of my cape, tiny flecks of . . . silver leaf. I stared at them.

Astonished, I picked them up on the tip of my finger. I was puzzling on the silver motes when I noticed some mud trails on the front outside of the cape, at hem level along the bottom. Not quite fresh mud, but not dried either: a few hours old.

I reminded myself, I should check Sally about wearing my clothes without asking me. Politely, almost casually, because she was my friend. But the speckles of silver leaf were what fascinated me. As if I must have started to dream about him already, and there – in a light scattering – amazingly was the actual evidence of my mind's fancy.

FIFTEEN

As soon as I walked into Satis House I knew something had changed. No riding cloak, no boots, no crop, none of Arthur's discarded effects. No stink of tobacco, or snuff. Arthur was living out.

'There's been a parting of the ways,' my father said.

The lawyer Mr Snee was involved, because my father had decided he must change his will.

'He's not disinherited outright. There's something for him. But only a minding.'

There had been terrible tantrums from Arthur, and those had put my father into a rage.

'I had no alternative. "You'll drain us dry," I said. His spending was much worse than I thought.'

'Is he coming back?'

'I have no way of telling.'

'It'll be like old times.'

Not really, I realised, a moment after I'd said it. In times past, I hadn't known my father was remarried, nor that I had a half-brother.

'He knows where to go to receive his keep.'

My father picked up items of correspondence which awaited his reply. He coughed his chest clear. Then he fixed his spectacles on his nose to read with, and reached out for his pen. Back to business.

———

Along the Backs. The willows drooped down to the water and skimmed the surface. Dragonflies hovered in the blue air. The grazing cattle lowed in King's meadow. Laughter, a woman's and a man's, trailed down from Clare Bridge. The bridge was beautiful but slightly askew, which made me think – as we drifted beneath it, through the small but suddenly dank tunnel of arch – that Moses had been right: beauty does always leave itself something short of perfection.

But my brief sobriety lifted as we re-emerged into sunshine. I felt I wanted to do no more than glance, dance, along the placid surface of this present time.

———

When we sat down to the play, on benches set out on duckboards in the college lea, the evening sun was still shining.

'Built for your Ease and Pleasure, Sirs, behold,
This Night, our little Stage its Scenes unfold.
Here, to the Muse, your fav'ring Smiles afford:
Bid Genius flourish, and on Fancy's wing
Mounted aloft, hear sweetest SHAKESPEAR sing!'

Time flew past. A wood near Athens. Another part of the Wood. Theseus's Palace. A room in Quince's House. I liked the Immortals best – Oberon, Titania, Puck, and the fairies – wearing their elfin green. I laughed as the love potion was sprinkled on sleeping eyelids, a juice to 'make man or woman madly dote upon the next live creature that it sees'.

Later, a chill started to seep up from the pasture-grass. A shiver passed through the trees. Act V. The conclusion was in sight, but all would not be resolved to every character's satisfaction.

Some of the players had to clear their throats, cough out croaks.

Dampness must have got into the scenery, because corrugations were appearing on the painted backdrop of Theseus's Palace. After the last lines one of the actors – Bottom unmasked – came forward to speak, to send us on our way.

> 'Precepts from hence with ten-fold Vigour dart,
> And seize thro' Eyes, and Ears, the captive Heart.
> Be VICE abash'd then, and be VIRTUE bold;
> Be honour ever free, and never sold!
> Protect the Stage on this determin'd Plan,
> And prove that Reason is the Test of Man.'

———

We started to make our way back to W'm's rooms, across the lawns. My feet felt wet through my shoes. A bright moon shone. The air was filled with our banter, our laughter, someone's philosophical exegesis. At one point I was walking beside W'm, but he seemed oblivious. Now I felt nothing either, and I wondered at that person I had been. He was busy talking to someone, not about Plato or Tibullus, but about one of his Surrey neighbours, Lucinda Osborne, teasing out information as adeptly as if he were playing a fish.

We followed the river. On the opposite bank, boldly illuminated by moonlight, I noticed a young woman stand listening to us. She twisted her head on one side to hear. Then she started walking. Down the embankment, to a small sliver of strand.

She continued to walk, and I kept looking, wondering why she didn't stop.

Into the river.

The water rose to her knees, then to her waist.

She kept on taking steps. A stumble on the stones at the bottom, but she stayed upright.

Now the water came up to the level of her chest.

(And the oddest thing, the detail I noted in these moments that seemed so slowed out of true, suspended from the rules of ordinary time: the young woman was wearing a hat.)

Moses was shouting down at her, then the others. Mouse screamed at her to stop, stop. Moses was first to go running down the bank, followed by two or three of the men. W'm held Sheba and Mouse close beside him. The woman had water up to her neck. Her face had a curiously seraphic and peaceful expression, she seemed to be smiling – smiling quite inconsequentially – over at us.

I was still supposing she was playing some queer game when her face disappeared beneath the water. (The hat on her head became detached: it was left floating while her face blurred palely beneath the surface. A straw hat with a scarlet ribbon and a white wax flower, adrift by moonlight.)

Moses had thrown off his coat and waistcoat and dived in. A hole exploded in the river. He swam out.

It was at the widest part of the river. By the time he reached the spot, the woman had disappeared from view. Moses reached down, tried grabbing, wrestled with the woman's limbs, which were becoming caught in weed.

From the bank it was all quite clear and candid to us. Huge events occupied only a very few seconds. Time stuttered.

Another two had gone swimming out, arms thrashing. They helped Moses haul the woman back ashore. The shore watchers were afraid to touch her. Her eyes were open, staring up at the moon in the sky. She still wore the expression of beatific certainty.

But the person she'd been was now a corpse. The skin seemed to be turning blue, like rich ripe cheese.

Moses, in sodden clothes, was praying for her soul. Something about the gesture, Moses's fervent bravery in the face of a terrible fact – or maybe the passion being wrung from a hopeless situation – moved me deeply. I was crying before I realised it. Sheba stared, transferring some of her horror at the night's tragedy on to me.

Next day we discussed it endlessly among ourselves.

While the others talked, I watched from the window. Suddenly Cambridge appeared very small to me. A collection of beautiful tended gardens, enclosed by high excluding walls. Beneath a high, vaulting, indifferent fenland sky.

> But yet the more we search, the less we know,
> Because we find our work doth endless grow.
> For who doth know, but stars we see by night
> Are suns which to some other worlds give light?

Moses was saying even less than I was. It was as if a part of him were temporarily absent, attending the dead woman's spirit.

I looked up at one point. He was staring across at me. Curiously, after his athletic heroism of the day before, his face now showed fear.

We avoided each other for the rest of that day and evening. By the *next* day he was coughing and sneezing, speaking through a blocked nose. I fetched him handkerchiefs and concocted a hot toddy for him to drink.

'Why d'you think she did it?'

I told him I had no idea. He seemed disappointed that I shouldn't know.

'A broken heart,' I suggested.

'Do people suffer so much?'

'For love? Oh, I imagine so.'

'To drown herself?'

'Why does that astonish you? Dido threw herself on the flames.'

'In legend.'

'And real life's different?' I asked.

'Cursed creature.'

'Hmm.'

'Bedlam Bess.'

'Aren't you meant to pity her?'

He was staring at me again, how he had done earlier.

More sneezes.

A knock at the door. Another friend's younger sister, asking if she could be of any help.

All this uncritical devotion to Moses. Even the memory of his vain dash to try to save the woman couldn't temper my impatience.

I thought of that seraphic face, prepared for death, and I made mine the opposite. I pursed my lips drily, crinkled my nose.

Moses was watching me, deeply confused.

I felt it must be magnetic repulsion, this failure of mine – which shamed me a little – to wreathe him with honour as his devotees did.

SIXTEEN

'*And* again!'

Sheba pointed.

'Your Mr Compeyson. Well, well!'

When it was time for us to pass each other, he was ready with a smile. He nodded at my fan.

'Hold on to that.'

Mouse whisked me away, with a vigour that surprised me.

'You haven't met all W'm's friends, have you, Catherine? Here're some more . . .'

There was an opportunity for a dance. I couldn't locate my partner on my card, and he came up to me shortly after the music started, telling me he had been let down by his, would I please do him the honour?

It was a fast gavotte. We managed to keep up. I was out of breath by the end, though; I felt that normally I wouldn't have been.

It was Moses's turn next, for a more sedate old-fashioned min-uet, and I wished it wasn't. He tried too earnestly hard, treating it as another abstruse subject he should master. But dancing takes a certain lightness, a spring in the step, an elasticity in the calves; a kind of *joie de vivre*, or alternatively a leavening element of self-proclaiming stupidity in one's make-up. It wasn't Moses's forte.

'*You* show me,' he mouthed at me.

I simulated incomprehension. He was trying to uncover my true talents, the few there might be, and buoyed up by the music and by my previous dance I didn't intend to be patronised. I made my steps so deft and elegant, so sylph-like, but so deceptively simple, that I knew he would appear all the more of a clod.

———

After that 'my Mr Compeyson' was at the majority of the Assemblies and house-parties I went to with the Chadwycks. I could see the pleasure he took from my companions' irritation, to find, hell and damnation, here was somewhere else *he*'d managed to get himself invited to. It was an entertainment for him, to see if the Chadwycks could ignore his presence for an entire evening. It was a divertissement for me, and literally, to continue acknowledging his presence, so that only he should be aware – furtive glances, and holding myself side on, and allowing a smile for someone else to become (over their shoulders) a smile intended really for him.

———

He wasn't au fait with Virgil, or *The Sorrows of Young Werther*, or Clementi's keyboard sonatas. But he had an incomparable mastery of racecourse runners and their riders. He had an infallible recall of their past showings, and on that he based his predictions of future form.

John Pond's daughter, Miss Pond. Captain Shafto. Hugo Meynell, 'Hunting Jupiter'. Lord Clermont in scarlet, Mr Panton in buff. Bunbury, pink and white stripes, the Dundas white with scarlet spots. Brown Queensberry, crimson Grafton, straw silk for Devonshire.

'I'm the memory man.'

I couldn't judge his tone of voice. I was a little flustered.

'Of course,' I said, obeying no logic, 'Dido, *she* couldn't forget.'

He smiled blankly.

'The queen,' I said. 'Of Carthage.'

'Poor old biddy. What couldn't she forget?'

'Oh . . .' I shrugged, embarrassed. 'It doesn't matter. It's just a myth.'

'Best left to the artists, then. Painters, sculptors, that sort.'

'Purcell.'

The name so revered at Durley Chase became entangled with nearby laughter. He was saved from having to reply, and I thought I caught a flicker of relief pass across his smoothly, evenly handsome face.

———

'Coincidences happen,' Sheba said. 'But not *that* often.'

'Sometimes,' Moses began, 'we're too close to something, it's really out of focus, it gets distorted –'

'Nothing's distorted,' I snapped back.

'It's all right, Catherine,' Mouse put in.

'*Something*'s got under your skin,' Sheba said.

W'm laughed.

'That's what friends are for,' Sheba said.

'I don't know *what* they're for,' I told her.

'So that we don't get out of our depth,' Mouse said.

'So they'll let us know –' Sheba leaned closer, '– if we're likely to make a tiny little fool of ourselves. Warn us if it looks as though we might be heading for a fall.'

I wouldn't have tolerated a remark of that kind from anyone except Sheba: and even then, scarcely from her. I was furious with them all. I could either let them see that, or convince them of the opposite.

I knew what they were thinking. 'My Mr Compeyson' wasn't *our* sort of person. Too forward, too familiar, and who had ever heard of a tribe with *that* name? I found myself smiling at them, but it was done with a cold heart.

Mouse slipped her arm under mine, then Sheba. W'm raised one eyebrow (as eyebrows always are raised) quizzically. Moses looked as unhappy as I felt; he was still thinking of the drowned girl.

———

But they couldn't stop me; they wouldn't keep me from him. There were always opportunities in an evening, and I was as adept as him at seeking them out.

A father who'd been a doctor at sea. A mother who didn't keep well. Several siblings.

A harsh school somewhere in the West, attended by sons of mainly naval and military families.

An anticipated inheritance from a Scottish relative reneged upon.

Introductions from old school friends. Other people's parties, in all the fashionable towns: Exeter, Salisbury, Nottingham, Chester, York, Tunbridge.

'I'm obliged to do a little work too, I'm afraid. Norfolk way. To earn a living for myself.'

'You shouldn't apologise. Work is honest and true.'

'That's your father's philosophy?'

'No. It's my own experience. I now realise that it is.'

And – before I could think to stop – I found myself telling him how it would give me no little pleasure at Durley Chase, but a private satisfaction I didn't declare to *them*, to consider how back home I saw wealth make itself: how I smelt it in the rooms of Satis House when the windows were open on the yard side and I could hear the men at their unremitting labour.

When I was physically close to him – as I used to be with W'm, only more so now – I was aware of an energy that was transmitted from him.

I felt like adamant, impelled by a magnet; the hardness of my substance no longer signified, against the power of that attraction.

———

He remembered whatever I told him. He had complete recall. It was uncanny. The memory man. He could anticipate what I was going to say next. He seemed to have read the libretto of my thoughts beforehand.

He knew things, as if I must have told him but had forgotten that I'd told him. Only Sally previously had been granted such a degree of intimacy as I realised – without quite intending it – *he* enjoyed now, with the most elusive details of my life: my most personal past, my feelings, my dreams.

No Latin, no Dido and Aeneas.

('Why learn to speak like people who've been dead for a thousand years?'

'Nearly two,' I said.)

No Purcell.

(He whistled tunes he heard at the theatre, or which he heard the travellers at the racecourses playing on their fiddles and squeeze-boxes.)

Again it was a reprieve for me, from too much sheer mental drudgery – not to have to come up with bons mots, or to weave the maxims of great men into my conversation.

'On the 20th, you see, Escape was at two to one. Field of four, over two miles. Coriander, Skylark, Pipator, they all beat him. On the 21st, field of six, over six miles. Escape was four to one and five to one. Chifney had twenty guineas on the second race, not the first. Both were his rides. Escape raced past the favourite, Chanticleer, came home well to the front.'

Now – and I was to tell him honestly – what did I think of *that*?

'But if he has all these friends . . .' I objected.

'Well, it's an art,' Mouse said, 'I grant you.'

'What is?'

'Collecting friends. Only, I should say, they're not.'

'Not what, Mouse?'

'Not friends, not properly. He drops their names, and they're too well-mannered – most of them – to show Charles Compeyson the door. They suffer him –'

'No, Mouse. That can't be –'

'– suffer him, because it seems everyone else does too, and we all *hate* to be different.'

'Don't they like him?'

'He just isn't one of them. He doesn't belong to the past.'

'*You* don't like him either.'

'I prefer to trust people.'

'And you don't trust him?'

'I need to *know* people to do that.'

'You know *me*?' I asked her.

'You're a friend.'

'But I've come too late. Remember – real friendships go back into the past. You said so yourself.'

'You're an exception, Catherine.'

'Why?'

'Oh . . .'

'Because I'm so foolish? Because I need your protection?'

'"No" to the first. But "yes" to the second.'

'Let's stop,' I said, 'please.'

'Only if you'll promise not to desert us. Your friends.'

'Nor you me.'

———

He didn't always tell me where he went between these re-encounters.

In a racing phaeton, I heard it said, a young fellow could put himself about over a weekend, travelling anywhere within a hundred-mile radius drawn from the capital.

He didn't have anything so fast at his disposal, that I was aware of. But he did have the healthy colour of a man who might well cover a lot of distance; and he certainly had the charm to assure himself of transportation, whether offering to drive a party or being given the use of a carriage for one or two days with an agreed time and place for its return.

He'd had his own life before I met him. Why should I expect him to account for the time when he was required to earn his own keep and was out of my ken?

I convinced myself that I *enjoyed* knowing as little about him as I did. I felt I was freer to fill in details from my imagination, when the picture was so sketchy; it gave me a bigger, not lesser, stake in his life, because I had to think myself into it more. And it occurred to me that he must be fully aware of this.

———

I told Sally things which, as soon as they had tumbled out of me, I realised I shouldn't have said.

(*Ah! how sweet it is to love.*)

About the jolts of excitement my body received from him; about waking up thinking of him.

(*Ah! how gay is young desire.*)

About dressing to please *him*, first and foremost. About finding him waiting for me in my dreams.

It was Sally who would remind me of what I'd said before, quoting my discrepancies back at me.

I laughed them all away.

(*And what pleasing pain we prove,/ When first we feel a lover's fire.*)

All the while Sally would be sewing or winding wool, even setting to some item of silverware she'd noticed hadn't been polished well enough.

(*Pains of love are sweeter far,/ Than all other pleasures are.*)

She was never still now, which made me wonder if she was losing interest a little – or was at the very least guilty, about the time I took up with my stories of Durley and elsewhere, my running narrative about a man I hadn't even mentioned to my father. But busy as she was, she must have been paying me very close attention, to be able to remember so much the next time about the Chadwycks and – especially – the fugitive figure of 'my' Charles Compeyson.

SEVENTEEN

The Osbornes had the neighbouring estate, Thurston Park. Lady Chadwyck and the second Lady Osborne weren't on the best terms, but their children were of an age and quite content with one another's company. The Osbornes had the loftier pedigree, but were never tempted to condescend.

There was an amount of come and go.

But we hadn't set eyes on *him* before . . .

A hooded figure was just visible under the trees. A man with a collection of books tucked beneath one arm. As soon as he saw *us*, he immediately turned his back and hurried away.

'Who's that?' we asked.

'Our new hermit.'

He called himself Nemo, 'No One', because he wanted to shed the manner of life he'd had.

He lived in a grotto, beyond the ha-ha's sunken fence. It was built like a two-thirds-scale gate-tower to a castle. The slit windows had been glazed, and a flue and fireplace put in, but apart from those the man lived with few creature comforts.

'Candles. A cooking pot. He draws water from the well; a well we dowsed to find for him. It's terribly quaint, don't you think?'

We concurred.

'My father has him write down what he wants – well, what he needs, since he tells us he doesn't have "wants" any more. And also there's a resume of his activities for the past twelve months he has to supply in return for his keep. Which takes about ten lines.'

So, this was what wealth allowed: the luxury of supporting other people's eccentricities?

We stood watching for a glimpse of him, taking care not to snag our finery in the cultivated wilderness of rough grass and nettles. When we spotted him, on the other side of the ha-ha, where the deer came to crop, *he* was watching us from the cover of the arboretum. Probably he was wondering at our own quirks: this show of sartorial vanity, and the herding impulse, our uniform fascination as we stared back stupidly with the white faces of showground sheep.

———

Charles told me that, following the report I'd given him, he'd come to an arrangement with Nemo.

'You've what? "An arrangement"?'

'That he'll make himself scarce every so often, and we can avail ourselves of his hospitality. He's quite well set up, you know. I thought it would be all sackcloth and ashes.'

'You've seen where he lives?'

'And so will you, very shortly.'

I couldn't stop myself from laughing, at the sheer effrontery. That eclipsed, for the moment, the question of propriety. He'd thought of that too.

'I've got the loan of a lad. He can serve us tea. If he's ever made the stuff.'

'Why shouldn't he know how to make tea?'

'Just wait and see.'

Boodle was a Negro, fourteen or fifteen years old, dressed in blue velveteen and gold buttons. (A snug fit, and the velveteen was worn, and the buttons tarnished, but the effect was all.) He had a smile of sharp white teeth, and wanted to show willing.

The lad's tea was inexpert, but I'd had a thirsty walk over and any refreshment was welcome.

The folly's interior was a little cramped, to be sure, with low ceilings. But it was decently furnished, with a fireplace where pine cones sparked in the grate; the fragrance of pine helped smother the underlying whiff of damp.

'Well, it's better than nothing, I thought.'

'Oh yes,' I said. 'Yes indeed.'

The shelves on the walls sagged with books. Some framed prints showed the grassy ruins of Rome.

From the (glazed) window I could see Nemo pacing about reading.

('I think he gets a bit lost if he strays too far. Don't let the house out of your sight, I told him.'

Was this another attempt not to offend the delicacies of *bien-séance*, I wondered.)

And there we would go, to the hermitage, once every ten days or so over half a year, whenever he could get away and I could make the excuse of a long walk *sola* from Durley Chase. We were waited upon by the black boy while, outside, Nemo strode back and forth in view of us.

We took tea. And we talked. I told him about life with the Chad-wycks, and he discussed none too respectfully the august company they kept. I was a little bothered that we kept Nemo out of his house, but I was assured that he was being adequately recompensed for the inconvenience.

'Some cash won't go amiss, I dare say. Of course those hermits always come from decent families who can provide for their own. But who knows what the Osbornes have taken from *him*?'

'Surely never,' I said.

'Never ones to miss out on a decent rental, the Osbornes.'

'I thought a hermit was −'

'A kind of decoration?'

'– to prove their intellectual qualifications.'

'Families like the Osbornes don't profit by their intellectual qualifications.'

'By what, then?'

'Their mercenary instincts.'

'No.'

'Oh yes. Come on, Catherine, that's the way of the world.'

The light playful tone of his voice puzzled me. If that was so, I said, then it was a harsh truth.

'A brewer's daughter like yourself too!'

'I'm meant to know all about the world?'

'*Don't* you?'

'This and that. But what it adds up to . . .'

'Well, you can just sit tight. In your cosy nest.'

'I can have aspirations, though.'

'Oh, heiresses don't need those!'

'Whose side are you on?'

He laughed, and I smiled, not because I agreed or even understood, but so that I wouldn't – if only for the sake of five brief seconds – be left behind and start to lose him.

———

The things he knew about me. Trivial, unimportant things. It seemed to me those must be the most difficult facts of all to discover. That I preferred fish to meat, and grayling to mackerel, and sole to grayling. That I slept with my window slightly ajar, and never on two pillows. That I wore away the left inside of my right heel before any other part of either shoe. That I carried a sachet of orange blossom in my portmanteau. That I wrote letters wearing a clip-on cotton frill over my cuff. That I gargled with salt water three – and always three – times a day. And let down my hair and brushed it with fifty strokes – or as near as – every night before bed. That my favourite poet used to be Gray, but now it was Cowper. That I had the knack of cracking a Brazil nut lengthwise, and split-ting an apple with just my two thumbs. That I preferred damsons, even bruised windfall, to a handful of sweet cherries. That I woke around seven o'clock every morning, whatever the season, however dark my bedroom was. That I always ran cream over the back of my spoon.

As if he'd been prying on me through the windows of the Chase.

His discoveries about me occurred in several quite different con-versations.

I made a fuss about not wanting to hear any more, although I was fascinated to learn how he knew what he did.

'I can't betray my source. Or sources.'

'I'm under surveillance by someone? Who?'

He shook his head.

'*You* can't know by yourself,' I said.

'Whyever not?'

'You'd need to be invisible.'

'A ghost?'

'No, ghosts are people who're dead to us. Over and done with.'

'Then I'm the spirit of curiosity. A locked door is no impediment.'

'Well, if you won't tell me . . .'

I was bemused, but not alarmed. He might have been guessing sometimes, he might have had good hearing for eavesdropping; the Durley staff were as liable to blab as any – and Satis House had em-ployed several loose-tongued girls in recent years. I wasn't both-ered enough to think about it much, let alone worry. It might have been telepathy that was responsible, his kindred soul exactly in sympathy – in imaginative conjunction – with my own.

We were perfectly decorous together. It took the will of both of us to be so. I trusted him with me, and myself with him. The blackamoor shuffled about just outside the doorway, his ears tuned and the whites of his eyes shining in the darkness of the corridor, all his native skills of the hunt reapplied to protecting our staunch English etiquette.

Maybe, a little bit, I didn't want to trust myself so implicitly. But then I would try that much harder, fastening down hard on myself, to drive mischief of that sort right out of my mind.

Dallying, once, while he was outside with the boy, I took down a copy of the *Aeneid* from the shelves.

I found a passage I already knew, from Book IV.

> But anxious cares already seiz'd the queen;
> She fed within her veins a flame unseen;
> The hero's valour, acts, and birth inspire
> Her soul with love, and fan the secret fire.

At his approach I closed the book and quickly replaced it among the others before he should see. Virgil, I felt, didn't fit in with this *modus vivendi* on our secret afternoons.

He seemed to sense the touch of damp or cold on my skin as soon as I did myself.

'You're a little chilly?'

'A little.'

'Here –'

'No, I couldn't possib—'

'Come on.'

He would remove his coat and drape it round my shoulders.

'I should wear warmer clothes,' I said.

So, when I knew that I should, why didn't I?

W'm's engagement had been announced. Sheba and Mouse were still recovering from the shock.

'We never thought . . .'

It wasn't to the young woman I thought I'd lost him to, but to one of her circle. The eldest Osborne daughter, and the plainest.

'Of course it's a very *good* match . . .'

Even Mouse had shown impatience with slow-spoken, slow-thinking Lucinda in the past; Sheba had neglected her, in favour of the younger three by the second Lady Osborne.

'I wish them well,' I said, not really caring if I did or not.

So much for a Cambridge education. All those people and places who were doomed to become my past . . .

———

'Catherine, meet my friend –'

'"Your friend"?'

'The Red Spaniard.'

I looked about me. He laughed, and clicked his fingers. Clicked them again. The black boy came into the room at a run, bearing a bottle.

'Like Canon Arbuthnot,' I said.

'Who's he?'

'In our town. Entertaining his friend from Bordeaux.'

'And glasses, Boodle. Glasses, please.'

So we spent that afternoon, untypically, drinking red wine. I wondered if he had some cause, either for celebration or on the contrary to cheer himself, but he wouldn't say. I grew a little silly, imagining I was dispensing wit.

'"In the shadow of the gods",' I heard myself saying, '"I approach opulent altars".'

'What's that?'

'What's what?'

'That nonsense you were speaking.'

'You're right. Quite right. You were never righter. It makes *no* sense at all.'

On my way home I stumbled into a puddle, but that was all part of the afternoon's charm.

Mouse saw me first.

Was I all right?

Here – She helped me upstairs.

What on earth?

I'm all right, I'm fine, really.

Your breath.

It's nothing, I stopped by a farm.

It's cider?

Yes, yes.

Which farm?

It doesn't matter, I forget.

Oh, *Catherine*!

I didn't make the same mistake twice.

Mouse and I exchanged private looks, but they weren't as knowing as *she* wanted them to be. Something was afoot, she realised. But I was too complacent, or too fearful perhaps, to take her into my confidence.

If I had – if I had explained to her where I went and who it was I met there, might the course of future events have been quite different?

———

Between my returns to Satis House I continued writing to Sally. Only she knew about the hermitage.

What I might have recorded in a diary, Sally received from me.

We play at cards! Stops mostly – Comet is v. fast – And Mariage.
They're games of bluff, he says – there's a game inside the game, you
have to get yr. opponent to declare – what you feel you never show,
never.

Sally wrote back. There was still no news of Arthur. She saw my
father about the town; he was improved, but he knew to work a little
less and to conserve his energies. Her mother spoke of sending her
somewhere further off, to London maybe. But it hadn't happened yet.

Some matters, though, I didn't confide even to Sally. I couldn't
have.

———

Whenever we accidentally touched at the gate-legged tea table or
in the narrow doorway – fingers, back of the hand, wrist – it was
like contact with sulphur. I felt that my skin was scorched for a minute or two afterwards. When he'd gone I would stare at the point
of contact, as if there ought to have been a burn. Nothing worse
resulted than some bright burnishing on my face, my neck.

I wanted to plunge into cooling water, immerse myself.

. . . and Joy shall overtake us as a flood.

He only had to reach forward, from where he was sitting, or to
pause a moment as we risked a stroll at dusk. And he set up those
nervous tremors again, spasms of excitement connected to feelings
I couldn't fully articulate to myself.

It was cruelty: I should have seen it was that. But I was the very
last person who would have.

He had me on a chain. No: on a silken halter.

EIGHTEEN

'And my mother thinks it will be good for me.'

'Oh, Sally – How could it be good?'

'The opportunity . . .'

'You'll have others.'

'Not just a lady's maid, though. I'm to have some housekeeping duties. The kitchen garden –'

'In Hertfordshire? Why Hertfordshire?'

'Why not Hertfordshire? It has to be somewhere.'

'Only if you want to go.'

'I have to think of the future.'

She didn't sound convinced. I told her so. She sighed.

'And what shall *I* do?'

'Your life is so busy, it can't matter to you –'

'Oh, *Sally*!'

It must have had to do with her mother always wanting more and better for her. Did Satis House have too lowly a status now?

'*You* must decide, Sally.'

'I have.'

'Won't you think again?'

'I'm sorry. Truly. But this is what I mean to do.'

I asked where I could write to her.

It would be best, she said, if I wrote to a female cousin of hers in

London. She wasn't sure that her employer would welcome correspondence.

'How ridiculous. What right has your Miss Stackpole –'

'Until I establish myself, that's all. My cousin can send letters
on –'

'From London?'

'Yes. When I know how I'm placed.'

'I'm off to the Hot Wells at Llanirfon with the Chadwycks. I'll
want to tell you all about that.'

'You will.'

'And the important news.'

'Yes?'

'About when I next see Charles, of course!'

A primeval swamp. Sunlight sifting down through high, dense trees.
The rush and swirl of hot water, clouds of steam.

A great water buffalo slowly submerges herself, covering her
wrinkled hide. Heads without bodies float past me. The mineral
vapour unpeels in curls off the surface of the bathing pool.

A crone stands beside a table of towels, to assist when you climb
the old smoothed stone steps, green from the spa's chemicals. For a
small rendering at the end of the week, she wraps you in towels, in
front of a small cabin she has prepared for you. You lie back and
look up at the oblong of open Welsh sky above the colonnade.

The Wells' was a strange geography to me, but not to the others.

In one of the steam rooms I lay on a cushioned chaise, anonymous in my brown linen petticoat and wrapped in towels apart
from my face, which was probably too red to offer much clue to my
identity.

I dozed off. Their voices somewhere behind me woke me: speaking not any louder than usual, but nudging me out of slumber simply because I recognised them.

'She *is* a funny little thing,' Mouse began. 'Catherine.'

'Well, hardly "little",' Sheba said.

'That's a term of speech. "Funny little" –'

'It would have to be. She's been filling out of late, have you noticed?'

'Moses doesn't agree, but she amuses *me*,' Mouse said. 'With those quaint country ways of hers.'

'That's what we're supposed to be getting rid of. Grooming her for a husband.'

'Every girl we know is being groomed –'

'That's *our* sort of girl, Mouse.'

'Maybe we won't be able to tell the difference, once she's finished.'

I told Charles why I was now less comfortable with them than I used to be.

I thought halfway through my account of Llanirfon Wells that he might find it something to laugh about, and he'd say I was making too much of it, how terribly sensitive I must be.

He listened to me until I'd finished, and then he said *he* thought they hadn't behaved like proper friends, and I had a right to be aggrieved. I should try to make my peace, certainly, but I wasn't to build bridges and suppose it was worth *any* cost.

'You have to think of yourself too. Your pride.'

'Oh, my pride!' I said.

'Well, think of the friendship *you*'ve given. And the amount of returns from them.'

'That all sounds very mercantile.'

'It's as much as I know about. Just like your father.'

I was treated at Durley exactly as I had been before.

But I knew now that there was less spontaneity in their actions. They had rehearsed their affability very well, which was why they were so good at it and why earlier I had been fooled.

The situation was also a test of my own powers of dissimulation: not to reveal any clues as to my degree of understanding. This was the other education, in expediency, which they were helping to equip me with.

Charles told me he'd been turning over in his mind the account I'd given him.

'And . . . ?'

'I think you should stick it out, Catherine.'

'With people who don't approve of me?'

'They could be useful to you. And anyway, they're good camouflage.'

'I suppose so.'

'Mark my word.'

'Very well, then.'

'Trust me.'

'Yes. I do.'

Moses was reading 'Jean-Jacques'.

'Rousseau,' he explained. 'His "Reveries".'

'And what are those about?'

'To me, Rousseau is about sentience. Feeling.'

'Like Goethe?'

'That is about wallowing in feelings.'

'I found *Young Werther* affecting.'

'Because the wily old dog meant you to find it so.'

'And Jean-Jacques wouldn't do such a thing?'

'I think not.'

Like two figures in a watercolour, we were seated on a fallen bole. Over in Thurston Park the hermit was back in his picturesque grotto, the chimney was smoking lavishly.

'Isn't it preferable', I persisted, 'to feel better for having read a book?'

'What about thinking?'

'But didn't you say Jean-Jacques was about feeling?'

'Feeling what it is like to be solitary.'

'Like Young Werther?'

'Solitude is natural. There's no surer means of perceiving one's humanity.'

'With no one to compare oneself *to*?'

'The brain has the company of all the books it's ever read.'

'Werther suffers too,' I said.

'And how he suffers. Delectably, exquisitely. It's just another appetite for him.'

Our conversation on solitude and the two authors got no further. I wouldn't allow any more.

He asked me, 'You think I'm too solemn?'

I was in a charitable mood.

'Too *young* perhaps. Don't we have to live a little first? And read later?'

'How are we to know to avoid the pitfalls?'

'Only by realising later. That they *were* pitfalls.'

'Don't you mind the prospect of suffering?'

'I don't intend to suffer. My suffering will be – thinking that I held back from life.'

NINETEEN

I would sit beside my father and, while I listened, he would address certain business matters, clearly enough for me to follow.

It had begun by my going to fetch the leather-bound records for him – tan or green or red – and finding the place he wanted.

I knew how beers were made, and something about the differences between them. But it was the arithmetic which he was quite ready and willing (to my surprise) to share with me, how the commodity purchases and the sales were calculated, how the profits and losses were worked out.

I attended, because I wished to, and more to the point because *he* wished me to.

There was a pleasing harmony to be found in the sums and subtractions, in ordering the balance of surpluses and deficits. I realised how intently my father was watching me, and I worried that I might have involved him in too much close work, in returning him too soon to what he ought to be taking a longer rest from. As it was, he was under doctor's orders not to be at his desk for longer than two hours at a stretch.

'No, no, Catherine –'

He put a hand to his mouth, before a sudden fit of coughing.

'If you're quite sure . . .'

'I need to tell a Havisham.'

'Then tell me, father, please.'

He took me into the brewhouse and led me through the stages of the brewing process. Grinding. Mashing. Boiling. Cooling. Fermenting. Racking. I listened carefully, I asked him questions about what I was seeing. Step by step, while he fought to curb his coughing.

Cleaning the malt, grinding it, diluting the grist with hot water in a mash tun, leaving the malt's sugars to dissolve. Draining the liquid wort; extracting final sugars with more hot water (sparging), then boiling the wort in copper vats, adding hops to sour the sweetness. Draining the hopped wort over used hops, and cooling it, before channelling it into fermenting vats and adding yeast. Leaving fermentation for five or six days, so that the yeast will convert sugar to alcohol and carbonic acid gas; skimming the film of yeast from the wort, once the sediment has sunk. After fermentation, diverting the green beer into tanks for several more days, while the yeast left further mellows the beer's taste. Conditioning: adding some caramel to darken the colour, adding finings (derived from sturgeon's bladder) to thin the brew's appearance. Storing the resulting beer in casks, introducing some extra sugar to aid supplementary fermentation, scattering dried hops for aromatic purposes.

After that I became interested to learn some of the tricks of the trade, and what might go wrong between one brew and the next.

Initially my father was uncertain: should he show me or not? But I wasn't afraid to know how we Havishams justified ourselves; and I had lived all my life within sight and sound and smell of the beer's manufacture, the source of our standing.

———

It seemed from her letters that Sally was also spending some time in London with her employer, and so she could simply pick up from her cousin any correspondence delivered for her.

I asked if there wasn't another address in London where Miss

Stackpole put up, where I could write to. But Sally replied that she thought the arrangement was working well enough as it was, and if I was still quite agreeable –

Her letters, I felt, were a little vague in content. It couldn't be the case that they were being read by Miss Stackpole. But perhaps Sally didn't like to dwell too much on her new duties, if she wasn't finding them altogether congenial; and she might have thought it would be disloyal to say so.

I realised I must simply put up with the situation for the while.

———————

In my father's office one day I noticed an unsealed envelope on his desk. Even upside-down the handwriting was recognisable, and con-firmed by the signature.

Charlotte Chadwyck.

He saw me looking, and pushed the letter beneath some other items of correspondence. He frowned.

I thought he looked grey and careworn.

'Some man will count himself lucky. When he first sets eyes on you.'

We had finished supper and taken ourselves through to the fire in the little sitting room. I was sewing; my father was sitting oppo-site, watching me.

'Yes?'

'Certainly,' he said.

'So . . . that is what my education's for.'

'It's the prospect for every young woman. To be married. Her responsibility even.'

'Or . . . ?'

'There *is* no "or". In your case.'

'Oh.'

He paused to cough some obstruction out of his chest.

'With all your advantages. Those you have and those you *will* have.'

'I see. I see.'

———

I consulted the racing news in the newspaper, and guessed where he would be. I walked to Durley Conquest Farm and asked, opting at the last minute for imperiousness instead of sweetness, to borrow their trap.

'Lady Chadwyck knows,' I lied.

'In that case, miss . . .'

They couldn't give me the mare. Solomon was properly too big for the task, and I'd heard he was grudging, but I only wanted to get away. I whispered in Solomon's ear as the trap was being wheeled out.

'We have to find him, we have to find him . . .'

I had heard reports about the place, its hazards. The horses racing pell-mell through the crowd, and the spectators galloping along behind. Cock-fighting, dog-matching. Thimble-rigging, crooked roulette.

But it was a quiet day. The dangers were largely out of sight. The sun was shining. I was dusty after my journey from Durley, a little light-headed on an empty stomach, but exhilarated just to be here.

An enchanted day, in my future memories of it, when no harm was meant to come to me.

The Epsom regulars pointed him out to me. I didn't even have to go searching for him.

I hailed him from the trap. (A humble farm trap negotiating parked gigs, chaises, cabriolets.)

The 12.30 race was over. A table had been spread for half a

dozen, with mismatching chairs fetched from wherever they could be found.

When I saw that Charles had seen me, his face made me think of a mask, another mask: features frozen in a smile, with only the eyes registering his perturbation. But his voice was remarkably steady and assured.

'Another chair for our lady guest, Spencer.'

A space was made for me. One woman now among six men.

I surprised myself by saying thank you, I would, and then sitting down.

(An umbrella was opened and placed above me in the tree, to provide extra shade.)

A plate was handed to me; on it were several slices of rich red beef and a plump duck's leg. The sturdy fare men enjoy. I didn't send it back, and started to eat. I was hungry. And I was intensely relieved to have found him again, so grateful just to be sitting feet away from him.

The company was jovial, and increasingly raucous. I didn't mind any of it, the loud abrupt laughter and the boozy imprecations to enjoy myself. (As a contrast and not a comparison I was thinking of Arthur and his roving gang of scapegraces, with whom I would *not* have been at my ease.)

'You're sure you're all right, Catherine?'

'I'm sure I'm sure, thank you.'

Charles would cover the tops of his wine glasses with his hand when the bottles were passed round. He was keeping himself sober. It might have been that he didn't want to be shown up, or to forget himself.

Later.

'I'll accompany you back.'

'Really, there's no need.'

'You *are* going back? You haven't abandoned them?'

'The Chadwycks? Not yet.'

'You won't, though?'

'One day I shall have to.'

He didn't come to Durley itself, or even to the farm. We parted on a back road.

'I've ruined your day,' I said.

'You've *made* my day.'

I smiled uncontrollably. I thought I was going to cry with gratitude.

'Every time I see you,' he said, 'it's the same.'

'I have to go now.'

He leaned across.

'Catherine, please —'

What was he going to say, or do, next?

Flustered, I picked up my reins before I could find out.

'Goodbye,' I called back at him.

I hoped driving off that I'd dazzled him with my last quicksilver smile. *He*, I felt, had spun my head around.

At least that allowed me to handle the Chadwycks, because in my mind I wasn't *with* them. I was only conscious of where I was at Durley when I fell behind at mealtimes, or dropped something, or had to be asked a question three times.

'Catherine, please —'

He'd leaned across from his saddle and on an instinct I had picked up the reins. Remembering, I stared down at my hands in my lap, saw how clammy they were, and I buried them into the upholstery so no one else would notice.

A long accumulating knot of some pleasurable pain corkscrewed through my stomach. I was corseted, to maintain my poise, but my breath was coming in shorter and shorter and more difficult birdlike sips.

TWENTY

I stopped hearing regularly from Sally.

I continued to write, supposing that there was only some delay in the delivery of *her* letters to me.

Finally one did arrive, but it was no more than a brief note. An acknowledgement of my last letters, and little else.

I wondered what reason there could be for her not being more forthcoming.

Was she dissatisfied in her post? Was she unwell?

Had my own letters sounded to her too much like exulting in my good fortune? To Sally of all people I'd thought I could confess these things. It might have been that distance and some little more experience had worked to change her.

I examined her note for signs of the former closeness, but there was too little in it to offer me any. Even her handwriting seemed more laboured, that script which she had – inevitably – had to base on mine; as if she had sat and written very slowly, very formally, only meaning to disguise what her true feelings were.

'It was extraordinary,' Mouse said as we went walking. 'Just this morning I saw a black boy running across that field.'

I stared at her.

'In a blue suit with gold buttons.'

She laughed.

I continued to stare. Boodle's return to Thurston Park was news to me.

'D'you think I've become too secluded from life, or something?' she asked.

I guessed that she didn't know who the boy was, or – more to the point – who hired him to chaperone at our snatched rendezvous.

She and I saw the hermit approaching in our direction, but this time he made no attempt to avoid us.

He waited for us at a stile. He held out his hand for Mouse's as she negotiated the steps. While I was climbing over and having *my* hand held, he dropped the book he'd been carrying under his arm. I took pity, and bent down at the same time as he did. I saw Mouse smile, then turn away. The hermit retrieved the book first. From between the pages he extracted a small folded sheet of paper and – once he'd checked my companion wasn't looking at me – he presented it to me.

———

The little hermitage had been got ready. There was tea, and a selection of small fancy cakes to eat. Boodle fussed with my cushions, unrolled a linen napkin.

'I would light a candle,' Charles said, 'but we might be seen.'

I agreed that it might not be the best idea. And so we sat on while the light faded across the park, across that assiduous reconstruction of Arcady.

I asked him what was wrong.

'Nothing, nothing.'

I asked again. And again. He wouldn't tell me. I let a few minutes pass. His mood didn't improve. For the fourth time I asked him if anything was wrong.

'You don't want to know that.'

But I persisted.

Another inheritance he'd been depending on wasn't going to come to him after all. His cousins were disputing the old man's will.

(In *Young Werther* the very same situation had occurred. Goethe described the wear and tear on the soul, and because my head was still full of the book I wasn't surprised by what he told me. Goethe's art was to take perfectly from the life.)

He said he had accounts to settle.

I told him off the top of my head, I would lend him some money. I could do it without my father discovering.

'No, Catherine –'

'Whyever not?'

'I couldn't take it.'

'I insist.'

I asked him how much he needed.

'Won't you want a little more?'

I suggested I double the amount.

He stared at me.

'At last,' I said, 'Charles Compeyson is lost for words.'

———

Out of the others' hearing, Moses asked me, 'How did Sir Thomas put it?'

'"Sir Thomas"?'

'Browne.'

'Oh.'

'"Love is the foolishest act. Which dejects the wise man's cooled imagination".'

'You'll have to explain.'

'Ah . . . You're joking, I see.'

He started to laugh. I shook my head.

'No, I *don't* understand.'

After he had put his argument, I offered mine.

Love, I said, took no account of any rules or ordinances.

'Your wretched Werther again?'

But really I was thinking of inflamed Dido.

'The more foolish,' I tagged on, 'the more instinctive, the more natural . . . Then the better. Surely?'

It was hard for me to tell just what Moses thought of my response. He was going to reach into his pocket for his portable copy of Browne, but decided to leave it there. I had a feeling I'd lodged a stick very firmly in the spokes of his poetic wheel.

Our hermit, it transpired, was being obdurate. The not-so-saintly Nemo.

> *Thought he wanted a bit more <u>cash</u>, made him an offer, but he said it wasnt going to be enough. 'Name your Price, then.' He couldnt. I dont know what the reason is, but he's not so green, our friend Mr N.*

I set off to call at the hermitage. But when I had it in my sights, its occupant came into view, talking with W'm. Why W'm? I dodged behind a tree, not to be seen.

Afterwards I thought that W'm must have seen me, he was watching me so closely at the dinner table, just as he used to do.

We spoke about inconsequences.

Wasn't there, though, an ironic curl to his lips? – as if he knew something about me I wouldn't have wanted to be more widely known?

At Durley we had unexpected visitors, a party en route to the coast from London. Among them was the silver-haired man, Garrick's double, who had hovered as silent witness outside the Temple of Thespis – called Calvert. And, with him, the woman I had once passed in a corridor who had seemed only half awake and yet, from under those heavy eyelids, had seemed to miss nothing. The two were now married.

Congratulations were offered to W'm, and Lucinda Osborne was put on display, to general disappointment and a deal of *Schadenfreude*.

I thought I would take advantage of their social activities to tackle the hermit again. Only steps away from his fastness I heard voices. Cries. The door was ajar. I went forward on tiptoe and looked in.

Two dishevelled bodies lay writhing on the floor.

His trousers were undone and his bare buttocks exposed.

Her dress and undergarments were hoisted high on her waist, and her legs were wide apart to admit him.

The pair gasped and moaned while he rode her like a wild thing. His buttocks thrashed and juddered as he plunged in and out of her.

It was W'm – and Mrs Calvert.

She let out a pained, ecstatic moan.

I stumbled back and fell against the door, which creaked. I rolled out over the threshold.

Outside I kept in motion. I started to run; I didn't stop, didn't look back, I ran on legs that seemed not to belong to me.

I continued running, back to Durley Chase, as fast as those legs would carry me.

TWENTY-ONE

That evening I was invincible.

I chattered with our augmented company, I laughed, I argued for and I argued against, I continued to laugh, I regaled the troupe with Rochester tales, I ate my veal escalope heartily and diluted my wine with very little water, I charmed and I cajoled, I sent my laughter shooting up into the top left-hand corner of the frieze in the dining room, I devoured all the fragrance in the bowl of roses, I made faces at myself in the table silver, I imagined myself a beauty for our extended party and for a moment or two perhaps I deceived them as well, I couldn't decide between syllabub and strawberry fritters and took both, I laughed as we ladies got to our feet and then I carelessly drifted from the room, I played a jaunty sarabande on the Broadwood and my fingers flew, I won a hand of vingt-et-un and a second of loo as I knew I must, I laughed as easily at my wit as all the others did, and all this time I betrayed nothing of myself. I let W'm see just what he had let go by him. I was even prevailed upon to sing.

'You have such a pleasing voice, Catherine.'

'Thank you, Lady Chadwyck.'

I sang while Mouse accompanied me, keeping me in tune. The song excused me.

'I'll sail upon the dog-star and then pursue the morning;
I'll chase the moon till it be noon but I'll make her leave
    her horning.'

My voice had never been more supple, or my pitch surer.

'I'll climb the frosty mountain, and there I'll coin the
    weather;
I'll tear the rainbow from the sky and tie both ends
    together.'

Afterwards, alas, came the fall. I didn't appear next morning. I couldn't move from my bed. I lay quite still, staring at the ceiling, like an effigy on a tomb.

Lost all my tender endeavours
To touch an insensible heart.

A maid tiptoed in and out. The housekeeper came and stood over me, and departed.

Sheba, then Mouse, asked if I was ill; answer came there none. I was lamenting my innocence, grieving for my naivety. W'm had caught me first.

Did you not see my love as he past by you?
His two flaming eyes, if he come nigh you,
They will scorch up your hearts.

I had allowed myself to be educated, so that I could be close to him. Any learning I acquired had been for his sake, to try to impress him. How little I had really known about the world's ways.

Ladies, beware ye,
Lest he should dart a glance that may ensnare ye!

A tall, hawk-nosed man introduced himself as the family's physician. He placed his hand on my brow and against my neck, before testing my pulse. He stood against the wall for a good while, and I sensed that all he did was watch me. Moses came to the door, asking after me.

'My estimate would be, this is an upset of the spirits. Where the distracted mind goes, the body will soon follow suit.'

'I shall tell the others. Lady Chadwyck is very anxious to know. I have a letter from her son addressed to you – *with* enclosure.'

'Please thank him. Few deal with the practicalities in such brisk fashion.'

'My cousin is quick, you're quite right, and methodical when he wishes to be.'

W'm must have felt he had good reason to sweeten the physician. *I'll lay me down –*
How easy it was for me like this.
– and die within some hollow tree.
I lay meanwhile on white feathers, layer upon layer, renouncing my folly.

The rav'n and cat,
The owl and bat
Shall warble forth my elegy.

I had flattered him with my attention, and perhaps because of it W'm had thought to ply his charms elsewhere.

Did I really think I might have been half in love with him? He and his friends were too sophisticated and too worldly for love. They sneered at it. I'd had to be rejected to know to look for love elsewhere, and to find it with another. The thing I had seen, at the hermitage, had been a hideous travesty. It had repelled me, but it fascinated me too. Now I couldn't put the obscene picture out of my mind.

I reached for the bell pull, tugged on the cord. The maid came running. I told her to bring me water. I needed to be up, moving about, keeping occupied, busying myself. Or – or should I feel sorry for poor W'm, I wondered as the girl helped dress me: oughtn't I to be pitying him for his ignorance of love?

In the mirror, I found myself again. Concentrating on my face, I worked on its colour. In front of me was someone who realised that this time at Durley Chase must draw to an end. The conclusion would come as it must, but the process had been accelerated within the past twenty-four hours.

At some point the name came up. We were sitting by ourselves, Sheba and Mouse and their mother, and Moses. Lady Chadwyck was talking about the London Set, who seemed to think that the county entertainments were laid on for *their* diversion. Now it was supposed that no event was complete without some representation from them. The Londoners in turn felt they could afford to be choosy about which events they attended.

'Mr Calvert's wife' was mentioned as one of the habitual offenders. I looked up from my book. Sheba turned towards her mother, while all the time darting her needle into her tapestry canvas.

'W'm isn't here to speak up,' Mouse said, blithely unaware. 'I'm sure he would want to defend her.'

'Your brother is a mere provincial to that grandee,' Moses told her.

'He says she has a false reputation.'

'Reputation for what, Marianna?' Lady Chadwyck asked. 'Or –' She hesitated. 'Ought I not enquire?'

'Who has *not* enquired!' Mouse laughed, dealing the last of the cards for a game of piquet with me. 'If that is how she wishes to spend her husband's money, gadding about –'

'She certainly keeps his name in circulation,' Moses said. 'That is one way of viewing her activities.'

At that very moment, at the word 'activities', Sheba caught my eye. I didn't look away in time, and felt the skin on my face heating. I stared at the spread of twelve cards in my hand.

'What is the matter, Isabella?' Lady Chadwyck asked.

'Nothing at all, mother,' Sheba said.

'Have you pricked your finger? Let me see what you've –'

'Don't concern yourself, please.'

It was clear to me now, as I prepared to exchange first on the baize, that I wasn't the only one to know this family's private shame. It felt not like a secret shared, however, but a secret twice hidden.

III

ROCHESTER

TWENTY-TWO

My father was found lying insensible across the desk in his office. He had collapsed.

A new doctor came and pumped out green bile. He told me as soon as I got back home, his heart had suffered, like last time, on account of his diseased lungs.

'His lungs?'

'I gather your father had no knowledge.'

'He had a winter cough. And couldn't shift it.'

'You've been away, Miss Havisham?'

'What can be done about it?'

'You both must exercise forbearance.'

What did the man mean, 'forbearance'?

'He'll recover?'

'I . . .'

I begged him to tell me. Quite frankly.

'His disease will kill him. Later I can give him opium, to dull his pain.'

My father aged quickly after that. Years in only weeks.

Those were his final weeks. I hated what I was witnessing.

Until this point I had seen him not just as he was but as a man who included all his younger selves which I remembered. A composite. Now I couldn't mistake him for anyone except this grey and ashen invalid (when he was in bed) or this stooping and sullen man with whom I shared a house (when he was up on his feet, but shakily), who forgot not to break wind when I was there, who was preoccupied still with the brewery but who looked as if he longed for nothing more than to be done with it.

I would try to remind him that he shouldn't exert himself. Clearly he thought it was extraneous advice; there was work to be done. Born a Havisham and reared a brewer, he had no choice in the matter, and who else to do his job if he didn't?

———

Arthur returned, with a jackal's timing.

My father asked to see him. Arthur alone.

'If you might leave us for a little while, Catherine. Please.'

I stood guard outside the room. It wasn't such a little while.

I went outdoors, into the garden to cool my cheeks.

When I came back in, Arthur passed me in the hall. No engineered collision this time. He was staring in front of him, he didn't seem to notice me at all. His face was quite white, but he was wearing the widest grin I'd ever seen.

I discovered soon enough that my father had repented.

Mr Snee was summoned from London. The will was going to be altered.

My father wouldn't discuss anything with me until the deed was done, until the new papers were signed and Mr Snee had gone on his way again.

Unequal shares, but Arthur's restored inheritance would be a fortune enough.

My father had woken.

I was sitting by the bedside.

'I don't know why you did it, father.'

He didn't reproach me for saying so; he didn't even sigh.

'One day,' he said, 'you may understand.'

'I want to understand *now*.'

'That's my Catherine. Still proud, eh?'

I drew myself straighter in the chair.

He asked me, 'Is it about the money?'

'Of course not.'

'You'll still be a rich woman.'

'I'm not interested in that.'

'You think *you* have first entitlement?'

'Arthur . . .'

'He's had a difficult start in life.'

'He didn't need to.'

'You'd have preferred I was open about my marriage?'

'I'd have preferred . . .'

That my father hadn't married the woman. I stopped myself saying it, but he could finish the remark for himself.

'It's about repairing divisions,' he said, speaking slowly. 'Before it's too late. It's about trying to complete my life – benignly. Benevolently. Making the past and the present consistent. Match up.'

I didn't speak.

'Come on, Catherine. Don't let anything come between us now.'

I placed my hand on the counterpane. He placed his on top of mine. I stared at the marks on the skin that are called the brown flowers of death.

I felt the terrible strength in his hand. I realised he was quitting this life fast.

'I wanted to do what is – truest.'

Through the window I could see Arthur down in the brewery yard, tightening the bit on his horse as a punishment for some misdemeanour.

'I know the truth about Arthur,' I said.

'What's that?'

I had spoken softly so that he might not hear, if he chose not to. 'Nothing, father.'

'I only wanted to do the right thing.'

———

I wished that I could hear from Sally again.

In her last letter to me she had said she thought Miss Stackpole would set off on her travels soon, with staff in tow.

I didn't see why that precluded Sally from writing letters, unless Miss Stackpole was such a tyrant that she didn't permit her servants enough time even to pen a brief note. What was the desirability of the job in that case?

But at least Sally must be having a taste of new places, and didn't she deserve to? It was what her mother had wished for, and I supposed – very reluctantly, though – that I must concede the point.

———

In the last fortnight my father just shrank away.

He curled up in bed like a starved bird, with his face to the wall. He lay without moving, quite still.

If I touched his hand, he didn't register the contact with as much as a shiver. He continued to keep his back turned on us all and his face staring into the plaster on the wall: here was a complete geography in its cracks and pittings, rivers and lakes and coastlines, an entire continent to quieten him.

Even the brewery, when I spoke of it by his bedside, that couldn't draw him back. He'd had his fill.

TWENTY-THREE

They wouldn't grant a resting-place inside the cathedral, let alone a brass commemorative plate.

While my father was alive they had taken his money; but now they didn't consider he justified any preferential treatment.

Born a commoner, he also died a commoner.

———

The modiste advised twenty yards of bombazine for a mourning gown (with long sleeves) and petticoat. (A father's death called for nothing less.) Plus, nine yards of wildbore, for a black stuff German greatcoat. (Please bear in mind, Mademoiselle Havisham, the gown must have complete front fastening, and not a glimpse of petticoat.)

She suggested, since it was the done thing for first mourning, a black paper fan. And black calamanco shoes, even though it mightn't be the latest fashion; but, Madame Morgan said, I wasn't in London, and the choice was dignified.

———

I had requisitioned a tame priest, a man with little faith who suited very well.

Carriages collected in front of the church. The building was respectably filled. Starting to walk to my pew, with Arthur behind me, I caught a glimpse of a small commotion in the porch, a figure in mourning removing stirrups from his boots.

Who else?

I mouthed his name. 'Charles, Charles.'

My spirits revived in an instant.

I glanced round. Arthur was watching the arrival too; I couldn't determine his expression – suspicion, alarm. I tugged at his sleeve, it was time to begin.

Somehow the service passed, and as soon as I had reached the porch I had already forgotten whatever easy words the priest had spoken.

By the graveside I was aware only of not raising my eyes in the direction of the straggling ilex tree, because that was the one *he* was standing beside. I glanced round again at Arthur, who was watching the pallbearers' efforts with disdain. (He hadn't offered to be one of them; his past was quite enough of a burden to him, without making an example of himself to all and sundry.)

It was only then that I forgot not to look over at the shiny jagged ilex tree, and when I did I found Charles quietly smiling: to encourage me, I told myself, to assure me he understood the very charybdis of violent emotions this day was putting me through.

He had arrived wearing deep second mourning. A black silk hat with crepe about the crown and a knotted bow. Black buckles.

I had no reason to be surprised. Perhaps it was the sight of him in so much black that moved me to tears: living and breathing and intensely alive inside his impeccable sartorial restraints.

'It was the death he would have wanted,' someone had the effrontery to say in my hearing, between noisy mouthfuls of tea, as I walked about the room.

People's faces were distorted as they tried to cram chicken legs and portions of pie and cake into their mouths. They drank quickly, before anyone else could drain the decanters.

They disgusted me. They had nothing to do with me.

I had *one* friend here, the truest, but where were the others who had called themselves my friends?

———

A letter of condolence arrived from Lady Chadwyck. But, it occurred to me on re-reading for the fifth or sixth time, the condolences might have been due to the sender.

> *– I feel this to be as great a Loss to myself. The Acquaintanceship of Mr Havisham occurred most propitiously for me, when my Trust in my fellow Mortals was deserting me. Your father had an undue Sensitivity – for a Man, I mean – as to the Wants of a Noblewoman (the which he insisted on calling me!) left prematurely widowed.*

The letter rambled on – written beyond midnight, surely – and skirted round the precise nature of the relationship with the departed. Lady Chadwyck was still shocked by the news, and trying to put her own thoughts regarding the future into some (cryptic) order.

No letter arrived from any of the others. They would have heard, wouldn't they? Or had Lady Chadwyck preferred to conceal the news from them for a while – until the mist of uncertainty obscuring, so to speak, the lawns and topiary of Durley Chase had cleared a little.

———

After the will had been read, my father's lawyer took me outside into the Cherry Garden.

'No surprises there, I dare say.'

'If you wish to put it like that, Mr Snee. No, there weren't.'

'Mr Arthur doesn't appear too pleased.'

He had just discovered that his inheritance was to be paid in annual instalments over ten years.

'It may teach him virtues of economy,' I said. But I doubted that very much.

Mr Snee was a small man, smaller than myself, with a face that might have been sharpened with a knife – and then treated with preserving vinegar. When my father first became acquainted with him, the lawyer was thought well of, but lean and hungry for success. Success soon came to him, and those clients he chose to retain were similarly equipped to do well.

My father had always been a little in awe of him; any meeting was preceded by an unusual degree of nervousness, even tension, in his manner.

'So you knew what to expect, Miss Havisham?'

'My father did explain to me.'

'To you both?'

'To us both, yes.'

His nose, when I inclined my head to the right and glanced a little down, looked sharp enough to cut my hand on. Then I realised that, without needing to turn *his* head, his eyes were swivelled sideways in their sockets, watching me.

I was embarrassed, and jumped in.

'But it's just *me*, is it, you want to speak to, Mr Snee?'

'Since it concerns yourself, yes, I judged it best.'

And he explained. (Before, he said, I should hear about it some other way.)

My father, he began, had been lending money for several years to a certain beneficiary.

'"Lending money"?'

'On such favourable terms, some might have judged the exercise foolhardy.'

'To whom?'

'That is the nub.'

'Someone connected with my stepmother?'

'There is no connection.'

'To whom, then?'

'You can't guess?'

'Not at all.'

'Really and truly?'

'I *can't* guess. Please, Mr Snee, tell me.'

Should I have been able to deduce the answer for myself?

'Your patroness, no less.'

'I *beg* your pardon –'

'The good Lady Chadwyck herself.'

I knew immediately how often I would return in my mind to these moments, how my memories of Durley Chase would be endlessly complicated by the item of information I had just been given.

What it had amounted to was this: my father, for his own reasons which *he* judged best, had gained the amity of the Chadwycks for me by the only means he knew. By buying it with his tradesman's ready money.

'Why, though?'

'You are a wealthy young woman, Miss Havisham.'

'I can't deny it.'

'I expect you'll have a wider circle now.'

'Very probably. But –'

'More friends than you ever knew you had.'

'What does this –'

'Your father craved – that isn't too strong a word – he craved you should have an introduction to that world. He wished doors to open for you. You needed to receive a training first.'

And the Chadwycks had obliged. My father had made it worth

their while to oblige. His association with Lady Charlotte had been mercenary from the outset.

'And the understanding with her ladyship? You'd like that to continue? Or . . . ?'

Why *not* continue with the arrangement? I could afford to do so. I wanted to prove to the Chadwycks, and also to myself, that I wasn't petty. (And maybe I wanted to savour too a little of my own glory.)

'Yes,' I said. 'Thank you, Mr Snee.'

'Have you seen any of them since?'

'No.'

'Or corresponded?'

I shrugged.

'We need discuss it no further. And my discretion in the business is naturally guaranteed.'

I nodded my appreciation.

Such attentiveness, from one whose erstwhile reputation for quick thinking and lawyerly subtlety had always been so considerable. I was bound to be paying for it, and heavily, but I was a rich woman now.

———

I concluded that money was capable of doing good and also terrible things.

It had brought comfort to Lady Chadwyck, but it had perverted relationships, making them seem what they weren't – and what they had no right to be.

I saw now, normally *they* would never have had the need to consort with the likes of me. Only my father's money had persuaded the children, at their mother's bidding, to entertain what must always have seemed to them an improbable friendship.

TWENTY-FOUR

Sally, Sally.

Maybe she had other interests now, and other loyalties? I presumed her cousin *had* received and sent on my own letters. Could it be that Sally had left Miss Stackpole's employment, or even been dismissed? If the latter, she would have felt embarrassed to write straight away; and time has a way of turning small procrastinations into habits. She might have felt it had got awkward, to take up where she'd left off, without the need of some explanation.

I was doing all I could to excuse Sally. Couldn't she get just an inkling of it, and respond with the briefest of notes, merely to keep in touch with me? Whatever her reasons for not communicating, I was only too ready and willing to forgive her.

———

Arthur was coming in at all hours. He had meals prepared in the middle of the night. He let his dogs have the run of the house, his boots left the floors in a mess. Things had gone missing.

'So, what is this? A house, or some private museum?'

'You treat it like a staging-inn. And sometimes like a farmyard.'

I heard myself raising my voice at him. Which only set him smiling.

'Don't go upsetting yourself on my account –'

'I'm not . . .'

'Save yourself for someone who deserves you.'

His smile turned to rude, knowing laughter.

———

I received a letter from him.

'*Most obediently, Charles.*'

It carried no address except '*London*'.

My Dear Catherine,

   I'm afraid that my Affairs are likely to detain me awhile. As you know I travel up to Norwich and whatnot, & things are at a head at the moment wh. makes it difficult to get away. You need all yr. wits for Business, as you will appreciate, & there is the possibility I shall have to venture further afield, wh. will be unplanned if & when. But I do assure you of my continuing concern, if I might presume so, & my best regards for your Success & Welfare.

Even allowing for his stylistic lapses, I concluded that the letter had been hastily written. He was telling me as much as he wanted me to know.

I read the letter over dozens of times. I wished I could reply.

Like Goethe's Werther, '*Today I put your letter to my lips and the contact of paper had me gritting my teeth.*'

———

I went into my father's office and sat down. I leaned back in the chair, and felt too small for it. The proportions of my back to the chair back and my legs to the shank of the seat were wrong.

He had sat here for twenty-five or thirty years, since he had inherited the private room – next to the general Compting House –

from his father. This had offered him his outlook on the world. The desk, the shelves of past ledgers, the view of the brewhouse, the roofs of the outhouses, a few trees, a church tower. With the window sash pushed up, he would have been able to hear snatches of gossip and tittle-tattle from downstairs, when the domestic staff had recourse to pass the brewery workers or the delivery men.

And yet I wondered just how much I had really known with any degree of certainty about him.

I opened a ledger at the final completed page. 'Purchases'. I read down the figures on the list, entered in his tidy hand.

Tears welled up. Hot spicy tears that nipped my eyes. They sped down the runnels on my cheeks, dropped from my chin on to the page, and instantly blotted the ink. My own mark of proprietorship.

———

Rates assessment:

£50 – Brew house

£70 – 4 malthouses

£26 10s 0d – 8 storehouses

£15 – 2 warehouses

£2 – cellar

£3 – cinder ovens

£10 – stock valued at £200

Twenty-four public houses had an average rateable value of £6 16s 5d.

I had to acquaint myself with the alternative accounting methods in the Compting House – and the twain didn't necessarily match, or were meant to.

Victuallers' Book, to register sales in butts to public houses.

A book to record country trade.

A Petty Ledger, detailing private dealings with favoured (personal) clients.

A Yeast Book.

A Grain Book, both specifying sales.

Additionally there were:

Brewing Books, noting every aspect of production, including each successive brew.

Letters Book.

Loan Ledger.

Bond Ledger.

Interest Ledger.

Rent Ledger.

Inventory Ledger.

Stock Ledger.

My father's office contained two other sets of records. First, the Rest Books: the yearly balance drawn up in early June, referring to debts and liabilities, and placing a value on the combined stock and trade. (Because my father was sole proprietor, answerable only to himself, he was under no obligation to keep these Rest Books. But since he had done, I deduced that he may have intended bringing in partners, or effecting an alliance with another sort of business than a brewer.) Secondly, the Private Ledgers: a register of every loan accepted and made that concerned the firm. These were kept in a separate locked drawer, intended for no one's eyes but my father's.

I had my clerks to assist me: the home clerks in the Compting House, and the abroad-clerks, who collected the monthly payments from publicans. Mr Tice was the brewery manager, whom I inherited. I promoted Mr Ambrose to be my chief clerk, which didn't please some of the others, not least Mr Tice.

I privately and confidentially asked Mr Ambrose if he would be a separate conduit to me of the brewers' and coopers' affairs, since –

he might have guessed, although I didn't state it so to him – I wasn't confident that I was receiving all the information I needed via the regular, formal channels.

—

Another letter arrived from Charles, from London, forwarded through a third party. He told me he was obliged to leave the country for a while – on a matter relating to business, he said, which had arisen quite unexpectedly. It wasn't clear to him how long it would be until he returned: not before there was a satisfactory outcome, at any rate. But he assured me of his most sincere best wishes in the interim, and every success in dealing with the affairs of the brewery, as a little bird told him I was doing.

I re-read this letter, as I had done the previous one, dozens of times. I imagined where he might be. If not the British Isles – France, or Holland, or further afield than either? How thoughtful of him to dwell on my own struggles here to make sense of the brewery finances when he had his own equally pressing concerns.

I was to hear from him four more times over the next seven months. Every communication was one to be treasured. It surprised me a little to think of someone so fond of the excitement of chance games – cards, racing – currently having to subjugate himself to whatever those 'business matters' were.

But now we had this new and unanticipated bond between us.

—

I wrote to Lady Chadwyck, thanking her for her commiserations, and those of the children that had eventually followed. I explained that I was necessarily detained at Satis House, that it wasn't at all clear to me when I might get away. I phrased my next remark with

care: hoping that their own lives 'continued as before'. (Meaning –
continued without any financial disturbance or upset.)

Once Durley Chase had seemed to me a fine and even perfect
place. The octagonal domed house on its airy knoll; the french
doors standing open. Family portraits, Greek maidens and their
suitors gambolling round the ceiling friezes. The lawns, the periph-
eries of long grass; the picturesquely convenient fallen boles, the
designed vistas.

Now . . . I felt now that I had outgrown it. That gracious but
stultifying existence, the proper – oh, always *so* proper – narrowness
of its scope. I was bored with it, the decorous routines, the never too
indiscreet gossip, even the theatricals where we pretended at nobil-
ity and legend we fell so far short of.

Everything, finally, had been play, which seemed to me not
enough for a life.

———

I found a forgotten garter halfway up the second flight of stairs,
kicked into the corner of one of the treads. I extracted it with the
toe of my shoe. A frilled, flesh-pink garter.

The scene inside the hermitage on that last day flashed into my
mind.

'Arthur! *Arthur!*'

'What in hell's all this noise about?'

'You recognise this?'

'I know what a garter looks like.'

'And its wearer?'

He shrugged.

'D'you forget so easily?' I asked him.

He raised his eyes. They were pink-rimmed, short-sighted, weak.

'*Not* wearing it, of course,' I said. 'That is the point.'

'Since when have I been accountable to you?'

I tried to field his question with a dismissive stare. A scowl. But it didn't silence him.

'Why should I listen to what a frustrated virgin tells me?'

That was too much for me.

'I won't have your harlots in this house. My father's house.'

'*Our* house.'

'I'll wear you down, I promise you. If *they* don't first. I'll prey on you, Arthur, until this is the last place you ever want to come again.'

I couldn't bear to have his company under the same roof after that. So, without consulting him but issuing my directive (as a command), I ensured that by partitioning the building into my territory and his, technically under *two* roofs, we shouldn't have to encounter one another more than once or twice in a week.

His friends were informed by him – with more accuracy than error – that I had planted spies among the household staff, and that he was treated as something of a criminal himself. Those same cronies of his were unsettled to be here, and came about much less often in this colder climate that prevailed.

———

I took solace in my work. It didn't bother me that Arthur remained uninvolved. Not in the least. The office wouldn't have been a refuge to me otherwise. An *active* refuge. I put in enough hours for the two of us.

Weeks passed. I hardly noticed. Just as I no longer noticed the smell of brewery hops in the air. Facts and figures, only those. A game of holding my nerve, when everyone else (except Mr Ambrose) thought I was bound to buckle at last.

———

The name HAVISHAM was repainted on the brewhouse wall. It had taken the weather; the paint blistered by the sun, the brick-work nibbled at by storms.

The letters remained green, and the same shape, but now they had a thin gilt strip on one side while, on the other, they dropped a small black shadow.

We were even more prominent now from the London road. We looked prosperous, singing our own praises.

TWENTY-FIVE

The brewery had its own malthouses. We bought our hops from four farms in a long valley near Ashford, at Burwell. My father would pay an annual visit, a few weeks ahead of harvesting time, to inspect the crop on its bines and to agree a price for however many hundredweight. Now the journey fell to me. I gave responsibility for the hop-buying to myself, but acting on sage advice from two of the firm's old hands.

It was arranged that they would ride there, and I would make my way in the curricle. We stopped to water the horses midway, at the inn where my father had always halted. The driver reminded me that my father had once brought Arthur, at the time when it seemed he would be working alongside him.

The owner of the inn presented himself. Would I do him the pleasure, the great pleasure, of resting in his best private room?

I thanked him, but told him we were late already, that I didn't –

'I venture to ask, ma'am, on behalf of another.'

'On behalf of whom?'

I discovered when I was shown into the room.

'Catherine –'

The blood rushed to my face.

'Charles!'

'Surprised?'

'How on earth did you know –'

'– you'd be here? Oh, I have ways and means.'

'But . . .'

'Never mind that now.'

He was dressed for a horse, but in dashing style. A waisted cut-away coat and tight breeches. What a handsome figure he –

I reached out for the support of the high mantelpiece.

'I'm not here,' he said. 'I'm far away. Officially.'

'"Officially"?'

'If anyone should ask.'

'Why should – ?'

He put his index finger to his lips.

'There's been a bit of confusion, that's all. Or there *might* be. It'll get sorted out, though.'

'Can I help?'

'You've been help enough.'

'That was nothing.'

'This is *my* doing,' he said, '*my* fault.'

'Your "fault"? What is?'

'No, Catherine. Remember what I said – ?'

I nodded my head.

Coffee and chocolate were brought into the room. He drank quickly.

'I'm so glad I was able to intercept you.'

'You could've called at the house,' I said.

'I think not.'

'No. No, I . . .'

My face heated again.

'I was waiting for the first sound of your carriage's wheels . . .'

He was gone before I was quite ready, taking a back staircase down. I had the touch of his hand on mine; I could still feel where he had brushed his lips against the skin on the back: speedily, but with great gentleness.

. . . and Joy shall overtake us as a flood.

The final moments were left so sweetly in my memory. I stood swaying slightly with emotion at the top of the staircase. I listened as his footfalls grew fainter, as the jangle of his stirrups faded; I heard the clatter of shod hooves on the courtyard cobbles, and five seconds later I could hear nothing of him at all.

It had been a decent year for the hops, I was told, with less disease about and less mould than last.

At Burwell we inspected the bines still to be picked. We compared the Flemish variety with the Kent. I was told the very best pickers were on two shillings a day, which seemed to me excessive, and I said so, but I didn't argue the point.

I was shown figures. Sixty-two hundredweight on ten acres last year, and a profit of £5 15s od.

'You're not complaining?' I asked them.

'Things could always be better.'

'These are hard times, Mr Foxton.'

'Indeed, Miss Havisham. But . . .'

'I shall look at my own ledgers. I can't make any promises, however.'

'That's most civil of you.'

Suddenly I was exhausted.

'Are you feeling all right, Miss Hav—?'

I saw again that scene inside the hermitage, the two bodies writhing at their pleasure on the floor.

My head was spinning.

'You've come over very pale, if I might —'

I was taken out of the sun, into the oast house. A chair was found for me. The hops were drying, and the air was hot and stifling from the wood fire. I could only manage a few minutes there, but that was sufficient.

Briefly I'd thought I was going to cry – I felt a sudden terrible sense of desolation – but just in time I pulled myself together, bundling my litter of wanton feelings back under cover.

———

An apprentice lawyer called Jaggers – in Mr Snee's practice – wrote to me, requesting the favour of my time on an issue – as he judged – of no little importance. He begged that I did not inform his employer of his communication.

I was intrigued.

I received a swarthy, sturdily built, bullet-headed young man. His wrinkled shirt collar strained to hold his muscular neck. Samson, I thought of, with the hair on his head cropped close to stubble.

He was far from disempowered, though, despite his subordinate position.

For a few seconds I was alarmed by this sizeable presence. He was tongue-tied at first, but I sensed the confidence he had in his own mission.

'We have something to discuss, Mr Jaggers?'

Indeed we did.

My visitor had discovered that Snee was an embezzler. He was defrauding me of this and that, but principally of the monies due to Lady Chadwyck. She had received nothing since before my father's death, since the time of his collapse.

'You're quite sure of your facts, Mr Jaggers?'

'I waited until there could be no possible doubt.'

'I see. I see.'

He had retreated to the other side of the fireplace. He stood chewing one index finger, clearly forgetful of everything except the gravity of his news. I liked that air of abstraction which was testimony of his diligence surely. His breath filled his bullock's chest, I could imagine the shirt buttons were ready to burst off.

'And you mean to gain nothing for yourself?'

The question appeared to shock him. I had asked it chiefly in play, in order to lighten the dark mood.

'Only to escape the infectious atmosphere of self-interest I'm forced to endure.'

'It really won't affect you too?'

'I'm young.'

'As Mr Snee was once.'

'You think the same is bound to happen to me, Miss Havisham?'

'Not necessarily.'

'It might, though?'

'Then I hope you'll prove yourself to me. As you have started to recommend yourself already.'

I confronted Snee myself. He denied my accusations more strongly than I anticipated. I called in my informant. Snee understood at once; there and then he wrote out a money order.

'To deal with this embarrassment, my dear lady –'

'"Embarrassment"? And how dare you "dear lady" me!'

I demanded that Mr Jaggers be allowed to gain his articles elsewhere. I would leave my affairs with Snee meantime. Thereafter, when he was fully qualified, Mr Jaggers would take over, representing my interests. If the transference was handled cleanly, I would *presume* that no earlier dishonesty had occurred, and forgo the pleasure of pressing criminal charges, as the older man must know very well he merited. With that I made the first of my enemies in business – Snee – and my first and trustiest ally – Jeremiah Jaggers.

However recompense might be offered, I would be admitting to the Chadwycks that I knew now about the financial arrangements that had pertained.

I could see no way around that problem.

No pretence of innocence was possible. Experience can never be undone, or knowledge unlearned.

Following my father's death, I had acted with the best intentions – not that they were ever likely to discover. Either I must simply let matters be, and hope other means were at the family's disposal, or I should pay them what was due.

The latter, I decided.

I wanted not to damage the past, even though I was acknowledging to myself that *that* part of the past was over.

———

War against France was pushing up taxation, and every brewer in the land had headaches.

Duty on hops was increased from fifteen shillings to 23s 4d per hundredweight. Duty on strong beer went up from eight to ten shillings a barrel. Malt duty was raised from 1s 4d a barrel to 2s 5d, then shortly afterwards to 4s 5d. The price of materials for pale malt almost doubled, from forty-four shillings a quarter to 81s 6d.

I got wind that some of the pubs were adulterating the brews, and I heard the idea being put about for ourselves too. (Substituting molasses for some of the malt. Mixing strong and light table beers, and marketing the result as 'strong'.) It would cut production costs certainly, but I felt it would be unfaithful to my father's memory to tamper with the recipes that had made us successful.

I tried to trim the labour costs, exchanging a few full-time for part-time jobs. I would have preferred to replace the voices that advocated watering down, but I was afraid of tangling with working practices at that level, at any rate before I had gained more expertise.

There's a silver lining to every dark cloud, however, and when it became too expensive for small house brewers and publicans to continue brewing, they turned to the common houses for their supplies. When one door closes, as they say, another one will open.

———

'How d'you know that?'

'Know what, sister?'

'About the Carnaval Ball.'

'Aa-*haa*!'

'Who told you?'

'Doesn't matter to you.'

'*Who*, Arthur?'

'Good God, I can't remember.'

'"Can't remember"?'

'No problems with your hearing, Catherine.'

'Or you *won't* remember?'

'What're you asking me for? I don't stuff my head with all that nonsense. Once something's happened, it's over. Gone.'

He was proud, like me. He took advice from no one, and would be obliged to no one. He thought he had his entitlements.

He selected what he wanted to take from the past: the past of his Havisham forebears.

He was aware that he had a role to play, and doubted that he had the talent for it.

He was afraid of revealing too much of himself.

For all that was different between us, we two had just as much in common, and this was my stumbling block, the point I could never think beyond.

TWENTY-SIX

One morning it happened: Charles was standing in the yard.

I had to look twice. Suddenly my heart was up in my throat, I was swallowing on it.

He was back!

. . . and Joy shall overtake us as a flood.

The blood was pounding inside my head.

I turned in different directions before I decided which. I wanted to change my dress first. Reset my hair.

A knock on the drawing-room door.

'You have a gentleman visitor, miss. He said he's come back from abroad. And you'll be able to guess who he is.'

He had been in Holland.

'Do you mean to absent yourself again?'

'It's not my intention. But life throws up surprises.'

He was complimentary about his surroundings. He noticed little details of the architecture and the decor, and I congratulated him for it.

'*Shouldn't* I notice? Have I forgotten my English manners?'

'No, no. But – it's more than I was . . . I'm glad, though.'

'Then I'm glad *you're* glad, Catherine.'

He didn't tell me what had detained him for all those weeks in Amsterdam.

'So, what's it like? Being a woman in a man's world?'

'I've had my honeymoon. After this . . . well, I don't know.'

'So much has changed for you.'

'In some respects, yes. But –' I lifted my eyes, '– in other respects, I haven't. Not at all. I'm exactly the same.'

———

I suggested that we should meet in London. Charles sighed.

'I'm not "tired of life", Catherine. But I do get tired of London. London belongs to everyone. Somewhere else. Somewhere that's just our own.'

It was always somewhere else.

Wherever we wouldn't be likely to cross paths with the Chadwycks, although of course we could never be sure about that.

On the Downs. In Tunbridge Wells. The Weald way.

I would take along a maid, for form's sake, but send her and the driver off for an hour or two.

Charles and I would walk. Sit before a view. Talk.

Happy days! I knew they were happy as we were living them.

Standing looking over the parapet of a bridge, down into a slow weedy river. Strolling through the fragrant shadows of a wood. Climbing, once, up the staircase of a windmill with its great sails revolving and cracking in the wind.

He saw how content I was. He told me he wished he could draw me well enough to take a sketch, but anyway he would always remember me like this. (Did he, very fleetingly, look a little troubled? Or am I mentally painting myself an idealised portrait of the man?)

I said to him, I could better appreciate this time we spent together because it was so precious, stolen from the timetable I had set myself at the brewery.

What a pity, he said in his turn, that we *had* to steal it.

'What d'you mean?'

'If we couldn't organise ourselves that this *was* our life.'

'No guilt?'

He smiled at the question. And pointedly didn't reply.

I thought quickly.

'I could give other people my work to do,' I said. 'Some of it.'

'I wasn't quite thinking of that. In the short term, yes.'

'"Short term"? You have a long-term stratagem too?'

'It's taking shape up here.' He pointed to the site of his brain.

'Can you tell me?' I asked.

'Might be unlucky.'

We were having our conversation on a river, in a scull. A faster river than the Cam. I sat looking up at the trees rushing past against blue.

'You'll tell me when you can?'

'I promise.'

'Then that will do me *very* well.'

———

But there was also Arthur. To begin with, he had been pestering me for small amounts: just until he could lay his hands on the next whack of cash from his inheritance.

'It's nothing to *you*,' he would say. 'You've got pots of the stuff. Don't humiliate me.'

'What happened to the last lot?'

'Got all used up.'

'Aren't I supposed to be *lending* it?'

'Oh, you'll get it back.'

'When?'

'This is to make sure I *do* get the money.'

'The money to pay me back?'

'Naturally to pay you back.'

But I knew better than to believe him.

He kept asking. I would put up a fight, and he never received what he wanted, or even half of it sometimes. But I did give in to him.

'There's no more, though.'

'It's not enough.'

'It's all you're getting.'

'*You* can afford it.'

'Did I miss "thank you"?'

'Would you like me to prostrate myself too?'

'That really would be stretching all credulity.'

'*You* call the shots, all-infallible one!'

Shortly afterwards something occurred to make me nervous, on that reprobate's behalf.

Loud insistent knocks rained down on the front door.

My visitors were looking for Mr Arthur Havisham. They had some business to discuss with him, urgently.

(Arthur had removed himself that morning – by no mere accident, I now realised.)

They frightened me, the trio, with their undertakers' black clothes and faux-solemnity and their grave-robber faces.

I performed at my most imperious. I thought of Dido and of Carthage. From a window I watched them leave the yard. Arthur returned late in the evening, when darkness had come down.

'I think you owe me an explanation,' I said.

'They go dunning. They demand money with menaces.'

'Is the money due them?'

'I would give it to them if I had it. All the interest adds up.'

'What's it for?'

'Past pleasures, let's just say.'

'For which you are duly contrite?'

'If I knew what being "duly contrite" entailed –'

'Those men put the fear of God into me.'

'And me too.'

'Something truthful from you at last. All is not in vain.'

'Please. For our father's sake —'

I sighed out my soul.

'Just — just tell me how much . . .'

When Charles wasn't there, I sagged. (Did the trees droop by nature's will, or because I told them what my feelings were?)

I should have been walking tall – and, doubtless, proud. But I was afraid every time he left me, not just unhappy. Fear cut me right down to size, and then it slammed an iron bar against my stomach.

My panic was that he wasn't coming back, or that I wouldn't see him again. My imagination threw a caul of gentle thoughts around him, to protect him, but all the time I was having to cope with my demons.

Wherever Charles might be, he would know that he wasn't alone. Where *did* he go?

There was a cousin in Suffolk, a farmer of some sort. Up in Norwich a friend sold land and stock. He visited this or that hospitable relative, or else he looked up a (temporarily, he hoped) ailing schoolfriend.

Here and there, hither and thither.

He had a sister in London, but he could only call at her home when her husband wasn't there. The man had heard false stories, put about by someone with a grievance. Charles claimed to be unperturbed.

'Doesn't worry me. I won't allow it to.' But he had to time his visits there carefully.

At last I received an address from him, in Blackheath.

'I've got some people staying.'

'Kin?'

'So they say.'

'Aren't they?'

'It's difficult to prove. Or disprove.'

We laughed at that.

'You don't pick your family,' he said. 'Unfortunately.'

'I wish, I wish.'

'But that's where my correspondence goes to.'

'That's all I need to know,' I told him.

'Is it so easy to please you?'

'You'd be surprised' – I spoke through my smile – 'just how little it takes.'

———

I would wake in the night, convinced at once that he was close to me, and naked, that he was a blaze on the sheets of my bed.

I reached out my hand and touched . . . only a very little warmth where I had been lying over on my flank.

And immediately I was ashamed of myself, and I wondered where these thoughts could have come from, how I was capable of bringing them to feverish mind.

I would settle back down. I was alone – of course I was.

I felt the tide of desire receding.

I closed my eyes and set about finding cool thoughts to think instead, safely stranding myself – as that troublesome tide ebbed and ebbed – on the drily ordinary and contingent, brewery matters and the soon-to-be needs of the housekeeping.

———

'Mr Compeyson will be passing through.'

('Tell your brother I'll be passing through.')

'I think you should meet him.'

('Say, you think he should meet me.')

'It's nothing to me,' Arthur said. 'But am I allowed to criticise the company you keep? As you criticise mine?'

'I thought you might want to see him.'

'Anyone who's taken with you, that *would* be worth –'

'He's not "taken".'

'Why's he here, then?'

'He's passing through. D'you listen to nothing I say?'

———

Arthur stood by the fire, with his boot up on the fender, eating cherries and spitting the stones into the hearth. He meant to leave our visitor in no doubt as to his own status in the house. He addressed him in his gruffest voice, calling him 'Compeyson'.

His purpose was as much to offend me, however, as to put Charles Compeyson in his place. (See, sister dearest, *this* is what I think of your choice of confidant.)

When he couldn't bear to look at me any longer, he kicked the coals back into the grate and stared into the flames.

I apologised afterwards. 'I'm very sorry about Arthur.'

'Not at all.'

'I've looked for redeeming virtues. I just can't find any.'

'Somewhere there must be.'

He shrugged Arthur off. What interested him, he said, was being allowed to see the brewery.

I asked Tice if he would show my guest round.

'*If* you'd be so good,' Charles said to him.

Tice drew himself fully upright. But of course, I told myself, he'll stand to attention for a man.

I waited until they'd finished.

'Don't pretend *that* was a pleasure!'

'But it was. You've known this place all your life, remember. It's an adventure to me.'

'Really?'

We had tea outside in the garden. I was a little nervous, in case Arthur appeared again. I chattered away, I spoke too much.

Arthur only appeared as we were saying our goodbyes. He might have timed it for that moment.

Another sneer.

But the two went off into the stable together, where Charles's mount was waiting.

I heard them talking. Arthur wasn't being openly insulting, I hoped.

I waited.

Something was said: '. . . a licence to print money, isn't it?'

It must have been Arthur speaking. Denigrating Havisham's, as ever.

Charles came out, leading his roan stepper which I had helped him to buy.

'I'm sorry about that,' I said.

'He's all right.'

'You don't have to say anything nice about him. On *my* account.'

'He's not so bad.'

'I don't understand him at all.'

'It's easier for a man, maybe.'

'That's what I value about you,' I said.

'What's that?'

'Oh . . . your optimism.'

'Is that how you see me?'

'Looking on the bright side.'

'In lieu of all the other trappings?'

'It's a spiritual gift.'

His eyes widened momentarily, as if my observation alarmed him.

'Money alone can't buy it,' I said. 'Or privilege either.'

TWENTY-SEVEN

A few weeks later.

'I hear', I said, 'that your knowledge is very impressive, Mr Compeyson.'

'Met a brewer once. Things've stuck in my head.'

'I'll teach you what I know,' I heard myself telling him. 'If that's any use.'

'"Use"? You're schooling me?'

I felt I was in danger of blushing.

'Well,' I said, 'I'll need your advice. I mean, I would appreciate if you –'

'I'd be honoured. Couldn't be taught by better, could I?'

———

Before my father's physical decline, production of strong beer was running at over twelve thousand barrels per annum. I made that my own target.

I was buying another five public houses, at prices between £230 and £480 each. Including another thirty-six tied premises, the number of publics we supplied had risen to eighty-six.

On his visits to the town Charles put up at the Blue Boar. He ate there, unless I had invited others to dinner at Satis House, when I would persuade him to join us. But in Cinderella fashion, he was the first to leave. All this punctilious formality, this terrible fear of committing an improper deed. All this intense frustration he let build up inside me. I asked him to stay on awhile in the house, so that we might walk in the garden or sit by the fire, talking, dreaming of life.

But no, he must be getting back.

'If you really have to.'

'We can't always do as we want.'

'No?'

'There are rules. Precepts.'

'You're right.'

But I said it sadly.

———

It occurred to me that perhaps they hadn't been what they'd seemed to me, those three men who appeared at the front door in their threatening poses, asking for Arthur.

I had no trust in anything Arthur said. All I could take as honest was his determination to embarrass me, to provoke my conscience, because it was I and not he who had inherited the greater part of the Havisham wealth.

Organising a few stage stooges to appear on the doorstep of Satis House, that would have been nothing at all to someone of Arthur's deviousness.

'It's only fifty.'

'*Another* fifty pounds you're asking me for. Added to the hundred.'

'I got my sums wrong.'

Here's yet another scene.

'How long d'you imagine this is going to go on?'

'It's just to tide me over.'

'You never tell me. What these "expenses" are.'

'That's because you don't want to know. Tell me you do.'

'Your life doesn't interest me, Arthur.'

'Maybe I'm keeping another household.' He laughed. 'I've got a nice little wife. And we're planning a brood of children.'

He continued laughing.

'That *is* a joke,' I said.

'What is?'

'You married. And a father.'

'And you see *yourself* married, I suppose?'

I looked away.

'All nicely set up?' (How bitter his voice sounded.) 'With the man of your dreams?'

First, Charles told me the house in Blackheath was shedding masonry. Then, that the building was being pinned up. For weeks the air had been thick with dust; the mortar wouldn't dry. The floorboards would have to be replaced. An elderly uncle was about to descend, needing to convalesce.

'From Norfolk?' I asked.

'Norfolk?'

'Your relatives. In Norfolk. Or Suffolk.'

'Yes, Norfolk. That's where he's from. From Norfolk. He needs looking after, so I've got someone in.'

'Oh.'

'Just a nurse. Sort of nurse.'

I nodded.

'He can get up to the river?' I asked.

'Who can?'

'Your uncle. You're close to the river in Blackheath?'

'He's a cussed so-and-so. I don't want to inflict him on you.'

'He's improving?'

'His health is. Not his temper, though.'

'He'll go back to Norfolk?'

'To Norfolk? Yes. Eventually.'

'Poor you.'

His spirits seemed to sink a little at that. His smile was wan. He shook his head.

'I don't deserve sympathy,' he said.

———

I found I was trying now to excuse Arthur to Charles. I didn't want anything to come between the two of us, even that wretch.

'But you told me he wasn't up to it – didn't you?'

'He lacks experience,' I said.

'He'd ruin the business, though. Given a chance.'

'His mind's on other things. He's younger than –'

'Catherine, it's useless. You can't go on defending him.'

'Couldn't he learn?'

'No. He'd be useless in a situation like this.'

'So, what can I do about it?'

'Look – Arthur needs money. Access to money.'

'Certainly he does,' I said. 'I can't tell for what –'

'Let's not enquire.'

'That's his argument, "you wouldn't want to know".'

'Take your pick.'

'Gambling?' I suggested.

'Very probably. But our concern is to get him off your hands.'

'Indeed.'

'So – so you have to pay him more.'

'No. No, I thought you said –'

'Wait a minute, Catherine. Pay him, in return *for* something. Something that you want.'

'What's that? What do I want?'

'His share in the business.'

'I beg your pard—'

'You heard me.'

'Yes, but . . .'

'If you pay – if you pay for his holding in the company . . . You see the advantages, don't you?'

'I'm trying to.'

'Then you wouldn't have the worry of his involvement!'

'How would –'

'It can be done in stages.'

'But the cost of it!' I said.

'It would cost you a lot. But think of the rise in profits.'

'It would mean – I'd have to take over all the running, wouldn't I?'

'Not necessarily.'

'"Not necessarily"?'

Might I not, he asked, think of engaging some assistance?

'What kind of assistance?'

'Sharing the responsibilities.'

'How?' I asked.

'Turning it over to a new senior manager.'

'I don't know who . . .'

He was smiling. He started to laugh.

'*Who?*' I said.

'Who do you think?'

It took me three or four seconds to realise.

'*You?*'

'Don't sound so aghast!'

'But I hadn't . . .'

'Why not? I know what I know. And I'll learn. Quickly. I promise you.'

I stood staring at him.

'Your father didn't have you mixing with the Chadwycks so that you'd come back to run a brewery.'

I nodded at that.

'*And*,' he said, 'it'll give us a chance to be together more often. Won't it?'

He reached forward and took my hand. His was warm. I felt the surge of energy in the fingers.

He raised my hand. Lightly, tenderly, he touched the back with his lips. How – how could I have thought to refuse?

'But,' he said as he straightened, as he gently let go of my hand, 'I shall ever be discreet.'

How could I have told him that I didn't care if he was not; that I secretly wished he wouldn't be – that he'd be anything but.

I wrote to Arthur in the fleshpot resort where he had taken up residence. I set out my proposals, the financial terms.

At first he refused me.

'Well, let *me* try dinning some sense into him.'

Whatever Charles must have said, Arthur was persuaded, and he agreed to my buying an initial portion of his interest.

The next time he was asked, the price of his remaining interest was doubled.

Charles reported back to me.

'That's just business, Catherine, I'm afraid.'

I sat down to complete another banker's order. I had never seen, let alone written, such a large figure before.

'You're hesitating . . .'

'It was my father's wish. For his son. His atonement.'

'Courage, Catherine.'

'If my father could've seen how much . . .'

'That's Arthur's asking price. He won't give an inch.'

'You're quite sure?'

'*Quite* sure.'

'Very well.'

'You'll recover it. And more. Much more.'

'It will take a while.'

'But if you don't act, if you don't do this – Arthur will be disagreeing with you about everything. He'll be saying you can't do this or that, you've no warranty, no authorisation –'

Charles unfolded a letter from Arthur's lawyer.

'This is *our* authorisation.'

'True,' I said. 'True.'

I started with a bold flying flourish to the first numeral of the total amount.

Charles was coming down from London each week, putting up at the Boar. He had asked me to appoint a works manager beneath him.

'For the hard graft,' he laughed.

'You work hard too,' I said.

'They'll think I'm pushing my way in. A cuckoo in the nest.'

'*I* appointed you.'

'You're the chief. I tell them that.'

'I know what they feel about having a woman in charge. Not that I am,' I added quickly. 'That's why I'm so grateful. Having you here. To deal with the men.'

'Man to man.'

'Yes.'

'Perhaps they're talking behind *my* back too.'

'Why?' I asked.

'They'll say – I don't know – that you have me on a leash or something.'

'Then show them you know your own mind.'

He came a step or two nearer. Very close to me.

'No,' I said, 'remember the hermitage –'

He stopped just in time. I had a memory flash of the two bodies locked together on the floor, passion sweeping all before it. A ferocious longing had welled up inside me, but now it collapsed in on itself again.

———

'I hear you've had a visitor,' Charles said.

'Yes. Yes, I have. Mr Jaggers.'

'At your request?'

'No. Not at all.'

'A social call?'

'Not exactly.'

'About the Chadwycks?'

'He was just – taking stock.'

'A general sort of taking stock, was it?'

'He'd been aware I was drawing on my personal funds.'

'He misses little, our friend.'

'That's what I'm paying him for.'

'To be your lawyer?'

'Everything tidily within the law. "Nothing to upset the King". As he puts it.'

'And is there?'

'No. Naturally.'

'Naturally. He confirmed that, I hope.'

'I explained about Arthur.'

'If that's any of his business.'

'I don't mind. I have a soft spot for the formidable Mr Jaggers.'

I paused.

'But you're not "soft" on him?'

'Good heavens, no!'

I had an item of information to impart, gleaned from my visitor.

'The lawyer Arthur asked us to use –'

'Yes. Crabbit.'

'Apparently he's a crony of Snee's.'

'Who's Snee?'

'Someone I once crossed.'

'Is this significant?'

'The coincidence is peculiar.'

'Coincidences always are. That's their nature.'

'Yes,' I said, inattentively.

Snee wished to do me no favours. If he was involved, it was to exact some revenge – blatant or, more troublingly, covert – on his former castigator, Catherine Havisham.

I came back one day to learn that Arthur had cleared out the rest of his belongings from the house. A few small *objets* were also missing from the downstairs rooms – a silver box, a silver tankard engraved with our 'H' emblem – but I wasn't bothered: it only mattered to me to be shot of *him*.

A note left for me announced that, all being well, I had seen the very last of yours truly. Now the two of us, he said, could have the run of the place. He wasn't sorry that he wouldn't be setting eyes on god-forsaken Satis House or this privy-hole of a town ever again.

TWENTY-EIGHT

Charles should look like a man of parts. I made him buy a supply of banyans for himself; Indian nightgowns. Waistcoats came curved now, with a narrow tail, and so I said he ought to have those too. A selection, embroidered as well as plain. And the new round hats with uncocked brim. And large buckles on his shoes, just as the macaronis used to wear.

He needed a manservant to take care of his appearance, and one was duly hired.

The roan was a fine pacer. I kept a closed carriage and also a curricle, for two horses apiece. But I thought it befitted him, and the dashing figure he cut, to be seen in a smarter sort of phaeton.

We discussed it. He demurred at first. However, as we talked more, I could tell that he was warming to the subject. He knew a good deal about the types available, the lightness of the bodywork by this or that coachbuilder, the speed you could expect.

'With a decent pair of horses, I mean.'

'Yes,' I said, 'of course.'

I dealt with the expenses as a practicality. It didn't occur to me that I – or he – was being extravagant or profligate. It cost a certain amount to live well. He had the easy manner of someone born to such advantage, for whom it was no more than a right, his patrimony.

Once I'd bought the phaeton for him, I would listen from the street side of the house for the first trace in the air of the wheels.

The response from the horses as he turned them first right, then left, and along the length of the brewhouse. The singing of the chassis springs. My heart would lift, soar. These were the most desirable sounds in the world now to me.

It was all money, impersonal and soulless. The more of it I gave him, the more I was trying to show him that it counted for so little against love. The value of money is the spirit in which we use it; otherwise it amounts to just the crackling of greasy paper, the piddle-clink of dulled coins.

Charles was too careful of my reputation, and of his own, to think of putting himself up overnight. It occurred to me that he could have one of the cottages at the back of the yard, but refurbished.

'You need more space.'

This would deal with the awkwardness of his presence in the house. I knew that the staff talked, and it irked me that they should suppose they deserved to have an opinion on the matter.

Charles saw the merits of having his own detached accommodation, but the cottage's occupant, Tice, was holding out.

'I can smell trouble with that fellow.'

'Oh, I've been having it for months,' I told him.

'There must be ways and means of satisfying all parties in this matter.'

'Which matter is that?'

'My home comforts, of course!'

A few days later Charles announced he'd found another cottage to let in Tap Street, suitable for the Tices, and he'd expertly beaten down the landlord on a price. He showed me the lease he'd had drawn up, awaiting my signature. I allowed him to persuade me that this was the best solution.

I was neglecting to include Tice in my calculations, however. I discovered that *he* felt he had been robbed not only of the cottage but also of status.

'Leave it to me, Catherine. I'll sugar him a bit. It'll be all right.'

Because I didn't hear any more about it, I presumed things were on a better footing. Tice habitually had a morose expression for me anyway, even though I would hear him laughing with his colleagues (*and*, apparently, with his new landlord in Tap Street): so wasn't it an innocent misapprehension on my part, supposing that order if not quite harmony had been restored?

Charles used the cottage less than I had foreseen, but it was a gesture: mine to him. I was also advertising to the workers just what the new system was, how Havisham's was being run now.

I was unaware of any complaints about my appointment of a new chief manager. That was either because there weren't any or because Mr Ambrose, being the sensitive man I judged him to be, was filtering them off (almost like one of the brewhouse processes) before I had a chance to hear.

He's on the other side of the yard from me, with his own housekeeper and a skivvy for that compact roosting box of his. He's so near, but the distance of seventy or eighty yards is crucial. I'm feeling something more strongly than I've ever felt it before – an urgency between my legs. It's like frozen heat.

An alarming, thrilling sensation.

When I clamp my thighs tightly together and concentrate hard on that hidden spot, the fear increases to terror. But my shameless pleasure increases too.

To exhilaration. Abandonment.

I roam beneath my shift. I lightly pass my hand over the fork, brushing the wiry hair there. I have a compulsion to dally. I press down with more force. I open my hand and let my fingers probe.

I part my thighs. My fingers reach their way in, not gently.

I move inside, towards my inner ache. My fingers explore deeper. Hot, wet, silky flesh. Untravelled, but knowing to yield.

I fight for breath.

From the crown of my head to my toes, I'm consumed by an unspeakable euphoria.

———

In the evenings we played cards. I learned the alphabet of Misère terms.

Alliance. Blaze. Cut-throat. Finesse. Ouvert. Pip. Renege. Ruff. Sans prendre. Skat/Widow.

Charles told me again, you have to play *against* the rules. Innocents to the game would think the cards were – literally – stacked against them, and that the outcome of a game was inevitable. He repeated, you needed courage, principally that: and the quality of clever, inspired bluff.

———

I wasn't expecting it. His first question came from nowhere.

'Are we going to continue like this?'

I was sitting at my father's desk. He was standing at the window. Above his right shoulder, across the yard, a signboard for strangers who still didn't know whose yard they were in, HAVISHAM.

'"Continue like" – what?'

'This arrangement.'

'I thought you wanted to know about –'

'No, not about the business. About ourselves.'

I frowned, quite caught out.

'I'm sorry, I –'

'The two of us.'

'Me in Satis House, you mean?' I tried again. 'And you over in . . . ?'

He shook his head slowly.

'No. No, not that.'

I saw him swallowing hard, so that the Adam's apple in his throat jumped.

'Shouldn't we be thinking of getting married, Catherine?'

It was as if I was in one of the Chadwycks' *tableaux vivants*, immobilised. At last, after a hiatus, I returned to my senses, in an approximate fashion.

'I'm sorry,' he said. 'I shouldn't have –'

I stared at him.

'What I said –' He began again. 'I ought to have asked someone –'

'Asked whom?'

'One of your relatives. Please – you mustn't –'

And then, did I panic? Because I thought he might be going to withdraw the question, undo the past moments, erase them –

'No. No, no.'

'Catherine –'

'I shall. I *shall* marry you.'

He didn't spring forward, didn't throw his arms around me. He wasn't even smiling. At first he just stood nodding his head, as if he had known I would consent.

'Charles – ?'

I felt that now I was having to pull *him* back from somewhere.

'Good! Good!' A smile broke out on his face at last. 'I'm so glad.'

'You've made me the happiest woman in the world. "Joy, joy shall overtake us –"'

'What's that?'

'"– as a flood".'

I told him how many times after that. On each occasion he would grow more thoughtful.

Self-deprecation, I felt, I couldn't allow in my fiancé.

'You should be proud of yourself,' I said.

'To be able to make a proud woman happy?'

'The most difficult sort to *make* happy,' I told him.

'All those beaks at school who thought I was a dunce.'

'Never!'

'Who was I to say they weren't right?'

'The more fool you.'

'Their point precisely.'

And somehow I would win him from his thoughts in the end, back to quiet laughter.

He would have kissed me. But I was terribly afraid of what I might have been allowing to happen next.

'Please,' I said. 'Not now.'

'Some time?'

'I want to wait.'

'D'you mean that?'

No. Of course I didn't.

'Yes,' I lied.

'It's important to you?'

'Oh yes.'

He didn't try to argue the point.

'I only thought –'

'It's all right,' I said.

'I know it's serious to you. If that's how you feel.'

Important, serious: yes, but not for the reasons he might be thinking.

I was melting between my legs, I could feel dampness on my underclothes, I was afraid the stains would show through.

'Later,' I said, forcing the word out. Nothing had ever been more difficult for me to say. 'Later.'

And he did the decent thing and concurred, nodding his head, oh quite agreeably enough, while I wept and wailed inside myself for want of him.

———

'When we're married...'

'Yes,' I said. '"When we're married..."?'

'Then I can allow you to lead the life of a lady.'

'Meaning –?'

'Meaning, I shall be able to take over the running of the whole brewery.'

'You'll run it on your own?'

'Why not?'

'Single-handed?'

'You trust me, don't you?'

'Of course I trust you.'

'And you can be wife, mother, grande dame, patroness, whatever you want to be.'

'And you'll have the grind of Havisham's every day?'

'Most days, let's say. It will be my job of work. You told me labour was honest and true.'

'Yes, but –'

'You don't think it's beyond my capacities?'

'No, no.'

'You don't think it's beneath me, either?'

'Not at all. But I *shall* get to see enough of you, won't I?'

'As much as you saw of your father.'

'My father wasn't always here.'

'Off on business? I should have to go too.'

'Yes, I've neglected that side of things.'

'Your father wouldn't have been disappointed?'

'About what?'

'About us.'

'Why on earth – ? No, I'm sure it's a great solace to him. If he's able to hear us. To know the brewery will be in reliable hands.'

'Then, that's settled?'

I nodded.

'Yes, that's settled. For when the time comes. Once we're man and wife.'

———

The engagement banns were read.

I surrendered myself to everything, and became –

that cherry tree throwing its branches

the flame leaping on the new wick

the water tumbling joyfully over the weir

the fragrant spring wind seeping through the window cracks

the yellow cart rolling down the street

the vigorous hyacinths sprouting from their bulbs, after a dark cupboard-growing

the old Roman bricks stuck into the flint wall at the bottom of the garden, when I would sit in the mild sun staring and staring in front of me.

I was still trying to believe my luck.

———

My only regret was that Sally couldn't be here to share my joy and to play *her* part.

I hadn't known where to write to her, to pass on my news, to tell her about the preparations. At one time she had been the person closest to me. It had seemed so curious to lose her, an inexplicable thing, but never more so than now.

Letters of congratulation arrived from the town. My Havisham cousins and second cousins queued up in the hall on a certain Wednesday afternoon to offer me, one by one, their compliments and felicitations. (Implicit was their presumption that now my spirit must be a more generous one.)

I woke in the mornings with an immodest delight at life, raptured back *into* life, realising what a deliverance from my past this was, to feel every surge of joy that I was feeling. I floated through the day, never so light or carefree, hopeful to the very tips of my fingers and toes.

—

We were to be married at St Barnabas's.

'You don't mind if it's nowhere grander?' I asked him.

'Whatever pleases *you*.' (He would have agreed to anything.)

'The cathedral, you see . . . I used to go there under duress. And when my father died –'

'No. No, that's fine. Really. Truly.'

'It'll be my birthday too,' I added.

He was about to look away, but turned back, did a double-take. He must have forgotten; he had known so much about me, the minutiae, but this greater event ahead of us had thrown a mantle over all the lesser.

'Now it will be a special day for a much better reason. Because every year on my birthday I shall share our wedding anniversary with you.'

I asked him another time – other times, plural – what about our honeymoon?

Would it be France, or Switzerland, or Italy?

'The choice is yours,' he said.

The sun, I told him. Please. But not too much sun. And antiquity. Beautiful antiquity.

It must have come into both our heads at the very same instant.

'Venice?' he was saying.

'Venice!' I spoke over him.

Where else?

We didn't discuss the expenses, because I didn't want to embarrass him. The bills perforce would be *my* responsibility. (This was the whole point of having money: recognising what it was destined for.)

And my trousseau? I asked.

That's *your* prerogative, he said. Surprise me.

(Sheba would have been the one to ask. But . . .

I'd manage by myself, though.

Mine would be the trousseau of trousseaux. My initials would be sewn into every article as finely, as meticulously as if enchanted fairy needles had worked the stitches.)

TWENTY-NINE

Charles was talking about the trade there might be in setting up friendly societies at our tied houses. Those would hold the funds of whoever might want to place them with us, Havisham's being a fully reputable local firm always running a healthy profit. Government stock was unreliable; we could offer five per cent, and do very nicely out of it – expand our own interests, bind our customers tighter to us, encourage others to come in.

'Just like a bank?'

'Offering credit. Money-merchanting.'

'*You're* ambitious.'

'I'm being ambitious on your behalf, Catherine. Havisham's has the prestige.'

'I'll think about it.'

'We should discuss it.'

I. We. It wasn't so simple any more, was it?

'Later,' I said. 'Yes.'

***

'I shall invite Arthur, though,' I said.

'You will?'

'Shouldn't I?'

'I hadn't thought about it.'

He had agreed to the list of guests I had drawn up, raising only a couple of queries.

'I'd do it for my father's sake. For no other reason.'

'Very well.'

'He mightn't come, I suppose. That'd be easiest.'

'Damn!' I watched him lean forward to inspect a stain on his boot.

'I won't if you'd rather not,' I said.

'It's all the same to me.'

I couldn't help wishing he would voice a sentiment, one way or the other. I didn't like to think of Arthur attending, too much drink in him, leering at us. But without him, much as it went against my better instincts, I felt I would be dishonouring the man who'd been father to both of us.

I had decided that the young Chadwycks – and cousin Moses – should be there at the wedding, notwithstanding all the reservations they'd declared about Charles. (They had misunderstood him, giving credence to stupid slanders; but I should be ready to forgive them, with my bride's magnanimity.)

I issued the four of them with separate invitations. I wrote four letters, as cover, expressing myself in much the same way to each of them. My life was about to change, and very *very* happy I was about it too, etc.

W'm replied from Devon. '... *quod bonum faustum felix fortunatumque sit* ...' He made no mention of the state of his own engagement; there was no reference to Lucinda Osborne. However, he did say that 'personal reasons' (Mrs Calvert, by any chance?) must detain him where he was, in the West, and that therefore, '*tristissime* ...'

Less promptly, Sheba and Mouse replied, in tandem, and sounding a little parsimonious in their congratulations. They very much hoped I *would* be happy ... Unfortunately at the time of the wedding they were required to be in Llanirfon Wells with their mother, who was hobbling now with swollen joints, and therefore ...

———

'See, Miss Havisham. What do you think, for the trousseau?'

'A la Turque', that's *the* style.

Muslin, gold India. Sashed and buckled. Gauze, ribbons.

We wear *this* over a light single petticoat. Very graceful, don't you agree? Capricious, even, I'd venture.

'Miss Havisham, you will feel you're walking a-float, inches off the ground.'

———

Charles had mentioned adulterants. One of the tricks of the trade, as others practised it. Or *mal*practised it. Using vitriol and copperas, to speed up the brew's maturing. Adding liquorice, quassia, wormwood, to give a hop flavouring; upping the beer's strength with cocculus indicus and opium.

'The law allows isinglass,' I reminded him. 'Nothing else.'

'The law's also clobbering us. Putting folk out of business.'

'Yes, I know.'

'The law doesn't *care*.'

'The law can take you to court. Fine you. The law could close this place down only too easily, and then everyone would be out of a job. And where does that get us?'

This was the most determinedly I had ever spoken to him. I knew what he was suggesting; the dissenters in the brewhouse had got to him. I had already been warned about this by Mr Ambrose.

'I'm just considering all the possibilities.'

'It's a solemn onus placed on us,' I said, repeating words my father had used. 'Supporting those men who come to work here every day. And their families.'

'It's not a charity we're running.'

'Yes, I know that.'

And, I wanted to add but didn't, it's *I* who still have charge of Havisham's. After we're married, then we shall attend to the transfer, but slowly, in good time, once I have assured myself.

Perhaps he could read from my face just what I was thinking. So be it. I had the name to think of, as always the name, because without it where was I, and where would he be?

I smiled at him, and waited – I kept smiling – until he finally responded in kind, with an easing back of his lips. We had never ended a conversation on a grumbling tone, and my mind was made up that we never would.

> Love to faults is always blind,
> Always is to joy inclin'd.
> Lawless, wing'd, and unconfin'd,
> And breaks all chains from every mind.

I didn't hear from Moses until ten days before the wedding. His letter was direct to the point of abject rudeness. I was incensed.

He had seen the notice of the engagement, and told the others. He hadn't written to me because he didn't know how he might be honest with me. Engagements don't always lead to marriage, do they? But now, in reply to *my* letter (for which many thanks), his profuse apologies, only it was going to be very difficult to alter his plans, when he had an extra parish in his charge at present. He did understand that my heart was set. He and his sister-helpmate Louisa were of an identical persuasion; yet they both sent me their best wishes, and wanted me to know that I should be in their thoughts. He would pray for me –

I tore up the letter. How dare he? How *dare* he?

All his sort amounted to were licensed meddlers; the loveless and unloved who cross themselves at the thought of other people's happiness; who couldn't in a lifetime of Sundays put themselves in the position of the beloved.

I tossed the letter into the fire's flames.

———

I attempted to exorcise the incident by having dinner served to us that evening before the same fireplace.

'Should we try to woo back dear Boodle?' I wondered.

'Boodle priced himself a little too high for my pocket.'

'"Dear" indeed!' I said.

'Must've been talking to whatsisname.'

'Nemo.'

At that instant a memory flash . . .

'He could be my present to you,' I said.

'You're dreaming!'

'I'm sorry –'

'Not Nemo anyway.'

'No. Boodle.'

It had been a silly, misplaced remark, I said. I apologised for it, and I drew my chair closer to his.

It was usually he, I felt, who was dreaming. How far away he got from me sometimes. Eleventh-hour nerves, was it? About marriage? Or about his duties at work? I couldn't always wait for his mind to clear, and I would tug at his arm to shake him out of his brown study.

'It'll be all right,' I told him. 'Everything will be fine.'

He would stare at me for a few seconds, as if he didn't understand what I meant. I would pull at his arm again.

'I promise you,' I said.

At that a shadow of sadness passed across his face: only for another moment or two, until he was finally released from his doubts and was returned to me.

———

'What I have will be yours,' I said. 'And what you have will become mine as well.'

'I have the better of that arrangement.'

'And I shall honour you and obey you. As I must swear to do.'

He would be in charge of the brewery. I should have the running of the house. When he had to be away, I would leave brewery matters until he got back, and I would learn to forget that once I had done what he was doing.

Anything. He might ask anything of me, and I'd surely do it. All for love.

THIRTY

I woke early, and it was the first thought in my head.

I marry this morning.

I lay for a while in bed. This would be the last time I took my rest like this, as a single woman. I felt a wonderful pleasurable confusion of anxiety, excitement and the comfort of my hopes achieved.

I bathed in my dressing room, in front of a fire, looking out at the blue May sky, at the martins' giddy zigzaggings. My helpers came and went. My bouquet arrived, not yet dried of its dew, tied with white and yellow satin ribbons.

I drank some tea and ate a coddled egg and a piece of toasted bread spread with cherry jam. The slices of cheese and ham I left untouched.

I felt just a little, gently dazed.

They dressed my hair first, which took half an hour, pomading and setting with silver combs and netting.

Then they powdered my body from head to foot.

Once I'd been wrapped in a peignoir, they went to work on my face.

My eyebrows were plucked to fine arcs. I was whitened again.

They painted my lips, and ringed my eyes lightly with kohl, turning them up slightly at the outer corners. My fingernails were buffed and glazed, and my hands were creamed.

She was a woman I scarcely recognised, the one in the mirror, looking out at me with increasing incredulity and fascination.

It was a carnaval mask.

Sophisticated, experienced, worldly, a little arch, a little ironic: all the things Catherine Havisham hadn't been.

And then, finally, the dress, without its train, which was to fall twelve feet behind me. French silk; but the silkworms had been brought from China.

Sprig embroidery on the bodice and along the edges of the sleeves. The neck and cuffs were trimmed with Bath lace. There was a delicate tracery of gold foil on the back of the dress. The miniature buttons were each painstakingly worked in silk.

It fitted me exactly as it should have. I could move my arms, and breathe easily. There was no straining. I saw no gathers anywhere.

How strange, that such a consummately made garment should be worn for this one day only. But, as every girl growing up understood, her wedding day was the most significant she would know: a woman's crowning glory.

———

They left me.

It was just after half past eight. We had made good time. I was due to arrive at the church two or three minutes before ten o'clock.

I found myself thinking of my mother. I wished she could have seen me, and I could have seen her expression of wonderment. I thought of my father; I felt it unlikely he would have been disappointed, since the brewery – what he had cared most for – was going to be under the management of the man very shortly to take me as his wife.

As I was fitting my left foot into its satin slipper, there came a knock at the door.

A letter.

It was placed on the side-table.

If I hadn't had time to spare I should have left it there. But we were ahead of ourselves.

I put down the other slipper, laid it on top of the dressing table.

I leaned across for the envelope.

I recognised his handwriting at once. It must be his last word on my single state, I thought, a missive of love on this sweetest of mornings.

I split the seal with my thumb, drew out the sheet inside, unfolded it.

I had read only the first few words when I felt my heart leap up into my throat. I couldn't breathe.

'*I cannot but expect that the Contents of this Letter must greatly aggrieve you –*'

I stared at the sheet of paper, my eyes fixed. The lines of script swam in front of me; white spots flared over them.

'*– because I do recognise how much your Heart was set on our Union.*'

No.

No, no.

'*What I must say will distress you, I am certain –*'

I felt wetness on both legs, a stream of hot liquid starting to soak my stockings.

'*– and I can think of no way of preparing you easily for it.*

In short, Catherine, I cannot be your husband.'

I couldn't control myself; a rivulet of piss flowed out of me. Suddenly, in an instant, my life had turned to tragedy.

'I hope that with the passing of the months, you will find it within you to offer me some measure of forgiveness.'

He was having a last joke, wasn't he? It was meant to be a test for me.

'– to offer me some measure of forgiveness.'

I closed my eyes for several moments, then opened them again. The letter was still there.

'You will recover your Spirits and find some worthier Suitor for you than I could be.'

My cries brought the others to my room. I had fallen from the chair to the floor. I lay in my own urine. They helped me back on to the seat.

Someone fetched smelling salts, and held them under my nose.

'No. No, no, no, no, *no* . . . !'

I flailed at them, howling.

One of them had found the letter and read it; she was whispering as she passed it on.

'It's not true!' I shouted. 'It's not true . . .'

They held me to the chair. I tried to fight them off.

'None of it's true . . .'

The rug was mopped at with old towels.

'None of it's true . . .'

'It's all right, miss.'

I stared into the woman's face.

'What?'

It was all right, it would be all right.

Then she turned and I saw the look of utter dismay exchanged between her and the others. No. No, it wasn't going to be all right.

She'd lied to me. I struck out at her with my arms, and she fell back. Her eyes widened in her face, staring and staring at the beast in its lair.

'Get away! Get away, all of you!'

Minutes passed, but I had no regard. Half an hour. An hour. Two hours.

People came and went all morning. Came and went.

Sometimes I screamed at them. Sometimes I said nothing. Sometimes I was unaware if anyone was there or not, I forgot . . .

All I knew, the only thing, was this: I had reached the end of the life I'd had. It was lost to me now.

———

They must have cleared the church, and the guests been dispersed. But they didn't ask me. I heard the whispers outside the door of my dressing room. Footsteps coming and going away. They knew they didn't dare disturb me again.

That was all I had. The letter. A sheet of paper. A message I couldn't comprehend.

Could he have thought that *my* love had dimmed?

Had he misunderstood something I'd said, or not said?

Had he allowed himself to be misled by what another person had told him?

'Lock the doors of the dining room, d'you hear me? Don't let them disturb the feast. The feast must be left, just as it is.'

> She last remains, when ev'ry guest is gone,
> Sit on the bed he press'd, and sighs alone;
> Absent, her absent hero sees and hears.

———

They tried to undress me, but I resisted them.

I felt . . . What?

I felt that if I was still wearing my dress, then the wedding would still take place. If I removed it, I would be denying myself the hope of a happy ending.

'I have to be ready, you see.'

They tried to persuade me, but I wasn't listening. I shook off their hands.

'When, miss?'

'Not yet, not yet.'

And shouldn't it have been 'Mrs Compeyson' by now? We ought to have set off on our travels, soon we would be enjoying each other's company in a strange foreign city, en route to the strangest of all, he and I intimately marooned together by its lagoon.

'Leave me as I am, will you? Just let me be.'

Frightened glances. Hands turned palms upwards, gesturing helplessness.

'Go now, go now!'

———

He needed more time, only more time, to prepare himself.

'He's taken cold feet, that's all. He's heard something, and it's quite untrue. There's been a dreadful misunderstanding. It's not serious.'

Wilt thou have this man . . . obey and serve him . . . and,
forsaking all other, keep thee only unto him, so long as ye
both shall live.
The woman shall answer,
I will.

The next day I wore the wedding dress, and the next again. I became used to having that woman with me, framed in the looking-glasses. I would stare at her, and it was like watching one of those (nearly) stock-still tableaux. When she was seated, she scarcely made any movement at all, except to draw and exhale breath.

I instinctively held out my hands to warm them at the fire, while my eyes passed over the Delft tiles on the hearth's surround. There were canals there too. Windmills, barges, locks. Hump-backed bridges, skaters on an iced pond. A street of tall, narrow-shouldered houses. Tulips – no, chrysanthemums, growing in a garden pot.

. . . then the solemnisation must be deferred, until such time as the truth be tried

The canals grew colder and colder, and started to freeze; the ice islands sighed. A bird flew low, between the Dutchmen's high gabled houses, on the spruce scrubbed streets of Leiden and Arnhem, while the chrysanthemums – no, the tulips – shrivelled and died.

———

'Tea, miss? Won't you try to drink some tea? Some toast? Here – You haven't eaten at all, miss.'

> The wretched queen, pursued by cruel fate,
> Begins at length the light of heav'n to hate,
> And loathes to live.

'You need to eat, miss. Isn't there something? Whatever you tell me you want to . . . Miss Havisham?'

Try to remember. When it was you felt most alive.
Try to remember who she was.
One morning, rising to a blue May sky. Pink blossom on the

cherry trees. The small flames of a new fire rustling in the grate, whispering excitedly.

Now,

      – brooding Darkness spreads his jealous wings,
      And the night-raven sings.

      The cards. Play the cards.
      Ouvert. Pip. Renege. Sans prendre. Cut-throat. Widow.

———

'She won't speak to us. Well, nothing to make sense of. She only talks to herself. It sounds like gibberish. But it must mean something. Something to *her.*'

———

      I'll bark against the dog-star
      I'll crack the poles asunder
      I'll sail upon a millstone
      And make the sea-gods wonder.

———

If...
   If...
   If...
   If I'd...
   If I'd...
   If I'd only...

If I'd only left the letter unopened / he might have been able to change his mind / somehow intuiting that I hadn't received his message / and returning to Satis House with me / he would have found a moment to remove the envelope / to slip it undetected into his pocket / and I should have been none the wiser / concerning those foolish, last-minute nerves / which is all they were.

———

'Tis folly
– where ignorance is bliss,
'Tis folly to be wise.

IV

CATHERINE REGNANT

THIRTY-ONE

I felt I had a fire beneath me.

Poor Dido . . .

And that I was lying pinned, spread-eagled, on a pallet of live coals.

. . . with consuming love is fir'd . . .

Every pore of my body was dripping sweat. The coals hissed under me and grew hotter.

> Sick with desire . . .
> And seeking him – him she loves,
> From street to street
> The raving Dido roves . . .

I kept asking for my wedding dress.

'I need to be dressed. It will soon be time.'

Time to leave for the church, to begin my new life, to claim my happiness.

> So shall their loves be crown'd with due delights,
> And Hymen shall be present at the rites.

No. No, that wasn't how the verse ran, not now.

It ran quite differently, raving and roving.

    – for still – for still the fatal dart
      Sticks
    – sticks in her side, and –
           and rankles in her heart.

There were poultices and balms, steam and ice, all to try to bring my temperature down.

They seemed to realise now that I was back among them again, that I had good money to pay those doctors and nurses for their attention.

I was sleeping more regularly. Long deep sleeps, as if I hadn't slept for weeks and weeks. Sometimes I would sleep through the whole of a day, and that day was then gone from my memory; nothing of it remained.

I got up from my bed, feeling like a paper person, the figure of a woman who'd been cut out of paper and unrolled. I felt I had no substance.

Just now and then everything is in its proper place. Objects fit their shapes, and are their exact colours.

And there are other times when everything will have been knocked out of kilter. Objects grow fuzzy around their edges, as if they've been dislodged: they can't hold their colours, the colours percolate out. (Where – but no one ever tells me – where have they put the wedding gown?)

Some days dawn with the trees and the rooftops already in situ, settled. The cranes in the brewery yard are cranes, the furniture in my room is solid and neither warm nor cold when I touch it. Other days, I roll out of bed and I'm in a tilting room. The floor runs away from me, and yet somehow – what magic is this? – the furniture clings on. The trees are gowned and stooped dons, and the rooftops are the lecterns they lean against, and the cranes aren't cranes but arcane hieroglyphics, devilish script like the positioning of the windows and doorways in the brewhouse.

A crack is growing in my bedroom wall. It eats the old green silk paper, and now the fissure is wide enough in places to push a finger into. Plaster pulverises and trickles down inside the wall, for an age. The crack is a river traversing some vast deep, dark forest. I call into the gap and the sounds are scattered for miles; they snag on the topmost branches of trees too tiny to see.

> How soon hath Time, the subtle thief of youth,
> Stol'n on his wing my three-and-twentieth year!
> My my . . .

A face rimous, crumbling, like the facade of an abandoned palace.

> My hasting days fly on with full career,
> But my late spring no bud or blossom showeth

Rain and wind have shaken the cherry trees to broken wire umbrellas.

And they haven't washed the powder off me.

It hangs in my hair, like a nest for rats.

The powder has gathered about my body in folds of skin, drifting, solidifying between my toes.

Perfumed and sweet has turned musky and sour. I smell of unassuaged longing, and of accumulated bitterness.

'If I'd worn green . . .'

'I'm sorry, I didn't catch –'

'Green. Like the Immortals. They wore green.'

'Who?'

Ignorance darkens the world, clouds of unknowing.

'Oberon. Titania. Puck. Living forever. If I'd worn green . . .'

'Rest now, miss –'

'Oh, there'll be time to rest afterwards.'

Decades of time. Centuries. Millennia.

———

I sit in the sun. The old walls trap the heat. Butterflies flit and flutter about the garden, scribbles of colour on the gassy air.

I sit in the sun watching the butterflies, and picking at a loose thread on my dressing-gown sleeve. The grass grows beneath my feet, and the earth sings.

A slow fly lands on the toe of my right shoe. I turn my foot in every direction, I stamp my shoe on the ground to shake off the fly, I shout at the interloper until it's finally dislodged.

A window sash is raised in the house. I angle my head to see. I can hear them talking about me, not what they're saying but the sibilant voices: droning, buzzing, cleverly drifting past my ear on the currents of air.

A ring of cathedral bells, carried over the wall.

I close my eyes. I command the bells to stop.

And lo, they stop.

The air clears of that complication. I open my eyes.

Butterflies are flitting and fluttering about the garden, like pastel scribblings. The air trembles. A slow fly lands on the toe of my left shoe, I turn my shoe in every direction, I stamp my foot on the ground, I shout at the fly . . .

———

I didn't want to think that the Chadwycks might have known better than I.

I didn't want to think at all.

But of course I would wake and catch him slipping out of my mind, with a backward glance and what might have been a smile on his face.

I asked if there had been any word of him.

'Of who, miss?'

'"Of *whom*",' I corrected them. 'Who else d'you suppose I'd be talking about?'

There was no message from him, no communication from any third party, no clue as to his whereabouts.

The trail had gone cold.

Nothing.

———

A man in a golden mask. He turns round. On the reverse of his head, which might be the back or the front, is another face, in silver.

'Eat, Miss Havisham. Can't I tempt you to a tasty morsel? No? Miss Havisham – ?'

'It's been a beautiful day.'

'I'm sorry – ?'

'Oh, so am I. My trap among the gigs. But now, gentlemen, I think I've had an ample sufficiency.'

'Please sit still –'

'I really have to go now.'

'– Miss Havisham –'

'They'll be expecting me.'

'Who will? Who is expecting you?'
'I . . . I can't . . .'
'No one, Miss Havisham.'
'But . . .'

———

Later.

They feed me *sorbet de crème*. Because it is considered strengthening for the digestive system. Eating cream ices will help me to live to a ripe old age. (Six egg yolks to two pints of double cream: can this be true?)

There's one flavoured with orange blossoms, and another with cherry kernel, and a third type with greengage.

The Italians stay clear of contagion this way. It's a delicious conceit, and almost worth getting better for. Almost.

Sitting in the cafes of Paris, which I've read about: the Dubuisson by the Comédie, or the Caveau in the Palais Royal, or its neighbour the Foy, where I perch on a chair in the palace gardens. Picking genteelly at my pyramid of ice while I wait, wait for someone who never comes.

———

'But leave the breakfast. Leave the breakfast.'

I must have had such fury in my voice, they knew not to disobey me.

The wedding feast remained where it was, set out on the extended dining table. If I were to lose that, I would be abandoning all hope.

———

In those first twenty-four hours, half of my hair had turned white with shock. I was left with a thick streak of white, which raced through the fair like a wave, roared like a flame. I had turned middle-aged overnight.

Nobody would have wanted to marry me. It was as if time had speeded up without mercy, and shown me the person who'd been hidden inside all along. I would have caught up with her, but not for another twenty or thirty years.

She was so cruelly different from me. The white bolt in her hair gave her eyes a hunted, obsessive look, as if the visible mattered much less than the mind's dark fancies. She terrified me, because I also knew (in a clearer part of my brain) that she had no separate existence behind the mirror's plane of wintry glass.

THIRTY-TWO

I ambled about the house, for hours on end, wearing only a loose sack gown and shawls. I waited for night, until I saw the watchmen's brazier lit, and then trod circuits of the brewery yard. From the garden I watched dawn come up over the rooftops of the town. I walked for many miles without leaving the policies. Ceaselessly I was turning matters over in my mind, the how and why and what to do next.

The news must have travelled far and wide by now.

About the Havisham girl down in Kent. Queerest thing. Left standing at the altar.

It would be talked about for weeks, months. Remembered from years away. A very rum to-do there was, once upon a time, a brewery heiress in a Medway town, jilted on her wedding day she was.

They wouldn't know *exactly*, but somehow they would never have forgotten.

I'd had my wedding dress hung on the hessian mannequin. The veil was draped over three chairs. Nobody had been allowed to touch the dressing table. My powders and combs were where I'd left them. The lid was still raised on the jewellery casket, and all the items to hand as they'd been that morning. Beside it was the other white satin slipper I'd been on the point of fitting on to my right foot.

Only the letter was missing. How it had been lost I didn't know, and wasn't going to enquire.

I had the dressing room locked. I removed myself to a bedroom on the other side of the house. I had no dressing room there, but all I meant to do with my life was work at brewery business. What time would I have now for the vanities of dressing up?

Once I was installed again in my father's office I put on a sober dress and a very little jewellery, to appear my most purposeful.

But I noticed straight away the change in Tice.

For one thing, the smirk as he sauntered into the room. He sat down without being requested to do so; I stared at him until my displeasure was fully plain to him, and he got to his feet.

In that conversation and the ones to follow he didn't allow me to forget that he'd taken on himself proctorship of the brewhouse in my absence.

He seemed to believe that we met now on altered terms: that he was privy to Havisham business as never before. (I realised he would have been able to acquaint himself with the contents of the ledger books in the Compting House.)

I attempted to put him right about that, without directly putting the man down. I couldn't decide if he was being deliberately obtuse, or truly didn't perceive my point. The former, I concluded, given that sly canny look of his.

I was obliged to be less subtle.

'I fear you may be under a misapprehension . . .'

He bit his lip, otherwise he might have spoken his mind. As it was, his remarks became terser, without the encumbrance of grammar: single-word responses sometimes, or a 'yes' or a 'no'. Not even a 'miss' to acknowledge my authority. Whenever I dismissed him, after informing him of my wishes, he would hold back for a few moments before turning to leave, as if he was awaiting some change of heart in me. I didn't care for his expression: a wily reminder to me, *I*-know-a-thing-or-two.

The men, I heard through Mr Ambrose, were wanting to be 'consulted'.

'Who's put that notion in their heads? Tice, let me guess.'

Mr Ambrose nodded.

'Did my father allow "consultations"? We'll have a revolution on our hands before we know where we are.'

I shook my head. It was the spirit of the times, but I was damned if I was going to entertain it here in Crow Lane.

'Quite out of the question. You might intimate as much to them, Mr Ambrose. However you judge best.'

'Very well, Miss Havisham.'

'*Someone* respects the name! Thank God for that.'

The ordinary labourers – the semi-skilled men (and a few women) – were the most docile. The cooperage foreman was a calming influence, and probably the chief storehouse clerk. They had too much to do perhaps, those stokers and yeastmen, the spare-men and drawers-off. (The draymen and horsekeepers were mostly loyal, but several wavered.)

However, our esteemed superintendent of the brewers, Tice, was winning over some of the clerks in the Compting House, including the abroad-men I used to patrol my empire.

I had books from the Compting House brought in to my office, and I pored over them, believing them less and less as I scoured the entry columns for signs of tampering. I scrupulously examined every blot, every repeated stroke of the pen. I compared single numerals for consistency. I checked and double-checked for errors in the sums and subtractions, which involved hours more of that close work.

They presumed I'd lost the knack, if I'd ever had it. I wasn't just a woman, I was a madwoman.

But the figures didn't add up, the entries on one page failed to tally with those on the next – and *they* imagined I wouldn't notice. The emendations appeared to have been made in various hands, so there must have been a more complex conspiracy afoot.

I might have banged the table and watched them jump out of their skins. Instead, when I was asking questions I dropped my voice and addressed my enquiry little louder than a whisper, and I hoped it made their flesh creep.

Who was responsible I couldn't tell. Maybe it didn't matter who. If I were to replace them all, I should have had to test the loyalty of their successors. But the brewery couldn't prosper on mismanaged figures, with a proportion of the profits being siphoned out by whoever was clever enough to get away with it. Now I was appreciating for the first time the magnitude of this endeavour I had taken on, which had the makings of a moral crusade.

———

I didn't immediately understand what he was meaning.

'I don't follow you, Mr Ambrose –'

When I did, I couldn't curb my temper.

'You *dare* to suggest such a thing?'

'But only Mr Compeyson was permitted to –'

'That's a slander.'

Why on earth was I defending the man? What possible reason could I have?

'Take back that accusation. At once.'

'I would if I could, Miss Hav—'

'At once, d'you hear me?'

'I can't. I'm sorry.'

'You *will* be sorry.'

'It's my considered opinion.'

Whatever else Charles Compeyson had been, and done, I hadn't doubted that he'd supported me here.

I told Mr Ambrose, with just a brief quaver in my voice, in that case – if he was refusing to resile – I must inform him that I, and Havisham's, had no further need of his services.

A notice in the newspaper. The engagement was announced between the Honourable William Chadwyck and Lady Frances Tresidder.

I enquired about the name 'Tresidder'. They were a Cornish family, owners of tin mines. For two generations they had lived in a mansion built by one of Queen Bess's favourites.

Satis House had once entertained Elizabeth. It was she who had given rise to the name, after thanking her host for his abundant hospitality. That Cornish mansion must have been grander than Thurston Park, and tin mines an even better prospect than brews of ale.

Had I seen W'm's fiancée-to-be when I was still accounted one of them, the Durley Set? Had she been persuaded to visit the hermitage with him? No, probably not; that was by very special invitation only.

Thespis had turned everyone into practised actors, all of us except myself perhaps: so adept at not betraying our private purposes and designs.

I wore the darkest clothes I had, short of mourning. I felt that *light* didn't involve me for the present, either entering me or being expelled. I was a woman of business and nothing else. I left off powder and my other applications. I dressed my hair plainly. I chose a few older items of jewellery, those passed on to me. Havisham heirlooms. Others might have judged that time had taken the shine of desirability off them. But their value to me now was as tokens of my lineage, unshowy symbols of the legacy I embraced.

I spoke for *les fondateurs venerables*, those original Havishams no longer with us.

———

The ledgers continued to divulge secrets from the time of the Compeyson stewardship, so called.

I requested that Mr Jaggers send someone to help me go through the books: he confirmed that, yes, there had been consistent meddling. An attempt had been made to disguise handwriting, but *he* would wager it was by the same person.

At first I told myself it must have been the work of an unknown, intended to reflect badly on the man I had elected to be in charge, my fiancé. But it took this Londoner, interpreting the evidence for me as he viewed it with outsider's eyes, to convince me finally of the unwelcome truth of the matter.

I had kept to the old method whereby surplus grains and the residue in the tuns were sold off, for cattle-fodder and as fertiliser. *He* – whose name I couldn't bring myself to speak – had terminated the existing and long-established arrangements and made his own, presumably more profitable, ones (although the figures were deliberately obfuscated in the accounts).

He might have attempted to affect the means of production – by cutting costs, by altering temperatures and quantities and durations, mixing brews – but I would have been bound to hear about that. (Using wild yeast, say, would have foxed the beer and caused infection.) Instead he had confined himself to petty frauds on the housekeeping: reselling returned (stale) beer, buying an amount of used oak casks in any batch of new, even – I had trouble believing it – having the draymen collect the horses' dung on their rounds and taking a two-thirds cut for himself on what was sold.

It was pathetic.

Worse, though. Mr Ambrose had suspected he was holding up on credit, and may have been dealing with individual publicans who had the misfortune of bad debts. That was the next matter I must investigate.

***

Meanwhile . . .

They wanted me to restore the full-time jobs. They also wanted the average of working hours reduced.

I told them we were fighting for custom with our competitors. Everyone was looking for ways to trim costs. If I reduced general working hours, there would need to be pay cuts.

Tice appeared with a delegation.

'We know what price the barrels are being sold at.'

'I can't think who's told you. But the manufacturing costs have risen, doubled.'

'Brewers are like farmers. They never run at a loss.'

'Who says? Look, beer duties up twenty-five per cent. Malt tax, three hundred per cent more.'

'But is there a loss – ?'

'Quart pot of ale. It's been fourpence for how many years. Now suddenly it's sixpence. There are breweries up for sale all over the country.'

'Not this one, though.'

'Because I'm looking for fresh suppliers all the time.'

'That's what *he* was trying to do. Mr Compeyson.'

'I'm in charge now.'

'Isn't he coming back?'

'No. No, he's not. *I'm* master.'

Tice spoke. 'Don't you mean...' He paused for full effect. '... "mistress"?'

All their eyes crossed tracks. Smiles, but no actual laughter. They will repeat the remark all evening long, and with each new mention the tone of voice will become more caustic.

'Whichever,' I said, 'there can only be one of them.'

They seemed disinclined to believe me.

———

I had written Mr Ambrose three letters. The third brought him back to the Compting House. I led him through to my office.

'Thank you for coming, Mr Ambrose.'

'You wished to speak to me, Miss Havisham?'

'Please sit down, won't you?'

He waited for me to speak.

'Mr Ambrose, I think I owe you an apology.'

I was as modest as a nun. My manner was my best statement of contrition. Seated where he'd sat in my father's time, he was persuaded by ghostly presences to give me another chance. I took his hand and shook it, while he stared in mild shock at the boldness of our two hands' behaviour.

———

I had another visit from Tice and his cronies among the workmen brewers. They wanted their salaries to match the clerks'.

'I'll think about it.'

But they were already getting their perks and gratuities. £750 for a second brewer, with a wife. Sixpence per hogshead commission.

'I don't see what you've got to complain about.'

'Mr Havisham, he wouldn't let us put money in.'

'You wish to invest? Although you say you don't receive enough?'

'It'd be a stake, though.'

And a means of applying stronger pressure on me. My father's original decision had been the correct one.

I could have increased the workers' wages a little. The additional price of their labour would have been quite insignificant set against the totals for purchases of materials and casks. I could have conceded something. But I was too angry to allow myself. They put a much lesser value on me, a Havisham born and bred, than they did on him, who had only ever been my appointee, and – strictly – a nobody.

To comfort myself, I asked Mr Ambrose to please make discreet enquiries about the rates of remuneration among our competitors. Just as I'd surmised, we were keeping pace very favourably.

'I've given this very careful and extended thought,' I told Tice.

'The pay?'

'Yes.'

'And the investing?'

'Both.'

'And . . . ?'

'I don't see any justification, I'm afraid, for what you're asking me. None at all.'

I had to let my ire with Tice and company cool. I consoled myself with the reflection that I'd remained guarded about the economic facts. We claimed seven or eight per cent return, after deducting interest charges on capital; really it was nearer fifteen per cent.

I had Mr Ambrose out interviewing those publicans who were closing their home mashers, and also calling by at some of the big farms and poorhouses where he'd learned ale was no longer being produced.

I needed two faces for this job. Perhaps I might have been left feeling guilty afterwards, if *they* – those bullyrags – hadn't insisted on bringing up his name still. The mention of 'Compeyson' wasn't spontaneous or accidental, but quite carefully calculated beforehand.

I would give just as good as I got.

THIRTY-THREE

I took myself off to Norwich.

'Where would I go if I wanted to buy land hereabouts?'

Wherever I asked in Norwich I was provided with a list of the same names. Two were sited in the centre. One, in Madder Market, was owned by a man in his eighties and managed by his son and grandsons. I couldn't envisage any 'friend' being given a worthwhile job of work here, in these amply staffed premises. The other I found at Charing Cross, in the lee of the Strangers' Hall. A brass plate by the door announced Calloway & Calloway. I waited in the parlour of an inn across the street to see who entered and left. I interrupted my watch to speak with the proprietor.

'I'm thinking of buying a little land,' I said.

'Across the way?'

'I've seen a young woman. One of the Calloway children, I suppose?'

She had been a little older than I. Well dressed, with rather severe features, as if she had undergone some strain of late in her life.

'But I've not seen any *Mr* Calloway,' I said.

'He's dead, Mr Calloway is.'

'Oh. Just one? It's in other hands now?'

'Her you've seen, that's Miss Jane. *She's* the Calloway now.'

'She has charge of the firm?'

'Does not a bad job of it neither, by all accounts.'

I enquired of a few customers about Miss Calloway. 'Plain Jane', one called her. Another said she must be worth a good deal. 'Drives a hard bargain' was another verdict.

'Doesn't put the men off, though. Not short of suitors, that one. I'd like to see him that gets anywhere, mind.'

One, I heard, had persevered and got further than the others. A couple of years back, after her father died, there had been talk of a secret engagement. But a pair of her friends had got to hear, and managed to talk her out of it, just in the nick of time.

'Those clever types, like she is, clever at her job anyhow – don't seem to see the danger – anyone could've told her *he* wasn't the one for her.'

A smooth talker, bit of a popinjay to look at. Father had been a doctor at sea, mother kept ill . . . He'd hung about racecourses apparently, made a bit of money for himself that way. Back he would come, though, to the Calloway house out on the King's Lynn road. At the last minute she saw sense, and sent the fellow packing.

Name like 'Cumberstone', 'Compston'. She had kept him from everyone except those two friends who got to find out. Maybe she'd guessed for herself it was just a forlorn fancy. One of those crazy notions that threatens to get the better of us. She wriggled free of him, though. And now look at her, running the business as well as her father ever did.

———

The church lay low in the fields. Fields of ripe corn, swaying voluptuously.

A parish of rich spinsters. It was ideal territory for him; it might not serve his ambition so well (although, on second thoughts, spinsters' word-of-mouth could work a wonder or two), but he would certainly be well fed and dined.

He had a voice to fill the space. It would dip and then theatrically rise.

'"Suddenly there came a sound from heaven as of a rushing mighty wind, and it filled all the house where they were sitting."'

The dowagers, warming themselves with their pugs and tiny terriers, lapped it up.

'"And there appeared unto them cloven tongues like as of fire, and it sat upon each of them."'

If they could have applauded him, they would have.

'"And they were all filled with the Holy Ghost, and began to speak with other tongues, as the Spirit gave them utterance."'

Anything he might have asked of them . . .

He raised both arms aloft, in inspired supplication.

God helps those who help themselves.

'Cold heaven, I've heard it called. Is the chill of your church a taste of it?'

'I beg your . . .'

'Good morning, Mr Chadwyck. Or it's just turned afternoon, if I'm to believe your bells.'

'It *is* Catherine? Catherine Havisham?'

'A little blue in the face. But it is.'

What was I doing here? Talking to Moses Chadwyck. (I still couldn't think of him as 'Frederick'.) Eating lunch with him, or trying to.

'We're delighted you've come. Thought to visit us. Aren't we, Aurelia?'

His sister glanced up from her plate, and when she couldn't catch his eye she smiled across the table at me. They had heard months ago that I wasn't to be 'Mrs Compeyson'; it wasn't being spoken of by any of us, but I sensed that at the time the news had come as a relief to him.

I dropped my knife, it clattered to the floor, and the maid darted over to pick it up. The housekeeper had been hovering outside, and she walked in, making straight for the canteen of cutlery to fetch a replacement.

They all doted on him, his women. What was his gift? Not physical attractiveness.

Those large hands, his big square cleft jaw, his premature stoop, his balding dome with its fringe of sandy baby-hair. An unbuttoned cuff; his necktie unravelling.

But his eyes, behind their rimless close-to lenses, were gentle, sympathetic, confidential: with a vision that saw beyond windows and pretty vistas, beyond self and immediacies.

'You were in the vicinity?'

'No. No, I wasn't.'

'You searched us out?'

'I was thinking back. To Durley Chase.'

'Well . . . My sister and I are very honoured.' It was said quite unironically.

I nodded an acknowledgement.

'You've changed, Catherine.'

'We all have.'

'Some fruit, Miss Havisham?' his sister asked. 'These are our own peaches.'

'No. No, thank you. I've had – an ample sufficiency.'

Petals shivered from an arrangement, falling to the table beneath.

'How have I changed exactly?'

'You seem – to live a little more inside yourself.'

'I don't see how – I'm running a brewery, aren't I?'

Aurelia looked with alarm between the two of us.

'*You've* changed too,' I said to him.

'How so?'

'You seem – to live *not* so much inside yourself.'

'Is that a good thing?'

'You're settled, I can see. Your sermons. The ladies and their lapdogs.'

'Oh, those dogs!'

'Do you still read your books?'

'Yes. But not so much perhaps.'

'And is *that* a good thing?'

'Maybe it isn't.'

'How well set up you are here. How comfortable.'

I felt unable to stop myself. I didn't know why I was repaying their hospitality so badly. I had drunk too much gooseberry cordial. But something about the house oppressed me: the regular mealtimes – no stranger to be turned away – when worthy tomes (if not as worthy as they once were; they had gaudier bindings) were laid aside with the bookmarks in place, and could be picked up again after a hearty feed and a doze in the high-backed armchair, positioned within reach of its footstool.

He played his role well, turning in a sterling performance in church and then retiring here to the semi-privacy of home. And yet . . . and yet the Cambridge books were still within his arm's reach, and the piles of papers, *those* weren't merely stage props, were they? His signet ring was engraved with a squared cross, + .

God, I felt, had managed to creep into the details. The white arum lilies. The demure chastity of Aurelia. The fruit remaining in the compotiers, strawberries for righteousness and pomegranates for resurrection. How the sun hit a green-and-blue glass bowl, spilling a holy potage of chapel-light on the rug.

We stood at the gate, he and I.

'What about the others?' I asked.

'I hear less of them now. The girls are married.'

'And their brother? With the tin lady.'

'Not yet. The engagement lasts and lasts.'

'None of you', I said, 'accepted my invitation to see *me* wed.'

'That is so. I do regret that.'

'Was it a conspiracy?'

'Not as such.'

'"Not as such". You're a Jesuit now!'

'I believe Lady Charlotte may have exerted a little influence.'

'Ah.'

'They're obedient children.'

'Adults, surely. Competent to think for themselves.'

'You were obedient to your father's wishes, weren't you? Aren't you obedient now to his memory?'

He surmised correctly. I nodded. The Chadwycks had been both wrong and right.

I heard skittering flints, and then the spinsters' voices as they approached. A lapdog yapped, sniffing a stranger. He looked away from them, directly at me. His eyes were filled with something more intense than tenderness. At the same moment I realised what it was I had never seen in another's eyes over all that time, up to my engagement and beyond. The vital absence: love.

'Catherine, I want to say what a pleasure, what a joy it's been –'

'Yahoo! Your reverendship!' a spinster called across to him. 'What a fugitive fellow you are! No more hiding from us *now*!'

I looked down at the dried mud surface of the lane, the flints' sharpness. God in the details.

At last I located my copy of the *Aeneid* on my shelves. I searched through the tracery of tiny ink cribs I'd marked in the margins. One passage was annotated in another hand. It must have been Moses's doing.

> The fated pile they rear,
> Within the secret court, expos'd in air.
> The cloven holms and pines are heap'd on high,
> And garlands on the hollow spaces lie.
> Sad cypress, vervain, yew, compose the wreath,
> And ev'ry baleful green denoting death.

I couldn't bear to read any further. I closed the book.

I was alone; there was no one else to hear. But I could only ask Moses for his forgiveness under my breath, confessing my misjudgements of the past in a penitent's whisper.

———

Then, later, came talk of having to contribute workers to the defence forces, if the French should invade. Mr Ambrose informed me that now some other big brewery-owners wanted to move in. They knew all about the state of morale here, or the lack of it. They smelt my blood.

An offer was put forward, to take over Havisham's, which was increased before I could respond. Then a second offer came from another source. I didn't want to hear what worth they put on the firm. I was indignant. I was ashamed of myself, that I had somehow permitted this dire state of affairs to come about. The brewhouse men sent in yet another delegation to argue their points, to try to harry me.

I'd had more than enough of it, too much, much too much. I was exhausted. I was at the end of my fraying tether. It simply *couldn't* be allowed to happen, that frail rope snapping for a second time.

———

I'd had an address – the one in Blackheath – where I could write to him in London. When I went there and asked, one of the tenants told me he was gone. The man gave me another address, at the Lewisham end. At that second house, the new occupants of the rooms made clear their distaste for the previous tenant, Mr Compeyson.

'We'd no idea the fellow *had* any friends. How his wife put up with him, God only knows.'

'His wife?'

'*She* seemed better. But all the more fool for choosing *him*.'

'You don't know where he is?'

'Nor care, frankly.'

I got out at the costume hirers in Covent Garden, and looked in through the windows.

There was a wall of masks, and a selection of period garments on hangers. A customer was leafing through a catalogue of items while an assistant on a stepladder was checking among drawers to see which were available. That life of pretence – that dream life – carried on just as before.

I went back to the second house, where the tenants of the apartment had been so candid. This was the closest I had come to him. But it still wasn't close enough.

I walked the pavement on the other side of the street. It was drizzling lightly. A woman with a child approached, keeping a careful watch on me. They stopped a few feet away. I ventured a smile, as much as to apologise for my presence.

Our umbrellas, it occurred to me, were going to collide. I stepped to one side.

'I was hoping it would hold off,' the woman said.

'No such luck.'

'It could be worse.'

'It might,' I concurred.

Now the woman was studying my umbrella.

'I knew someone with a blue umbrella just like yours,' she said.

'Yes?'

'Quite envious I was.'

He had bought it for me, when I once expressed a fancy.

'Is it so unusual?' I asked.

'I'd never seen one. Not that shade. What would you call it, a greeny blue?'

'I suppose it is.'

'She had one just the same. The lady across the way, I mean.'

I looked across to where the hand was pointing, the very house I'd had in my sights.

'Who used to be there, I should say. Mrs Compeyson.'

'You knew her?' I asked.

'Oh yes. We were neighbours.'

'D'you know where they've gone?'

'The Compeysons? Yes. Only, I wasn't to tell anyone.'

'You can tell me,' I said.

'I can?'

'We – we were well acquainted, he and I.'

'Not from Kent?'

'Yes.' I was startled. 'Why d'you ask?'

'His wife was from there. And he had something to do with a brewery in those parts. Only it didn't work out for him.'

'No. No, it didn't.'

'You know something about it?'

'I'm just – an observer. Now. But I would like to find out.'

The little girl was pulling on her mother's arm.

'I would like to find out very much,' I repeated, not certain whether I did or not. I thought the woman's eyes were kindly, for this cold and uncompassionate city.

'How to get hold of him,' I said. 'Can you help me? Please.'

They live in a tall house of flaking stucco, in a not insalubrious or inelegant quarter. Milborne Street in Wandsworth is hanging on to the coat-tails of genteel respectability that graces Putney to the west. The Compeysons are trying to move on and up in the world.

I stand beneath a dripping ash tree to watch, with my blue umbrella raised.

Drops of rain run down the back of my neck. I can feel dampness through the soles of my boots. My bones ache with exposure.

It's all for just a sight of him. He knows the quick ways home, and – I can guess how it is – he's able to make an exit from the house so furtively that he seems to be no more than some temporary readjustment of the light falling on a wall, or the momentary disturbance of vegetation at the side of the path.

She doesn't appear, either. Maids come and go, but not their mistress. Meanwhile I'm Lot's wife, a pillar of bitter salt. The cold brings tears to my eyes; my eyes sting with them. The house blurs, as our watercolour sketches for Signor Scarpelli used to do when a drizzle came on.

What am I doing here? It's an elderly woman who's asking me, her voice stretched long and taut with social pretension. That clears my eyes. I stare at her with the full eviscerating steeliness I can muster from my predicament. She takes several steps back, staring at me as if I am an unnatural sight.

The rain has passed when the front door of the house, once a more imposing residence, opens.

A figure begins to descend the flight of steps.

There's something familiar about her. And then I recognise just what it is.

Of course. The cape: a travelling habit. Broadcloth, donkey-brown.

It's identical to one that I had, a few years ago.

The coincidence interrupts my train of thought. Now she's at the foot of the steps, starting to walk on the path. She pauses, turns to look back, then sideways, down into the submerged area. Perhaps it's to check if their maid's at her work. She stands still for several seconds, offering a profile to me.

No. No, it can't be. But it is, surely. How could I have forgotten? Her nose, brow, chin. The thickness, the copperiness of her hair. More than that, though. The walk. The clothes: the cloak I gave her. The air of aloofness, even a disdain for the ordinary. Everything that I taught her. My apprentice, only – now – more convincing than the original.

THIRTY-FOUR

I followed her along the drying street. She walked straight-backed, with her head set square on her neck, gaze directed in front of her. Her heels pecked busily at the paving stones. From that street, round the corner, on to the next.

Suddenly she stepped off the pavement and crossed over on a diagonal, negotiating the cobbles, to the other side. I did exactly likewise. She rounded another corner, with me in pursuit. She started to walk more quickly, and so did I.

She wasn't carrying herself with such confidence. She had lost a little height; her head craned forward – she might have had a stoop. Her heels were scraping now. She was proceeding at an untidy scuttle. She was less and less myself.

'Sally!'

I didn't mean to call out. But the word flew out of my mouth before I could stop myself. Hearing her name she slowed, stopped. She hesitated before turning round. Her eyes widened. Her mouth opened, but she didn't speak.

We stood staring at each other.

'It *is* you, Sally?'

She shook her head, as if she would deny me. Then she must have thought better of it.

'Why, Sally?'

I couldn't think what else to say. It was the only question I had in mind to ask her, because the answer would have to explain everything. I took a few steps closer.

'Why?' I said more softly, to tease the truth from her.

She stood in silence, coiled, sprung. She was holding her ground. Apprehensive she might be, but she wasn't afraid. I couldn't match her. It was I who was faltering. I had to reach out my hand to the wall, to steady myself.

She still hadn't answered me. I was none the wiser. On the edge of my vision, a cart passed along the street. A hawker cried out somewhere; a dog barked. Other lives were being lived: workaday, unsuspecting, uncaring.

I took my hand away from the wall, and wobbled slightly. I was so weary now – exhausted. I would have sat down if I could, on the pavement's edge. Only the dim consciousness of who I was kept me from doing so. ('Imagine! Old Havisham's daughter, slumped over a gutter!') I stayed up on my two legs, but barely upright. She was no more stooped than I was. I was curling like a leaf.

I tried to read her expression. Disdain? No. Pity? No. Fear? Embarrassment? No. Had I taught her this too – to give nothing of herself away? If I had, then the teacher had forgotten the lesson. Disdain or pity I would have tolerated. What I couldn't suffer was her silence, and her refusal to show me any feelings at all.

A leaf. A husk.

'*Why, Sally?*' My voice cracked on the words.

Her voice when she spoke was quiet, collected, to the point.

'No reason. Things just happened as they did. I wasn't meaning anything.'

She spoke without any emotion.

'There was no scheme, no plan. That's just how it is sometimes. One thing led to another.'

My eyes began to lose their focus on her face.

'Believe me,' she said, in the same flat tone.

It didn't matter to her, I knew, if I believed her or not. This was what *she* had come to believe. She might tell me there was no malice aforethought, but surely there must have been some guilt, some remorse, even some shame?

She was able to speak to me in the unimpassioned tones of one who is the victor. Her life was settled, so she could spare me her condescension.

It was I who turned away first: I wouldn't have her see my tears. I didn't wipe my eyes until I had turned the corner. What had possessed me to go after her? I had gained no satisfactory explanation, no knowledge of what had really taken place between the two of them.

I saw her in my mind's eye as I continued walking, with the street liquid in front of me. I'd had this last sight of her: turned into a very passable imitation of myself. An imitation or a parody? Cruel and heartless as she seemed to me, she would have considered herself without blame.

I returned by the river.

She would have told me that she had merely followed the current, gone with its flow. That was no excuse. I had the prerogative, surely, to feel betrayed.

I couldn't take my eyes off the river. My feet were being drawn towards it, across the bank's sward of green. The water ahead ran fast and dark and deep.

Who would not sing for Lycidas?

I was held, transfixed.

The lines, memorised in the schoolroom at Durley Chase, recurred as my own epitaph.

> He must not float upon his wat'ry bier
> Unwept.

I could even pity Sally now, not envy her, for feeling so little. At interludes I had dwelt among legends, in the knowledge of mythical beings. They are the archetypes, the bearers of their own fates and larger than life. In her complacency, safe and snug for the moment until that man grew tired of her one day, Sally would experience none of the surfeits. To taste the absolute joys, you also have to suffer absolutely for them.

I took a step forward.

> So Lycidas sunk low, but mounted high
> Through the dear might of him that walk'd the waves.

Another step and the bank would start to crumble beneath my feet, one further step and I would tip forward through crumbling air –

'Catherine!'

A hand had grabbed hold of my arm. It was drawing me back.

Two hands, one clamped on each elbow, guiding me gently but firmly up the grass banking.

I was shaking. I turned and looked into Sally's face. She didn't speak, and neither did I.

This was us even, she was letting me know; we were quits.

She waited, as quietly and dutifully as she used to be with me, until I had composed myself. I felt again the hardness of paving stones through my soles.

We parted.

'Goodbye,' Sally said.

'Goodbye,' I replied.

One simple word apiece, and then we turned in our different directions.

I didn't look back. (Is she watching *me*, I wondered.) I carried on walking, getting my strength back slowly. Already I knew that we should never meet again. I went on my way with gathering determination, trying not to think about what had nearly happened at the river's edge – how it was that, for once, my pride had failed me. Later I passed a building topped by a pediment. There carved figures, classical deities too high to distinguish, lolled and disported. No one noticed them on that busy street except myself. They were beyond time and the earthly, beyond chance and the accidental.

The Immortals. The Hesperides, the Furies –

I smiled with recognition. I matched my fate to theirs. By the triumph of the will, I should become just like them.

THIRTY-FIVE

Goose & Cabbage, Blade Bone, Noah's Ark, Bull & Butcher, King Lud.

('Things could always be better.')

Lion & Adder, Plow & Sail, Half Penny House, Cocoa Tree, Bombay Grab.

('These are hard times.')

Swan & Maidenhead, Swan with Two Necks, Swan & Sugarloaf, Swan & Hoop.

('Sixty-odd hundredweight on, was it, ten acres, profit five pounds something.')

Whistling Oyster, Three Nuns & Hare, Copenhagen, Two Chairmen, Mother Redcap.

('You've come over all pale, miss –'

'Still? Not still pale?'

What about my mastery of my untidy emotions, my self-command? My pride?)

Foul Anchor, Ship Aground. World Upside Down, World's End.

I knew what they wanted, which was to have a man in charge, however they could effect it. Either I should appoint a man to manage Havisham's, or – their alternative wish – I should sell the business.

(Did I detect the hand of Snee behind one of the hostile bids?) They all misjudged me gravely.

I defied the brewhouse, which was where all the trouble had begun. They could go hang. I accepted no new orders. When we had exhausted the stock, I ordered the brewing to be halted. I dismissed the workmen.

I heard the rappings at the front door, and then the door being opened a crack from inside and the person sent away. Another worker's wife thinking she could appeal to my humanity, my womanliness.

But I waited. I held my nerve.

I had the gates to the yard chained.

No capitulation.

I had been paying for the upkeep of the horses, and the services of an ostler or two, but I sold the horses and told the stablemen to search elsewhere for work.

I boarded up every window in the brewery that could be broken from the street.

'So . . .'

I watched from the room which had been my father's office and then my own. The ledgers were piled up on shelves behind me, gathering dust.

'. . . so, they haven't the courage of this poor paltry woman?'

I smiled at that.

They had forgotten the stock I came from: that I wasn't just any woman, but a Kent Havisham: proof and tempered, through and through.

Intrepid Fox. Fetterlock. Marrowbone & Cleaver. Tom o' Bedlam.

That scream.

Mr Calvert's wife lying beneath, and those thrusting buttocks as her lover drives up into her.

The woman was transported beyond her pain, enthralled into a fourth dimension.

Run aground, stuck fast as I was, how could I not be riven by envy of that outrageous metaphysical adventure?

———

They burned me on Iden Meadow.

My effigy was hoisted on top of a bonfire they'd built. A straw woman, wearing a wedding dress made of newspaper.

Put together from dry kindling, I went up – so I heard – magnificently.

Cheers, catcalls. Flames ten feet high. I exploded in a reveille of sparks.

> Wild through the woods I'll fly,
> Robes, locks shall thus be tore.
> A thousand deaths I'll die,
> Ere thus in vain adore.

I shall defy you again.

I shall hold out against you all.

He isn't coming now.

He will never come.

I can do whatever I like.

I might put on a wedding dress if I choose to, just to laugh at all those innocent virgins. Hear how I'm laughing at them, cruelly and without pity. How it *matters* to them, much too much, and yet they see nothing of how the world contrives to delude them.

Giving yourself in love, you give yourself as a hostage to fate. The less you think to think of yourself, the more easily you'll be betrayed.

Wearing white silk and a veil and satin slippers for a day will change nothing, and couldn't make a false man true.

You break a superstition only by challenging it.

There *is* no sorcerer's charm for happiness. You won't find it in the Book of Common Prayer. It's only a dress, and they're only slippers, sweated over in some dingy workshop.

Look at me, in my train and veil. Tell me what magic you see. This is the awful damage that men do. And still the foolish, forlorn virgins go on believing.

Look at me. Let your blood run cold at the sight.

Take heed. Beware.

Or you will suffer just as I have suffered.

Love, devotion, married bliss.

They're dizzards' dreams, that vanish with the dawn.

I returned to the bedroom and dressing room that used to be mine: I reclaimed them.

'Fetch me my wedding dress.'

The veil disguised my hair. From a distance, seen from across the room, no one would have known my age; they would have presumed me young.

'Fetch my slippers. The spare pair.'

They hadn't been worn. When I put them on, they took the shape of my feet.

'Leave me now, will you. Go.'

I seated myself before the glass. I pulled back the veil. With my face scrubbed clean, the true ravages were revealed. I had to conceal them again. It was the face that held everything together.

So . . .

Paint it white.

Powder it, and sweeten it with perfume.

A slash of colour on my lips, a rim of black kohl round each eye, and a tiny upturned hook etched on the outer corners.

I did this twice over, to make sure, applying a second layer of everything.

From this point forward, Satis House would be a memorial to the real Catherine Havisham; a repository of holy relics.

Fresh air invades and destroys.

Keep it out.

Keep it out; then everything can be preserved. The contents will be encased exactly as they are. We shall be impervious to change.

I issued my instructions.

Doors should remain closed, except for immediate ingress and egress. When leaving or entering the house, the doors must not – must *not* – stand open for a moment longer than required.

Window sashes have to be kept lowered. Sunshine, another destroyer, comes falsely smiling; and so the curtains and shutters should be drawn at all times in those apartments I mean to use.

('The sun was now Inned at the Goat –'

'Miss – ?')

For light, candles will be lit in the candle sconces.

Fires might be kindled, but not allowed to roar, which would agitate the stillness of the air. The servants stared at me. But it was only sound common sense.

> Where there is neither sense of life nor joys,
> But the vast shipwreck of my life's esteems.

I also had the clocks stopped. At twenty minutes to nine, when it was the fatal blow had been delivered. Those metal hearts would never beat again. A mausoleum demanded the solemnity of silence.

I was merely the one who tended the altar. I would perform the rituals of devotion, in order to disprove devotion. I wore my ostentatious wedding dress in order to become a shadow; I was nothing more.

THIRTY-SIX

Day for night. Night for day. In this sepulchre there were to be no distinctions.

I did as was done on that morning. I powdered myself, applied colour to my cheeks, highlighted my eyes, teased a stubborn hair from the plucked arcs of my brows.

On the dressing table I had two candelabras, one on either side of the triptych of mirrors, with five candles apiece. By the bright light they cast I saw what I saw.

Not the woman sitting here, but the young woman who sat here one morning long ago, a bright May morning, making the final preparations before exchanging her old life for the new.

———

I had described him to Sally with so much awe and admiration in my voice, she must have doubted the reality of the man. The only recourse I'd given her was to see him for herself, to discover just how much of what I'd said could be true.

———

In the colder months – the *mois noirs* – water was stored in a lead sarcophagus, so that it didn't ice over. In winter and early spring my hair acquired a greenish-yellow tinge, and the shock of white was less shocking.

I still had my hair, the flyaway sort and only fair for half the year, a reckless aureole around my head. It unwound from the back like a plaited rope; then I hoisted it back up again, pinned it haphazardly into place with old silver and diamond clips.

The dress had needed to be taken in. Even with that, the seamstress had been too optimistic, and the dress ended up hanging. The silk better suited curves, and that fleshiness which used to be considered a sign of good breeding. But that woman was no more. Now the bones of my rib cage showed through.

The girl banked the fire high.

'Sawn ilex?'

'Please, miss – ?'

'It's of no consequence . . .'

She built a fire to last me a couple of hours, which would allow her to slip off to meet her young man. She would pretend that she hadn't heard me when I rang for her, or (her usual alibi) that she'd looked round the corner of the door, but I was napping.

When the coal heated and the flames deepened, I sat looking at the golden palaces of the moon. Soaring domes and minarets, invincible ramparts. Shining seas running beneath them.

Out there, beyond the closed shutters, everything changed and nothing changed. Sacristy Gate, Prior's Gate, Chertsey's Gate. Pilgrims' Passage, Minor Canon Row.

The Corn Exchange, the Butchers' Market.

The Theatre Royal, at the foot of Star Hill.

Chalk Church.

And the publics. The Leather Bottle, Crispin & Crispianus.

The shoals by the bridge.

Day for night. Night for day. There were to be no distinctions.

I wore the dress – except when I bathed (I did bathe) or when the dress required freshening (I still recalled the delicacies of that pampered child who used to live here).

When the powder thinned, I made my face up again: I ringed my eyes, rubbed rouge on to my cheeks and coloured my lips.

I should always look the same.

I couldn't go back; to be the woman I had been before the letter reached me, on the morning of what should have been my wedding. Now I lived in the present, where an event happens repeatedly and eternally. I couldn't get any younger: why should I need to grow any older?

THIRTY-SEVEN

Town rowdies had thrown mud at the name on the brewhouse wall, and pockmarked the 'V' and the second 'H' and the final 'M'. (The same youths who once climbed on to the house roof and tried to block up a smoking chimney, until Mr Jaggers – by good chance, he was visiting – kicked away their ladder and gave them a verbal thrashing they'd clearly never forgotten.) Lazy swallows picked at the mud to help make their nests, and so time and nature did their work, and life went on, and on.

And, I didn't know why, I failed to die.

Just as before, I told the modiste, it will be very fine work. A second dress. An identical dress. Silk from the same source, and the style copied exactly. Sprigged and trimmed with Bath lace, as it was; and embroidery of gold foil on the back. Repairs to the twelve feet of train. Another Honiton veil. A headband of entwined silk roses. Two new pairs of ivory slippers, with silver lacing, ten eyelets on each.

I was still inhabiting those places, the ones where my feelings were keenest. It was as if my feelings had imprinted themselves on the air there.

For animals, everything happens in the present.

Again and again I replayed my life, on a long continuum of time, where my future was nothing other than the past. I was living through events once more, with the same intensity they'd had for me then: it was the first time, and it always would be, over and over again.

———

Nine faces, which seemed to have materialised through the fabric of the wall. My dressing-room wall. Carnaval masks from Venice, which I'd had bought for me in London. Several were pensive, one (shaped out of a sickle moon) smiled enigmatically. Some wept, so that the black kohl ran from their eyes, streaking the white faces. My wailing wall.

> exiled from light, To live a life
> half-dead, a living death, And buried; but O
>   yet more miserable!
> Myself my sepulchre, a moving grave;
> Buried, yet not exempt,
> By privilege of death and burial,
> From worst of other evils, pains, and wrongs.

———

They were living in accommodation which *my* money, Havisham money, had provided them with. He had married on an income donated by me, and what he scavenged. I had set them up, and in no little style.

How droll it must have seemed to him. Was *she* now sharing his laughter? No, I preferred to believe he'd kept her in the dark: that Sally still believed he was a man of business who had earned the wherewithal by his honest toil.

The way he had of pressing back on his heels before he walked forward. A habit of stretching his neck and straightening his head before he said anything meant to be of greater consequence.

How he smelt. The oil of bergamot on his hair, and the tar soap he was diligent about washing his hands with. The spicy tobacco in his snuffbox. The saddle-soap rubbed into his boots.

> T'was dead of night . . .
> Unhappy Dido was alone awake.
> Nor sleep nor ease the furious queen can find;
> Sleep fled her eyes, as quiet fled her mind.
> Despair, and rage, and love divide her heart;
> Despair and rage had some, but love the greater part.

After Gold and Silver, I had continued to keep a pair of cats, pedigrees, about the house. Now I was told that the tom, Mace, a replacement for Gold's successor, had been found nailed by his paws to a tree. Thankfully he died a few days after he was taken down. I kept the tabby indoors after that. She seemed quite lost not to have her companion, and grew thin.

But later in the year there was a very curious development. The tabby, Saffron, spayed – or supposedly spayed – at an early age, gave birth to a litter of kittens. She was too weak to provide the survivors with the milk they needed, and I told one of the girls to look after them.

Saffron regained some weight. Her spirits revived. She took a critical interest in the four kittens left, and was gentle or sharp with them just as they deserved.

Had you deferred, at least, your hasty flight,
  And
And left behind some pledge of
Our delight,
Some babe to bless the mother's mournful sight,
Some young Aeneas,
   To supply your place,
Whose features might express his father's face,
I should not then
Complain to live bereft

I found the image of Mace crucified on the cherry tree with rusty nails was starting to fade. Instead I was distracted by the rivalry of the kittens for their mother's attention, scrapping with one another and rolling themselves into a large amorphous fur ball with at least a dozen legs.

I understood that, mysteriously, life will assert itself even out of despondency and despair.

'In my end,' Mary Stuart said of herself, lying on the executioner's block, 'in my end is my beginning.'

V

ESTELLA

THIRTY-EIGHT

The little girl stared at me.

She would always remember this occasion.

Seeing me for the first time, she was also entering what was to become her normality.

The rooms where it was neither day nor night. My attire, in celebration of an event that hadn't happened. The mouldering breakfast feast spread out on the table, and the high-backed chairs standing to attention, as if at any moment . . . The flames licking at the grate, the slivers of white light balanced on the candle wicks suddenly jumping in a draught, shadows flaring up the walls.

'Don't cry,' I said. 'Don't cry, please.'

I stretched out my arm, but the child turned away quickly, raised one shoulder to protect herself.

Her mother was a Romany, a felon defended by Mr Jaggers on a murder charge; it was claimed she'd strangled a rival for a man's affections. The father was native-born, with a misapplied intelligence, fallen into bad ways and transported.

'Not the most auspicious start, Miss Havisham.'

'The child cannot be responsible for their sins.'

'But she is their child.'

'She will be *my* child, Mr Jaggers.'

'And you can be sure to set her to rights? When the rest of the world would condemn her?'

'She and I will live apart from the world.'

—

She was to have come the next day, a Tuesday. Then she would have been 'full of grace'. By default she was a Monday child. 'Fair of face'. That was enough for me.

I chose her name.

> *Estelle. Estella.*
> *Or sometimes Estelle for Esther.*
> *Esther, Hester* fem., *poss. Persian 'star';*
> *or* der. *Babylonian, Ishtar, the goddess Astarte*
> Dims. *Essie, Hetty.*

Estella she would be.

—

I tried again to touch her, but I fared little better. She was astonished that I should want to, and she would shy away. It was as if any contact at all caused her physical pain.

If I then smiled, I did so out of embarrassment; not because I felt any pleasure at her confusion – but she may not have understood this. A wild look would flicker in her eyes; she seemed to be searching for an escape.

And it was because I was afraid of losing her that I had Mrs Mallows take her – resisting, crying at the woman to let go – to her room and lock her there for the next hour or two hours. I always unlocked it myself, and brought her in a little treat, either something sweet to eat or some coloured paper scraps for her to paste into her album. Usually this brought her round, because she liked sugary flavours and the gaudy colours of the paper angels and grandees.

I watched how she would grab at things, and hoard them. That was the gypsy in her.

'No one is going to take them from you, child. Now put them back. You will have much more given to you than you ever dreamed.'

She would keep a fierce hold on the object until I could prise her fingers apart.

'Who is going to deny you, you little fool?'

She still recoiled from me, afraid I was going to strike her. She would drop whatever it was, on to the floor, at my feet.

'No. *You* pick it up. Estella, do as I say.'

On the third or fourth time of asking she would pick it up and hand it back to me.

'*Now* we trust one another. Thank you.'

She would run off and hide; she was the one embarrassed now, and ashamed. That was good – it meant she was starting to see that the deepest feelings are the ones we do our learning from.

I had her taken out into the open air. I instructed her to run about. She must grow healthy and strong.

I supervised her diet. I arranged the buying of clothes, extra warm for winter and light and cool for summer.

I ensured that *her* rooms were daylit and ventilated well, that it shouldn't ever grow too hot and her skin dry out, or the temperature drop too low and slow the blood. I wanted her to have a perfect second start in life.

I required that she play in front of me.

'Play, child. Amuse yourself. Go on!'

She brought me flowers from the garden. And, later, chatter overheard from downstairs but not comprehended.

'Show me how you play. Let me see, Estella. Play away, *now* . . .'

———

There were always petitioners. My cousins and second cousins. Every Wednesday afternoon. They sat in the hall until I was ready to receive them. If I wasn't in the mood for an audience, they went away even more disappointed than if – as was normal – I'd refused their request, but they would return with the same promptitude the following Wednesday, ready for more of the humiliating ritual.

If I mocked them, they said nothing by way of complaint. I might be as rude as I liked, and they wouldn't raise a single objection. So, there was no pleasure to be had from them. It was no more than a tedious necessity: a rich woman being supplicated to.

They were dismissed, and even if I had been agreeably disposed that afternoon no one ever believed that I'd been as generous as I might have been. ('Her belfry's chock-full of bats, that one.') I thought they would actually *despise* me if I didn't offer them, so infinitely remote as it was, the hope of seeing me throw gold at their feet.

———

Estella knew that I was not her mother. I told her that I didn't want her to call me her mother. If she must call me anything, then why not . . . why not 'Nana'?

She should look on me as her provider in all things else.

'But I had a mother?'

'She gave you birth.'

'Do you know about her?'

'What I know is that I shall take care of you. *This* is your home.'

'But you're not my – the thing I mustn't call you –?'

'I'm better than a mother. Mothers can vanish. You're here in this house because I wish you to be. I mean no harm to come to you so long as we're living under this one roof together.'

I ensured that my growing Estella should want for nothing.

Clothes and shoes. Books. Dolls. A wooden barrow for the garden, and a set of tools. A leather horse on which to perch sidesaddle.

I would have bought her a model theatre, or looked out the one I used to play with so long ago, but she expressed no interest in that idea. Instead I gave her some jointed shadow puppets on sticks, which she articulated – indifferently – against a lighted wall. She didn't much like the little carriage for her dolls, but she asked me (coyly, prettily) if she might have a parasol for herself – and some cups and saucers, such as adults use for entertaining, so that she could play host to those invisible friends she preferred to the flesh-and-blood young companions I now and then asked to Satis House.

She was oddly casual with her possessions. She would leave the barrow out in the rain, or her dolls. She didn't fold the parasol as I showed her, and the china cups and saucers acquired cracks and chips. Sometimes she eyed the things quite hostilely: resenting the demands they made on her, to play dutifully.

I didn't chide her about her negligence, her indifference. I had a fear of provoking her. In time I came to see that I was wrong, and guilty of neglecting my duty to *her* by not remonstrating. But by then we were settled into our routines, in the perpetually shuttered and candlelit reception rooms, and it seemed too late to jeopardise this slender harmony.

———

She had been sitting at my dressing table, hadn't she?

There was a trace of powder under her jaw line, and by her left ear. She smelt sweet.

Even though she'd had the guile to be careful, I knew from looking at the dressing table – shifting the candelabra about to see better – which items had tempted her. There was a place for everything, and the tiny disturbances to the dust told me just how she had proceeded.

'Well, Mr Jaggers . . . ?'

I'd had a single shutter inched back in his honour. I stood close to him, shading my eyes, as he watched Estella through the grimy window glass.

'. . . what do you say?'

He liked a little silence to expand after any question I asked him. Perhaps it was a courtroom trick, compromising a witness into thinking she had to speak and letting her say too much.

I wasn't going to be put on trial in my own drawing room, though. I waited for his reply.

'Coming on. Coming on.'

'Is she recognisable?'

Pause. He put his head on one side.

'To ourselves.'

'And not to anyone else?'

Pause. He considered the flattened tip of his index finger.

'Surely not.'

'I'm glad to hear it.'

Pause.

'You've quite remade her.'

As he chewed at the fingernail his eyes didn't move off Estella; they grew smaller in their sockets with the keenness of his concentration.

'It's a beginning –' I had started to say when he interrupted me.

'That woman would have killed her. She wanted to. With her bare hands.'

I shuddered involuntarily at the thought of it. But Mr Jaggers was smiling as he unrolled his white handkerchief.

'What would she have deprived us of?' he said. 'Thanks be to God.'

I corrected him. 'Thanks be to Havisham money.'

The children I invited to Satis House had to come singly. I selected
those with parents or guardians who would regard it as an honour
of sorts to be asked, who wouldn't dare to refuse me. The idiots
delivered their offspring, blinking, all of them, at the candlelight
and shadows. I left the rest to Estella.

'Speak, Estella – why don't you?'

Estella would be sitting with whichever child I had chosen for
her. In the drawing room like this her manner became quite stately.

'Say something, Estella. Tell me, is our visitor today your favourite of the ones who've come to see us?'

It was hard for me to keep the laughter out of my voice.

'Tell me, visitor,' she asked, 'do you play at dominoes?'

The answer was invariably 'No'.

'Then I must show you.'

At which point she would rise.

'Come along –'

Already her voice had a ring of majestic impatience.

'– what are you waiting for? Follow me.'

To your doom, you poor noodle born of nincompoops.

The Misses Wilcox had their great-nephew staying with them:
Master Drummle, a lumbering boy a little older than Estella.

With the two women he was charm personified, keeping a couple
of paces behind them except when he jumped forward to open a
door or a gate. But once his great-aunts took up talking – gabbling –
again, his face would fall, and two deep and prematurely adult lines
fixed on either side of his mouth, advertising his discontent and
boredom.

I said to the Wilcoxes that they might take a turn about the garden: I would sit with the children for a while. It was spoken as a directive, not as a suggestion. The two women didn't want to risk offending me, and went waddling off, into daylight.

I sat down to spectate.

'Tell me, visitor –' Estella emptied the box, '– do you play at dominoes?'

'Dominoes? Why on earth should *I* play at dominoes?' Even if he had a lagging gait, the boy's wits were quick enough. Estella stared at him.

'"*Why*"?' she repeated, and sounded mystified.

'That's a game for publics. Not for well-born types.'

Quite flummoxed, Estella swept the pieces back into the box, scarcely looking at what she did.

'If *you've* got a better idea . . .'

'It's too stuffy in here.'

I had a timely hunch I should pretend to be asleep. Eyes closed, I let my head tilt to one side.

'It's a rum place, this.'

The boy had dropped his voice, but Estella was shushing him.

'Why does she wear her wedding clothes?'

Estella whispered, 'That's just what she wears.'

'Is something wrong with her?'

'"Wrong"?'

'Don't tell me you haven't noticed.'

'Noticed what?'

'C'mon. I'm going outside.'

'Outside?'

'D'you have to repeat *everything* I say?'

'Why on earth – ?'

'Look, are you coming or not?'

'Where to?'

'Anywhere'll do.'

———

Estella told me afterwards how he had teased and baited whatever he could find out of doors. Two of the cats, a dog, a squirrel, a horse standing in its harness.

There was no tone of disapproval in her voice as she told me. At nine years old she merely stated matters of fact. One visit from young Drummle, I felt, had been quite sufficient.

———

She was looking at me queerly.

'What is it, Estella? Why the big eyes?'

'Didn't you ever want to wear your old clothes again?'

'Instead of . . . ?'

'Instead of your wedding clothes.'

(It was the end of something. Her naivety. Her uncritical acceptance. And what was I to say to her? Because – because everything is symbols and gestures. I knew that now. Because we only play and declare at life. Because true life is too awesome and terrifying to bear.)

'Were you going to be married?'

'I thought I was.'

'But you didn't *get* married?'

'The man who was meant to be my husband . . . he decided . . .'

'It was *his* fault?'

I started to nod. Then I stopped myself.

'It wasn't to be. That's all.'

'Were you sad?'

'Oh, I was too angry to be sad.'

She continued to stare at me. At my wedding dress, at my greying hair shot through with white. She was staring in the same way I used to stare, myself, at the strange sights I saw when I was being walked about the town. The poor souls, people would say of them, they'd lost their minds.

———

I wouldn't have anything changed, even though my dimensions were bound to have altered.

Just as before, I told the modiste's niece, it will be very fine work.

A third wedding dress.

Silk, Lyons silk, in that same old-fashioned style. Sprigged and trimmed with Bath lace, as used to be favoured; and – on the back, as delicately done as gossamer – gold foil, which was the taste at that time too.

Repairs to repairs on the train. A Honiton veil. A headband of silk roses. Three more pairs of ivory slippers with silver lacing, ten eyelets apiece.

THIRTY-NINE

The blacksmith Joe Gargery had brought up his wife's little brother, and I requested that he deliver the boy to Satis House.

Pip Pirrip kept apart from other children, I'd heard, which was to the good. The children from the better homes knew that Estella was my ward, and brought their parents' prejudices with them. *This* boy had no such expectations.

'Play,' I told them. 'Play together.'

Estella treated him roughly.

'Why do you keep staring at me? Are you slow-brained?'

I laughed. Estella so trenchant, and the boy – dressed up in his starched best – so out of sorts. They played with marbles, and then Estella showed him her articulated wall puppets, but the boy tangled the limbs of his and Estella snatched the puppet from him and flung them all back in the box.

'They're ruined now.'

'Take yourselves off into the yard,' I said. 'Or the garden.'

I heard them from my window.

'*I* don't know why she dresses like that. Why do you dress like *that*, boy?'

They returned, and played Beggar My Neighbour.

It's called a game of chance, but I knew my Estella would win.

'Hear him! He calls the knaves "jacks", this boy.'

I watched him. How his face crumpled whenever she said

something to hurt him. Then, between times, how he got a little of his confidence back, and tried to recommend himself to her. And how cleverly and instinctively my Estella would put him down again.

Even a blacksmith's stepchild may have some little pride, and Estella was set on puncturing it. But a cat will kill its mouse, and so I had to ring the bell and summon Mrs Mallows, before my entertainment was ruined. I had to prolong the pleasure.

'You will come to us another day, Master Pirrip,' I said – I commanded.

At that he looked quite shocked. But I knew it was also exactly what he'd been hoping against hope to hear.

———

For a while Estella had been aware of her attractiveness.

It was precocious in a child, but her associations with other children had been of a kind – brief, and to the point – that enabled her to sum them up quickly. She could read their opinions of her from their faces.

She felt as isolated on that score, I guessed – because she carried the stigmata of beauty – as she did because I kept her to myself. Later she must want to let more people see her, a different sort from the ones who saw her performing her piety in the cathedral on Sunday mornings; that was bound to make my task easier when the time came. She might become haughtier than she currently was, but that would be her strength and her safeguard.

———

The Pirrip lad had returned to us, for more of the same.

Further visits – in response to my summonses – followed.

He was quite willing, and Estella didn't object. And I was curious to see what would happen.

He had clever eyes. He'd been born, as some are, out of their proper locus in life. His manners were still crude, he had all a country boy's gaucheness. He would *learn* manners, though, that was the easy part; natural intelligence will take anyone far.

'So, Pip, what do they say about me?'

He told me, eventually, when I had worried at him and worn him down.

That I was crazed in the head. I didn't ever bathe, ate as little as a sparrow, and drank only French champagne. I could sleep standing on my feet. My belfry bats were allowed to fly about the house.

> The loud report thro' Libyan cities goes.
> Fame, the great ill, from small beginnings grows:
> Swift from the first . . .
> Soon grows the pigmy to gigantic size . . .

'Well, Pip, you've certainly been keeping your ears open.'

'I didn't mean to hear.'

'And you've got a good memory, I'm thinking too.'

'Yes?'

> Talk is her business, and her chief delight
> To tell of prodigies and cause affright . . .
> Things done relates, not done she feigns, and
> Mingles truth with lies.

'And what do they say about the fair Estella?'

They said that she was an angel for looks, but as conceited by nature as I was. She was inclined to society ('Aa-*ha!*'), but not sociable. They wondered what she was doing in such a town as this one, when it was clearly her destiny to dazzle on a larger stage.

'And she's still only a child!' I said.

Some folk, the boy added, foresaw an unhappy end for her.

'Then we must prove them wrong, mustn't we?'

'Must we?'

I laughed.

The door opened, and Estella walked in. She didn't look at our guest, but her question was directed at him.

'I suppose you bring the local scandal about me.'

I looked at Pip, and he looked between me and Estella.

'No,' he said. 'No, I haven't.'

An inspired fibber, even if not one by forethought. I smiled at him. I'd been hoping to find some complications in him, some density, and now – thank God – I had. With some *esprit*, but also with some mental ballast in reserve, he might be able to put up a challenge to Estella, to test her as any weak reed would never do.

He expected to see my hands like claws. But my hands had always been judged one of my better features – a lady's hands and not a brewer's daughter's, pale and etiolated (a word Moses taught me), elongated and tapering. They had a way of arranging themselves, hanging loosely over the end of a seat arm, like the gently winnowing fronds of some sea plant.

How he stared at the flashing stones of my rings.

'Play, boy, will you? Play!'

I watched the two of them, the forgeman's charge and my Estella. Her behaviour with him was natural at one moment and then artificial the next. She ran skidding on the gravel like a girl, threw her doll to him like a girl, but she spoke to him – proudly, dismissively – and flounced past him like someone twice her age.

The boy was losing his bearings with her. How he stood with his shoulders hunched and his arms gawkily loose and limp by his sides, and his eyes not so clever that they could disguise his dejection as he stared after her.

He could write his letters very neatly. He multiplied and divided quickly in his head.

'Would you like to learn Latin?'

'I don't know if I should have need of it, Miss Havisham.'

'That depends on what you want to do in life.'

'I'm bound to be something in Mr Gargery's line, I think.'

'*He* is . . .'

The boy looked awkward, ashamed to admit it.

'. . . the blacksmith, isn't he? Out Lower Higham way?'

'Yes, Miss Havisham.'

'And what do you *want* to do?'

(Those good hands, not made for the anvil. His clear skin would coarsen in the forge-fire.)

'I haven't thought, Miss Havisham. Not really.'

'A doctor? A lawyer?'

'*Me*, Miss?'

'Or a teacher? A scholar?'

'I don't know – Mr Pumblechook, in the High Street –'

'A shopkeeper, you mean?'

'No. He's a corn factor, Miss Havisham.'

I nodded.

'Yes,' I said, 'you're quite right to correct me. I was wrong.'

He shifted from foot to foot, raising his eyes and then, whenever he caught mine, lowering them again.

In the dragon's den!

He laid temptation before me, to give my leading-lady performance – to act Sarah Siddons off the stage and into the wings. He was my perfect audience.

He was remembering this, all of it. One day he would attempt to make sense of the experience, meaning to tell himself that Estella couldn't have been as unbenign as she appeared – so implacably hard on him.

The boy with the absurd name and the clever eyes. Pip Pirrip.

———

Estella liked to search through the clothes presses in my dressing room.

'And this?'

'A *chemise de la reine*,' I explained. 'I wore it in the mornings. There's a sash for it somewhere. Blue Persian, that was the fashion.'

A history lesson.

'And my riding habit.'

'I've seen that.'

'My summer one. Nankeen.'

How important it had been to be *comme il faut*. It must be stone-coloured, lined with green, and matching green for the waistcoat.

'*"Habillée en homme". Jolie comme un cœur.*'

And hats. The wide brims had buckled and creased, but Estella tried to uncurl them. I fitted her with the little cane undress hat, and straightened the festoon of ribbons which hung down at the back. The pink had faded; some of the strands in the weave were quite colourless now.

I thought of another straw hat with scarlet ribbons and a white flower, afloat on the Cam. In my memory it floated forever on that surface of darkening water, like a wreath.

'*You* wore this hat?'

'There are always rules,' I said. 'And those were the rules in the ancient of days.'

———

I watched her sleeping. I stood back, in case my shadow falling across her should wake her. Seen like this in profile, her peerless features cried out to be touched, but very very gently. The merest contact of a finger skimming over them might wake her; better the most evanescent shiver of a feather.

I dreaded disturbance, causing her to open her eyes, having her stare up at me not able to comprehend for the first few moments.

Oh, Estella! You don't realise the reach of the power that lives in you. You mustn't let it be squandered through ignorance.

———

I woke once more in my bed, in the night or the day, convinced a man was close to me, lying naked, ablaze on the sheets alongside me.

I stretched out my hand and touched only a very little warmth where I had been lying over on my flank. I was alone. Of course I was.

It didn't happen again. I felt no shame, nor regret either. My life was now spared those fleshly embroilments. I rarely felt those surges between my legs which I used to, and the want was less urgent.

I lay back. The tide of desire was ebbing quickly, drying off to traces, and I was left safely stranded, among my reliable shadows and with the same tried and proven air I had been breathing in and breathing out for long months, for years.

———

'Hand me my stick, young Pip. I have an ache today.'

He did as he was bid.

I pointed ahead, across the passage, to the circuit of the dining room we followed.

'You know what comes next?'

'Yes, Miss Havisham.'

I held on to his shoulder.

'Very well. Walk me, walk me.'

We proceeded along both sides of the long table.

He stepped on a dead beetle. The husk crackled under the sole of his shoe.

Cobwebs covered everything, draped like spun sugar over the

feast and the chairs. The disintegrating bottom layer of cake had started to subside, and the other three above leaned tipsily.

He stared at this rich woman's indulgence. But he must have known that the worst disgrace to befall a woman was not to be abandoned before she was married, but to be jilted while she was wearing her wedding dress. My shame excused my capricious ways: my lunatic ways, if you will.

How he stared.

'Come along! Walk me, walk me!'

We had bewitched him.

But he had fallen under our spell, I could believe, before he ever set eyes on us. Out at the forge he would have heard all about us, and been set wondering. I pictured him walking past the high walls and looking up at the shuttered windows. He had imagined the secret garden that must grow behind the house. He had envisaged the rooms ill-lit by candles, rooms as vast as sea caves.

And now – it was his original enchantment he was trying to recall. The reality, or what we offered him, couldn't ever match the pictures of us he'd carried in his head. He used his politeness – his unctuousness – to try to conceal the disappointment, but I saw right through his cover.

'This is my birthday, Pip.'

'Happy –'

'No, I don't suffer it to be spoken of.'

I stared at the mouldering food which lay strewn with spider silk and dust.

'And on this same day my wedding breakfast was set out. The mice have gnawed at it. And sharper teeth – fangs – have feasted on me too.'

His shoulder had stiffened under my hand as he concentrated harder.

'Maybe my death day will be on this day also?'

I didn't mean it as a question, but he answered me very earnestly.

'Oh, I should hope *not*.'

I meant to smile at that, but for some reason my lips wouldn't oblige. As he looked round at me in the gloom, he must have thought I was grimacing. I made out the expression of disquiet on his face.

'But I have much to see achieved before then, Pip – you've no idea. I have my curses to lay first.'

'"Curses"?' he asked, right on cue.

———

It was always twenty minutes to nine in Satis House. The passage of the weeks was marked for me instead by the Wednesday afternoon arrival and departure of the cousins, on their petitioning business that was never satisfied.

I was annoyed by their myopic clock-watching regularity, even though I insisted on it: presenting themselves, I presumed, at the same minute of the same hour every week, staying not a moment longer than I had demanded of them. I was relieved that they were so compliant, but I felt the differences between us were exemplified by their servitude to time: time as it was measured out to the artificial dictates of a pendulum swinging (as is the clockmaker's tradition) on a length of gut, the tube that carries semen from a bull's testicles.

———

'And now, madam –'

Estella jiggled forward in her chair with joy decipherable on her face. I heard it in the sudden breathlessness of her voice.

'– for the first time –'

She threw down her last card, the Queen of Spades.

'– I have beggared *you*!'

I sat back. I couldn't withhold a smile.

She wasn't expecting me to smile. Her own pleasure faded from her face. Those petulant furrows reappeared in the middle of her brow, drawing in her eyebrows. They were the only blemish she had, but they bothered me. (How was I going to eradicate them? Not by my smiling.) It seemed I had ruined her moment of victory: the 'daughter', as through the whole of human history, managing at last to trump the 'mother'.

'You've trounced me, Estella.'

She pushed her chair back.

'It's only a stupid game of cards!'

It was always when the game excited her that she took colour to her face. Now her anger was burning her, from the inside out. But that, poor child, only aided her beauty, like refiner's fire.

FORTY

The passing years had done no favours to the fabric of the house. Thieves attempted to break in several times, at the back, and once they succeeded. I had bars put up at the windows.

I couldn't take myself into my father's office now, nor the Compting House. It pained me too much to remember . . . I had those windows bricked up. Inside I locked the doors, and placed the keys somewhere for safe keeping, and later I wasn't able to recollect where. The maids occasionally spoke of hearing noises from behind the office door: surely not ledgers being opened and shut or papers sorted through, as they liked to frighten themselves by thinking, but whatever had happened to fall down the chimney, maybe a bird with a broken neck beating its wings on the hearth stone.

A carriage had stopped across the street, and its two passengers had stepped out.

They were watching the house closely.

The woman was dark and compact. My contemporary for age. The girl who accompanied her was dark also, and a little shorter than Estella.

The woman was speaking. The girl listened, following the direction of the other's eyes.

Was it really her? Marianna Chadwyck? Mouse?

With – whom? – her daughter?

Mouse's appearance was now of the sort (kindly) called quaint. She was wearing a melange of mismatched pelts and feathers, lacking Sheba's ready advice.

We entwined our arms, and she failed to do the obvious, by *not* commenting on how I was living, by candlelight, in unaired rooms, and dressed as I was for a wedding.

I saw tears in her eyes, but I couldn't tell if it was with pleasure or sorrow: with both perhaps. I was introduced to her daughter, who had to be prompted forward, and who offered me a hand tense with misapprehension.

I heard Mouse lightly gasp when Estella entered the drawing room. Her daughter, alarmed, drew closer to her side.

Estella was intrigued, I could see, because these were grander visitors than our usual, as the lit chandeliers announced. Only I would have been able to gauge her reaction, from my experience, because as ever her looks were triumphantly unmarred by the evidence of superfluous feeling.

Mouse and Eveline admired in silence. Estella had lost that original dusky tincture, but the passage of time had enhanced the colour of her eyes: violet eyes, which added to her strong presence in a room. Hers were the ideal proportions of my youth, the high narrow waist and long arms, with a deep bosom to come. For the last two or three years she'd been able to fix her own braid of hair, and to roll and pin it on top of her head in increasingly complex arrangements, as if the touch of others offended her for its clumsiness.

Estella and Eveline went off together, into the garden.

I didn't ask Mouse why she'd come, but at one point she mentioned the name 'Jaggers', and I wondered if she had picked up something about the true circumstances concerning the payments to her mother.

Lady Charlotte had gout, and she had become short of memory.

'Her forgetfulness was amusing, to begin with. Then a little irritating. Until now . . .'

Mouse expressed sympathy for my own past 'predicament', using a tactful choice of words which I pictured her rehearsing to herself on the journey over.

W'm was finally married, she said, although it had been touch and go. Sheba up in London never had an evening unaccounted for in her social diary; and few mornings or afternoons were left spare either. Mouse herself had another three children, and sometimes took in Sheba's two, when she felt particular pity for them.

I mentioned the name of Mrs Calvert (last seen by me on the floor of the hermitage).

'Oh, her husband's become someone terribly important, and I expect she'd look down her nose at us now. I always thought she did that anyway.'

(I didn't remark.)

Lucinda Osborne shared Thurston Park with a fearsome female companion, and gave generously of her time to the church.

And what of Moses? He was where I'd left him, eleven or twelve years ago, only busier than ever now.

'He's kept his faith?'

'I think so. Why do you –'

'It must've been truer to him than his inheritance.'

'His inheritance?'

'Not that there is,' I said. 'For the youngest son.'

'Oh no, Moses isn't the youngest. He'll get a title from a favourite uncle. And what comes with it, lucky man.'

'This is a recent development?'

'No, no. He's known since he was a boy.'

'But I thought . . .'

It had always been there in my mind: the notion of his (comparative) poverty. I'd thought that God's ministry had to be worn like a badge, signifying one's humbler status.

'Oh no, Catherine. You have that quite wrong.'

And so, on the flimsiest of social pretexts, I had been content to judge him. I avoided Mouse's eyes for a little while.

'I used to feel you didn't believe me,' she said. 'But Moses is a fine man. I have no doubts about that at all.'

'I see so now. Only, it's taken me too long.'

'Better late than never.'

I smiled, but not as confidently as I wanted to.

We didn't speak about my father's payments to Lady Charlotte, and Snee's malversation. I knew that she knew. At another mention of Mr Jaggers's name she took my hands in hers.

'Has it been very hard for you, Catherine?'

'Round about here, they used to think I was a girl who had everything. That has been the hard part: realising that I didn't.'

'I thought you might have left. Taken yourself off somewhere new.'

'Twitch'd my mantle blue?'

'I'm sorry – ?'

'I felt I could hold on to more by staying here. If I'd gone off . . . I'm not sure I would have known who I was. I would have come apart perhaps.'

How reasoned I made my behaviour sound, when I couldn't remember it having been so. I had surely depended on something much closer to raw instinct.

'Perhaps,' Mouse said.

'But I made my choice.'

Or did I really mean the opposite – that events had chosen for me? And because I'd needed to be practical, what had been more necessary for me than to try to save as much sanity as I could?

We parted. I promised Mouse that I would keep in touch.

'For Estella's sake, Catherine.'

'For Estella's sake, yes. She has become my life now.'

———

By coincidence, shortly after Mouse's visit, past matters came to be spoken of again. I'd had no word of the subsequent life and career of Charles Compeyson, following my visit to Blackheath. When I was finally enlightened, my source was Mr Jaggers.

As ever, he was circumspect, enquiring merely as to whether or not I wished to be apprised of certain reports on 'not incontiguous matters' that had come his way.

I indicated that he should go ahead for the nonce.

'You will understand to whom I refer but shan't name?'

I nodded. Mr Jaggers paused only to ease the tightness of straining shirt collar round his wide neck.

'To be brief . . .'

Following three 'iniquitous offences' (forgery of documents, falsely claiming on a charity, passing of stolen banknotes), where the wronged parties had elected not to prosecute, the (nameless) man's luck had run out. He was charged and found guilty of a fourth – a sustained programme of embezzlement – and sentenced to a couple of years in jail. Or rather, on board a prison ship.

'Moored not so far from a shore you will be familiar with.'

(Why did I feel *that* was Mr Jaggers's true condemnation of the man: the fact that he'd been fool enough to get caught.)

'I can supply a few more salient details, should you wish.'

'I would rather *not* hear, thank you.'

I didn't feel it was either a release or a vindication to me to know this, the man now touched me so little. Along the way he had become abstracted, as he fully deserved to be. I hadn't forgotten a single one of my own humiliations; but I had turned my ire since then on men – all of the genus who conceitedly, smugly supposed that they were indispensable to a woman's personal completeness, her felicity.

Mr Jaggers's news – as scant as I wished it to be – confirmed my own thoughts, but also consolidated, *hardened* them in the following few nights of insomnia.

A woman can only satisfy and fulfil herself, I understood, when she establishes her own authority, and sees beyond equality, realising how terrible and damaging her own power – if unleashed – might be.

But there was more. Something to do with Arthur, I gathered.

I was confused. All these pronouns, 'he', 'him', 'his'. I begged that we revert to names. I needed to get this sorted out in my head.

'It seems that they've all been living together,' Mr Jaggers told me. 'Arthur. And the . . .'

'Let names be named.'

'Arthur and the Compeysons.'

'"Living together", you say?'

'Off and on.'

'No!'

'Indeed.'

'Arthur couldn't stand the man.'

Pause.

'So your half-brother claimed.'

Mr Jaggers stood holding his unfolded handkerchief, but he didn't apply it to his nose.

'Arthur got bought out, though,' I said.

Pause.

'Exactly.'

'I'm sorry, I don't . . .'

'Would Compeyson – would it have occurred to him to buy Arthur out if he hadn't known that was what Arthur wanted too?'

'What?' I found myself thinking aloud. 'They – they'd discussed it first?'

'In quite a detailed way, I should think.'

'Before it was suggested to *me*?'

'It was important that you should be the last to know.'

'A plot, you mean? Between the two of them?'

I stared between the unused handkerchief in Mr Jaggers's hand and the unblown nose.

'I think you'll find it makes a kind of sense, Miss Havisham. Criminally speaking.'

A name, 'Charles Compeyson', and so little else. The years had rubbed away at the physical features. If the facial details had surrendered themselves so easily, it must have been that they had lacked some definiteness to begin with.

If the set of a face can give clues to the firmness of a personality, I had to doubt that I'd read him properly.

It had been enough that he was a man who attended upon me, and who lightened the mental load I was carrying at that time. *Who* he was had mattered less to me than the fact that he was there, and so often.

I renewed my concentration, and then details did return to me.

The exact hue of his eyes, their cerulean blueness. The precise degree of brownness of his hair, the evenness (too much evenness?) of that brown, and how it had curled around his head. How one eyebrow would rise and arch higher than the other. His chin had shown a small cleft, almost apologetically small; that had saved it from being a wholly anonymous chin.

But his nose, his mouth, those eluded me. Likewise his teeth.

His hands had a sweep of brown hairs on the backs, and neat clusters on his knuckles, but I couldn't bring to mind the shape of his fingers.

He evaded me now because, I realised, he always had. I had been in love with someone I had half imagined to life, half invented for myself.

FORTY-ONE

Mrs Mallows sketched in what had happened. Blood stains on the rug in Estella's room. On her sheets. On her nightdress.

Estella looked pale and strained; she was getting through the small actions of the day by rote, without thinking. Her replies to my questions, which were harmless enough, were all delayed, and sounded irritable. I stopped saying what was unnecessary; Estella relaxed in the longer silences; she even allowed herself to smile faintly, as if aware that she wasn't any more the child who'd been brought to this house.

———

Because Estella was filling out, and my old clothes didn't seem so oversized, I had a seamstress tack a few items with pins and take them in.

Estella asked if I wouldn't be wanting them again.

'I have nowhere to go in them,' I said.

'And where shall *I* go?'

'You will have your own toilette made when we send you out into society. As it calls itself. Polite or otherwise.'

'When will that be?'

'Oh. Soon enough. Once we're ready.'

'Are you coming with me?'

'In spirit,' I said. 'In spirit.'

She could read and write well, and count less well, but ably. Her history was only so-so. She could point to no more than half the countries I asked her to find on the turning globe. She muddled poems she had to memorise, splicing lines from one into another, and then forgot them quickly. Academically she was *not* going to prove exceptional.

It occurred to me to have her speech worked upon, to remove the local giveaways she had picked up from the servants. An elocution teacher was hired. Mr Jaggers helped find me a good instructor in French, also fluent in other languages, who came to the house three times a week.

Pianoforte.

Singing.

Sketching.

Needlework.

Deportment.

Dancing.

All that she might need.

Before too long I was observing new aspects of behaviour in my Estella in the presence of visitors. A way she had of being coquettish without ever forgetting herself. A facility for listening to an interlocutor, so that all her attention appeared to be given to that one person, out of all the persons whose opinions she might have been receiving in that room. Taking leave with one long backward glance, which spoke eloquently (or appeared to) of caring and loss, and so imprinting her image on the person's recollections. The trick of rounding off a conversation with a concluding *trait d'esprit* so that all the previous wit in the repartee seemed to accumulate to her, like gamblers' money. She was learning how to sparkle and how to cast an allure, and how to make the business look nothing at all like the machination it really was. I wish I had known such tricks when I was young.

She was also a creature of moods, especially with her peers. I could spot the dangers, for them but perhaps for her also.

She teased Pip shamelessly. If he was discouraged, he struggled not to betray it. I admired his pluck. I forgave him his folly. How entertaining it was.

'What do you think, Pip? Does she grow prettier and prettier?'

'Yes. Oh yes.'

Estella devoured his praise, but she was a mistress of disguise. Such adeptness at subterfuge! Obscurantist supreme! She would have her rewards.

'Does she suit diamonds better, Pip? Or rubies?'

I would hold the stones against her.

'Or fire opals?'

Estella's eyes would catch the gleam of my jewels.

I watched them play cards. She still beggared him. He was learning, but he wasn't fast enough yet. He imagined that it was only a matter of time, and so he supposed he could be more beneficent in defeat.

(And he thought, did he, he was going to get away with his precious heart intact?)

—————

I lamented now my fine hands. They had never been *delicate* hands. Strong hands, which I also used to communicate with. I would see how approvingly Lady Chadwyck watched them ply knife and fork and, in the saloon, shape the air to help express the meaning of some remark I was making.

I had stopped the clocks of Satis House, but I hadn't stopped time, and this was its handiwork: these thickened (sometimes bloated) fingers that were starting to point in different directions. Here and there on the back, a first trace of the marks that will grow to become those same brown flowers of death that danced across my father's hands.

I'd had the rings widened; the rich deep lustre from the stones distracted the eye a little, their radiance reminded whoever saw them of the Havisham money that had bought them, and the respect formerly owing to us.

———

Estella continued her Sunday morning appearances in the cathedral. On her return she had difficulty telling me which anthems and psalms had been sung, or which Books the readings were taken from. It wasn't because she was devout that she carried on going, I knew that.

When I asked her about the gathering there, she was better able to answer. But I judged that there were evasions too, and she wasn't disclosing all that she might. Her colour some Sundays was a little high, as much before she left Satis House to walk there as afterwards. (She always took care that it should be the dullest girl in the house who accompanied her, both as a screen and against whom she was seen to even more startling effect.)

My Estella, I realised, was acquiring depths: shadowy places where I was not allowed to follow. But I also understood how it had come about, because a similar need used to occur to me, and I'd had to stake those secret corners just as she was doing.

———

Pip had a sixth sense as to just where Estella was in the house at any moment. He sensed her presence, above us or below us, or out in the garden.

Even if she was about the town somewhere, and she kept us waiting, he was with her there – wherever she might be – in his thoughts.

If Estella was cognisant of the hold she had over him, she didn't acknowledge it. That was her craft.

Pip looked pained: still a youth, but somehow understanding more, and at his wit's end wondering how he was ever going to win her approval.

I pitied him standing there. I suffered to watch him, because I was remembering . . . But it also filled me with anger, to see someone – this lad, or myself as I used to be – so unprepared, so unprotected.

Equip yourself! Get sword and shield and helmet! Or you will have no means of defence.

Quick – go arm yourself, boy!

———

Gradually my bones had grown stiffer and stiffer. It hurt me to move about. Some days I felt I had hot wires pulling inside my legs, my ankles, my feet. I was off-balance. I had to be assisted in and out of bed.

My money bought me labour, whenever in the day or night – it was all one to me – I required it. The maids took no pleasure in their work, but they were paid well enough to show willing.

I tried not to be a burden to Estella. I wanted her to remember who I'd been, when I could stretch straight and stand tall and move freely. This wasn't who I wanted to be, so I made sure that at least she stayed out of my bedroom and didn't have to witness me at my very worst. She had the tact – or was it only distaste? – not to look at me when she might have done, sneaking covert glances instead. When we were together, talking and eating, I hoped she was seeing me in the plural, a synthesis of her recollections, someone I preferred should be half a fiction of her past to this sorry extant fact.

FORTY-TWO

Have I o'ercome all real foes,
And shall this phantom me oppose?

Estella didn't care for Purcell. Too morbid. Give her Lockwood's or Renshaw's jolly tunes. She sang those prettily enough, but their music was too sweet and too flowery for my ear.

'I sing to enjoy myself,' she said. 'Not to have gloomy thoughts.'

'Purcell can be joyful too. When I was your age we –'

'Oh, he's just a curmudgeon. I can't think he ever wasn't old.'

———

Attached to a piece of correspondence on another matter, Mr Jaggers begged to inform me that a youthful acquaintance of ours – he named names this time; it was none other than young Pip Pirrip (estranged, as my correspondent would have it, between the states of 'Master' and 'Esquire') – had recently come into a sizeable and unforeseen legacy. Mr Jaggers was representing the benefactor, who wished to remain anonymous. The fortunate but still callow recipient was to be educated rigorously to the standards of a gentleman.

'I see myself playing the role of a physician, engaged in a surgical experiment on a living being that cannot be undone.'

Mr Jaggers had been requested, by the aforementioned (name-naming lapsed for the interim), to communicate his sense of honour and gratitude . . .

The boy's feelings on his situation were of no concern to me. Or – or did he suppose *I* was the one responsible, and so Mr Jaggers was only fulfilling an instruction he knew to be quite mistaken?

At least Pip's recent absence from Satis House was now accounted for. Yet the nuisance was twofold. He had been a gauge to me of the changes affecting Estella; and I should want for exercise, without him to lead me round the dining table. Once he was educated – Mr Jaggers mentioned that the benefactor ('the fountainhead') was in favour of Pip's 'prolonged sequestration' – he would judge he was above and beyond us.

I should need to make alternative arrangements.

I showed Estella a necklace, a heavy gold chain with an opal pendant. It had been one of my father's gifts to me. Her eyes lit up with interest.

'Put it on.'

She did so. The necklace complemented her beauty, perfectly served it.

I passed her a hand mirror, so that she could see.

It was hers to keep, I told her.

She took my hand and grazed my wrist with her lips, an awkward gesture which embarrassed us both.

'But we must give you places to visit,' I said. 'So that you can wear it and be seen.'

'In the town?'

'No, not in the town.'

I had been musing on Pip's rise to good fortune, which didn't so much cast the seed of an idea in my mind as affirm other thoughts already germinating there.

I wrote to Mouse. I told her, 'in confidence', that I meant to give Estella some extra polish, and then to introduce her about.

Mouse replied at once. She was shortly sending her own daughters to an establishment on the coast, by Eastbourne. Might Estella, she asked, benefit from the same?

Estella wasn't effusive at first, that was not her way. But I could tell from the manner in which she returned to the topic, and the frequency of her enquiries, that she was very curious, and that she would eventually agree.

'My friend writes that you will receive invitations,' I explained to her. 'You must take advantage of those. It is a responsibility now. To let others "in refined circles" – which is her term – to let *them* see Estella Havisham.'

I organised a new wardrobe for her, to her taste rather than my own. I had the carriage refurbished, so that she might arrive in some style and not be ashamed.

And so . . . Away!

One nervous wave of her gloved hand as the carriage lurched forward, then – for myself – ne'er a backward look.

Without her there in the house, I sat in a great deep well of silence.

I sat and I thought.

I schemed. I plotted. I manufactured the future.

Each time she came back home, she was somehow *more* Estella-ish.

Hands closer to her sides, she walked taller and straighter. Yet she was even more feline, with a cat's ability not to make contact with any object she was passing, to leave the stale air undisturbed.

What if Pip were to see her now? But he'd been taken off, by altered circumstances, and was only a memory – if that – to his persecutor. She had discovered the world since then, and the world could count itself very fortunate to have discovered *her*, a paragon, my darling Estella, the Havisham girl.

We would sit by the fire, she and I, long into what she told me was her night.

I asked her to describe the people and places she'd just seen. I built pictures in my mind.

(I knew who the families were she spoke of, with whom she mixed now on equal terms. I had their recent genealogies mapped out in my head, from the talk at Durley Chase or on the Chadwycks' circuit. A mention to Mr Jaggers, or to Mrs Bradley in Richmond – a sister of one of my father's early colleagues in trade, and a devotee of Debrett's *New Peerage* – and I received confirmation by return.)

Sometimes it seemed to me that those mental scenes remained clearer for me than for her. Because I had to put them together for myself, the effort ensured that they stayed fixed, whereas Estella gave her characteristic indications of casualness, forgetting from one telling a few days back to the current one.

Every little chip was fitted into the mosaic, and maybe she thought I was too fastidious about it, but this was my method, to repeat her words – to turn them over, scrutinise, test them – and then to refashion them into the images I saw with my mind's eye.

When she'd retired to bed at last and I was left alone, to sit on until the dawn chorus sounded outside, I worked on the scenes, to put a glaze – a lacquer – of familiarity on them, so that they would stay vivid to me and not dim. I transformed them into my memories, and the process left my brain hurting, as if I'd literally embedded them there.

My life was bound up in Estella's. When she was at home with me, I planned where she should go next, and whom she should meet there. If she showed any signs of resisting, I threatened to cancel her next dress fitting or postpone the next purchase of shoes, since she didn't have the same need of them. That always brought her round.

When she'd gone off, I spent the time envisaging what she was doing now, and now, writing notes to her and awaiting her replies, reading her scratchy despatches.

She fleshed out her accounts on her returns.

Details, details: I needed to hear the minutiae. About their clothes, of course, and their equipage. But also about how many dances she managed with A or B, and how many people B or C had introduced her to, and to which events C or D had invited her, and meanwhile what was happening to A and B.

'I forget, I forget,' she would claim sometimes. 'Does it matter?'

Oh yes, it did. Indeed it did.

I would sit up long after she'd left me for bed, and I would have to remind myself – when a coal fell in the fire and the other coals shifted – that she'd been gone for an hour, or perhaps two hours, and that the last expression I'd seen on her face, turned on me from the door, was petulance or boredom or grudging pity: or, on good nights, the wry humour – that puckish and conniving air of irony – which convinced me she was reading my mind very well.

———

I received a letter one day.

The handwriting of my name and address was familiar to me: *a*s and *d*s and *m*s as I wrote them myself.

I had a baleful premonition before I picked up a fruit knife and split the seal on the back.

Dear Catherine,

    It is a cause of regret to me that I must be the bear of Sad Tidings.

    YOUR BROTHER ARTHUR HAS PASSED AWAY.

    Relations between you were never quite favourable, and I have to confess that I often found the demands he made on my Patience very great. But he fell a victim of his own Weaknesses, and latterly he was able to see this for himself. He was an impressionable fellow, susceptible to Persuasion, and frankly unable to resist Strong Temptations. The opiates he took were the worst of it, and an Infernal Sentence.

    I should offer my Condolences, if I felt they were appropriate. But, as you used to tell me, Arthur had forfeited the Right to your Respect. He had his Virtues also – he might be cheerful company when unbefuddled, and his Prodigality hinted at a Generous Spirit unfortunately gone awry.

    Arthur, I shall merely say, was well cared for during his Final Days, and his Dying Pains eased as much as we could dispose.

    It is my Earnest Hope that this should, notwithstanding, find you in Good Health and Settled Spirits.

    Obediently,

    Sally C.

I sent no reply. What could I have said?

Oh Sally, Sally, why did you do it?

You don't speak of the other man, of *him*. How often has he betrayed you? Have you received any joy at all?

Was marrying him worth the loss of my friendship?

Like the 'I' of the name once painted in green on the brewhouse wall, it's I who have been the sentinel, the one who kept my senses (whatever they've put out about me to the contrary), to sound the dire warning.

– Give a man your love, and he'll abuse you for it.

– Promise him everything, and he'll leave you with nothing.

– Sleepwalk into marriage, and you'll wake in purgatory. Then he'll steal your heart, and let you rot in hell.

The house leaked, but no puddles on the landing floors yet. Loose drainpipes banged against outside walls. Indoors, dampness was a louring presence on several walls, and had warped some of the woodwork. But more than the substance of the house was damaged.

Pain collected at my joints, then shot into my hands or along my arms and legs. My fingers were knobbly and twisted, like vegetable roots.

I moved in response to my pain, jerkily, like a doll, like a puppet on ravelled strings. I was like a woman who couldn't make up her mind. So I broke my own rule in trying to lessen the pain: shouting at the servants to remind them who was their mistress. Sometimes I talked too briskly to Estella, and she took (silent) umbrage, removing herself to another room.

If I couldn't walk, I perambulated in a moving chair with wheels, rather than sit grounded to the spot.

My head was like a bulb of intelligence, pure mentality, trying to float free of the rest of me: this soon-to-be cadaver, with its misshapen joints, a knee that was swollen to twice its size, the unremitting and grubbing pain.

'Well, the place is no dustier than it was.'

Estella's voice had the pure pristine chime of the best crystal.

'Is *that* how you've remembered it?'

'Satis House is many things in my mind.'

'Yes? Sit by me, Estella.'

I indicated which chair she should take, but she took another, beyond it and four or five feet further from the fire.

'Aren't you cold – ?'

I couldn't call her 'child' now, a young woman gifted with such graces.

'A little.'

'Draw closer, then.'

'A fire is no friend to the complexion.'

'Ah.'

The Greenwoods and the Welbys were off to France, Estella told me another day. They were to be 'finished'.

'"Finished"?'

She let out a long sigh. I was meant to hear it as an exclamation of her envy.

She came over and lowered herself on to a stool beside me. She even allowed me to trace the outline of her cheek with the tip of a tuberous finger.

'And would *you* like to see France, my darling?'

She replied without a moment's hesitation.

'More than anything in the world.'

FORTY-THREE

'And now,' I said, when France had 'finished' her, 'you are to be my ambassadress.'

'What must I do?'

'You will represent the Havisham name.'

'But what must I do?'

'Impress them with your beauty, your *savoir faire*.'

'How?'

'Captivate them however you can. Talking with them, dancing with them, laughing, staring into their eyes.'

'Who are "they"?'

'Those you meet. But the ones who will appreciate your talents best.'

'Who, though?'

'The young men, of course.'

'Which young men?'

'Haven't I said? The ones you see eager to respond.'

'And what is the point of it all?'

'The point?'

'Of being an ambassadress? Representing the Havisham name?'

'To win their hearts, my darling. To make them unable to forget you.'

They were hardly older than boys, the first ones, wet behind the ears.

Then, as they aged by a couple of years, they learned more seriously what it was to be hurt: expecting more from someone – my precious Estella – than they were due, and watching her reject them, humiliate them.

Names, I always wanted names. Parents or guardians, grandparents, great-aunts and uncles. I liked to know with whom we were dealing.

'And . . . ?'

'And he looks at me with his big doleful eyes!'

'What is that like, tell me –'

'Like being trailed by a spaniel!'

Or, 'He is so arrogant and superior.'

'Isn't Estella Havisham his match? Then give him the proof. He is only a fondling, a cosset who has never known what it's like not to get his own way.'

'What proof? How do I . . . ?'

'That is the amusing part. Answer him back. Question what he means, everything he says to you. Laugh at *him* and not at his jokes.'

'What if I scare him?'

'Arrogance never runs away. It stays, it'll put up a fight.'

'And if he wins?'

'He thinks he wins if he has your approval. *Almost* give it to him, and then trump him – beggar him – when you snatch it away.'

Estella would take her hostages – I trusted her to do it – and, by some instinct, by the contriving genius of my laboratory, she would know how to treat them quite unmercifully.

———

A Mr Pirrip was waiting in the hall.

'Who did you say, girl?'

'Mr Pirrip, miss.'

'The boy from the forge,' Estella called over. 'Who had the good fortune.'

'And now – and now he threatens it.'

'Threatens it how?'

'Send him up,' I said to the maid. 'Send him up to us.'

A couple of raps upon the door.

'Come in, Pip.'

Enter – a young gentleman. Most presentable, and prosperous-looking.

I told him at once, before he would mention it, that I was aware of his altered circumstances.

He kissed my hand.

'I'm a queen, am I?'

(He still considered *me* the unnamed person responsible, did he?)

Estella was seated on a stool at my feet. He stared at her, almost as if he was having difficulty recognising who she was.

Estella at last held out her hand. He bowed low to kiss that too.

'Do you find her much changed, Pip?'

His mouth fell open.

'She hurt you with her pride,' I said. 'She insulted you.'

'That was long ago.'

'Do you see much change in Pip?' I asked Estella.

'A good deal of it.'

'Not the blacksmith's boy any more?'

Estella laughed.

I sent them both outside, to take a turn about the garden.

When they came back in, I had Pip to myself for a few minutes.

I thought he looked hot, and agitated.

I asked him to please push my mobile chair.

'Now explain about yourself –'

He told me he was being educated, an education to set him up for life, and he was *most* grateful for the opportunity. Whoever his benefactor – or benefact*ress* – might be, craving anonymity . . .

Anonymous benefactions, blah-blah, gift horses be damned.

'Enough!'

'I do beg your pardon. I've been at fault, I apolog—'

'Well, is she not beautiful, Pip?'

He comprehended straight away.

'Miss Estella? She is indeed, Miss Havish—'

'Do you not admire her?'

'I do.'

'Tell me, how does she use you?'

He didn't reply. I repeated my question.

'How does she use you? How?'

Before he could speak, I had another question for him.

'Could you love her? Whatever she does to try you and test you – are you the man to love her?'

He nodded at me.

'Tell me, Pip. Say it.'

'Yes. Yes, I would.' How dry his voice sounded. 'I do.'

'Would *what*? You do *what*?'

'Love her.'

'And you know what love is?'

'I *think* so.'

'I shall enlighten you. It's devotion. It's submission. It's giving up your whole heart. It's sacrifice.'

'You – you know this, Miss Havisham?'

'It was so with me once. And to what purpose – ?'

My voice broke. Pip, pushing my chair, stopped quite still, drew sharply on his breath, as if he'd heard a banshee cry.

I listened to a falling echo of Estella's voice in my own. And then I realised she was speaking to us from the doorway.

'What's this, what's this . . . ?'

She was smiling brightly: too brightly, as if she also was on edge.

'. . . Is this how we welcome back Sir Hotspur?'

———

'One day, he told me, he wants to write a novel.'

Estella paused to laugh.

'Imagine – once a blacksmith's boy!'

But she was giving him her time. If he were just a blacksmith's boy, what would be the sense of that? It was because he could talk of such things, of writing a book, that she was exercised by the possibilities: just what he might make of himself in the future.

'A novel, you say?'

'*He* says. Yes.'

'He's got all that going on inside his head?'

'Well, I expect he would base it on something.'

'Such as?'

'Something real. A place. The people he encounters. That academy he attends. If he ends up at university, or becomes a lawyer. *Us.*'

And so Estella helped me put my finger on it: why at another level I had instinctively distrusted Philip Pirrip. He had the ready charm of one who would betray you.

I'd been able to tell straight away that the forge was no more than an accident of birth. He was clever, he was one of that sort who can think themselves out of their initial lot in life, he learned quickly from watching others.

Our lives are fictions. How others interpret us. What we allow others to do with us. What we make of ourselves. What we fancy, make believe, we *might* do.

———

Now Estella wouldn't automatically launch into an account of her travels. I was required to ask her questions, and she would reply. Some answers were quite full; others came slowly and were incomplete, I had to try wheedling them out of her.

She made me wait, playing on my curiosity, baiting me. She did it with a semblance of inattention she had been cultivating in the Assembly Rooms of southern England and northern France, all the while smoothing out the travel creases on her dress and twisting the ringlets of her hair round one finger.

In France she'd come of age, and the party had gone on long into the night; I was dealing now with someone, a bona fide adult, who considered me – not warmly – across a metaphorical channel, from the other far shore.

Why did she wound me like this?

All that I had given her, and the little that I looked to her to give me in return . . .

Where was the justice?

But who ought to have known better than I the uselessness of such reasoning? There was no fairness, there never is, so I shouldn't seek to find it.

———

She mentioned a name I recognised. 'Drummle'. It jarred with me. A few sentences further on, I took her back to that earlier point in the conversation.

'Drummle?' she repeated. 'Yes, that's right. Why?'

'The Somersetshire Drummles?'

'I've no idea. He didn't mention anything about –'

'You didn't enquire? Afterwards?'

'No. Should I have?'

'Not if it wasn't important to you.'

'It's important to *you?*'

'Whatever concerns yourself, Estella . . .'

'You know of him?'

'It's only the name.'

'Am I to pay him attention in the future? Is that what you mean?'

'I didn't mean anything –'

'I dropped my fan, and he picked it up for me. There.'

Fans, gloves. Oh Estella, don't you realise, that's the very oldest trick in the book.

'He once came here,' I said at dinner.

'Who did?'

'The Drummle boy.'

'Are we still on about *him?*'

'I merely point it out to you.'

I watched her push the food around on her plate. Doubtless we didn't provide fine enough fare now.

'He came with his great-aunts, the Wilcoxes.'

'Why?'

'Why what?'

'Why did he come?'

'He was brought here. To play with you.'

'I can't remember it.'

'You were very young at the time.'

'He didn't say.'

She turned away.

'Didn't he?' I asked her.

'No.'

'I wonder why.'

'Because he must've forgotten.'

'Surely not. Surely not.'

'I don't see why –'

'How would that be possible?' I said.

'What be possible?'

'That he could ever have forgotten meeting *you*? Not Estella Havisham.'

———

Pip assisted me to my feet. I could feel the vigour of youth in him, it passed along his arm. He smelled of soap. He scrubbed his skin, until it shone. He washed his hair before he came. Brushed under his fingernails.

He was a picture of cleanliness and good health. I watched him, smelt him, felt his vitality. He was no taller than average, carried no excess weight, but he was robust, foursquare. If I leaned more heavily against him, he didn't waver. He volunteered every time, proffering me his arm, and we would set off, around the dining room. Round and round.

The table was a tempest sea of cobwebs, rising like waves over crystal jugs and plate-stands, all breaking around that great lopsided scar, the centrepiece, the cake which would have been kept until last at the feast.

The cobwebs tugged over skerries, layers of cobwebs, tides and riptides. I clung on to my pilot, and he steered me. We would discuss Estella. He thought she was ridiculing him, pillorying him. But he was taking her abuse manfully, or he pretended he was. I could tell that he had already forgotten what his existence had been like without Estella. She was an exquisite addiction, one that was slowly poisoning him.

———

I said the name to Estella. 'Drummle'. But she immediately started talking about something else, a family quite unconnected, as if she hadn't heard me.

When I repeated the name, she couldn't ignore me.

'Have you encountered the Drummle fellow again?'

She hesitated, and looked away.

'Which fellow is that?'

'His name was Drummle, you told me.'

'Did I?'

'You haven't crossed paths with him again?'

'I can't have.'

She was looking past me, at the tubs and phials on my dressing table. Everything was in its customary place. She knew that the powder was replenished, and the fragrances in the bottles replaced. The presentation on my dressing table was a *symbol*. It would be twenty minutes to nine for ever, but – in order to be symbolic – the moment had to be reconstructed, and that meant replenishing and replacing but taking care that the containers weren't moved, that the unworn slipper remained where it always was. It wasn't a lie, what she saw: it was an artful illusion.

She had learned from my example. Her insouciance was what she intended me to see at this juncture, but she was having to work hard to maintain it. Perhaps she *did* resort to blatant untruths, but youth will always lack the subtlety which experience can bring to its cunning.

———

'It's Mr Pirrip again, miss, downstairs. Says he begs your indulgence.'

He came because he adored her. His eyes followed her everywhere, they didn't let her alone for a moment: unless I knocked my cane on the floor, and spoke so loudly that he couldn't fail to hear.

'I'm sorry, Miss Havisham – ?'

You will be, sir, you will be.

A navy was launched for the sake of one woman's face. So why shouldn't a facsimile gent risen from a blacksmith's forge be turned head over heels?

I sometimes thought that I disappointed him. He would have liked me to be more of a 'Miss Havisham' than I was. Had he been directing me in a play, he would have heightened the effects. I should have laid the whole house waste, and not just the dining room. There wouldn't have been any retainers coming and going. He would have had chains on the front doors. Every room in the building would have been shuttered. I would have treated Estella as my prisoner, had her permanently under lock and key.

Not all was left to the imagination, though. A sapling protruded from a window in the old brewhouse. Birds flew in and out of the building. The debris of smashed rooftiles from many storms lay in the yard.

The lettering on the wall had worn away; the green had washed out. The name was on the point of disappearing; it seemed to be doubting its own existence, or its ever *having* existed.

At first I hinted, but Estella was clearly being obtuse, and then I had to address the issue more directly. The Drummle men had never been known for considerateness to their women. They didn't look after their money. They had hearty appetites.

'Appetites?' she repeated.

'For life,' I said.

She looked at me for a few seconds, puzzled. Something occurred to her, and her brow corrugated in folds. Then, just as suddenly, the folds vanished as she sent those moody thoughts packing;

her face lightened because she had already – so soon – forgotten the need of my minding.

———

To Pip, *I* was his benefactress. Who else could it have been? I was the only wealthy person of his acquaintance, and he supposed he must *know* whoever had chosen to fund the lush mode of living he enjoyed.

He came back, to be humiliated again and again at Estella's hands. Did he think this was the penance to be paid for his progress in the world?

———

I was on the street side of the house, by a shuttered window, when I heard the high-stepping trot of a brace of harness horses. For several moments I was returned to the brewery days, when I would stand by an open window waiting to hear the first footfalls of *his* sleek horses, and the singing springs of the phaeton's suspension. My heart would be wound tight like clockwork, so tight that it hurt.

The horses this day stopped outside the gates. The bell on the wall was rung, impatiently, three, four times. A pair of feet in outdoor clogs hurried across the yard to open the gate.

I heard Estella's voice, clipped and peremptory, before she turned to whoever had delivered her to me in their fast carriage. Perhaps she was explaining that I was a recluse, or was ill, and apologising for me, and all the time hoping her driver wouldn't persist in wanting to meet me. She must have been persuasive on this occasion, and in my mind's eye I saw her enter the yard alone behind her luggage, snapping her orders.

The carriage was being turned in the street. The horses whinnied on their close reins. A blasphemous cry, 'Jesus wept!', not in any coachman's accent. Then the man made off, at the same brisk trot and, past the first narrow corner, whip-cracked the horses into a young blood's madcap canter.

Her charioteer had brought her all this way.

Could his name be Drummle, by any chance?

She must have made an impression on him. With anyone else I would have been glad; in this case I was more troubled, to dwell on the risks I ran in sending out such an accomplished and desirable young woman to do my old witch's sorcery for me.

———

In Estella my love lived on. But I imagined it as a love grown wise in its own dark way.

She knew not to make the mistakes that I'd made. She knew now to keep her love pure and – because no man was deserving of it – her own secret.

She would play at love, like the actress she was. She would convince her admirers, but it would only be a performance, a charade.

Take them as far as you can, Estella – and then, beautifully, abandon them.

Use your will to, finally, deny them.

Make them endure agonies.

Rule their hearts, and savour your sovereign victory.

You will only ever know your own strength through the spectacle of others' weakness.

———

I was greedy for whatever news she might give me. I snatched at it, I wolfed it down.

My ambassadress, with her irrefutable credentials. Furred and bejewelled, and on her face an expression of the most professional inscrutability.

The cruel warrior that she also was laid out her scalps before me.

The names were all recognisable to me from Durley talk. She had no compunction about who they were, her admirers, how high she reached: no family was ineligible by their lofty rank.

But who, in all honesty, could have resisted her?

This was what the Havisham fortune was *for*. Estella was its creation. Every penny clawed in from each of those drinking-holes stinking of beer-slop and the huddle of poor folk, their piss runs on the alley walls. All of it was done in *your* name, Estella Havisham, so that you will never have to know a future like my past.

Pip's voice was thick and croaky; his throat sounded parched. His eyes burned with the sight of her, but he couldn't tear them away.

He stood stock still while Estella serenely catpawed around him. She aimed her laughter at his face, and he didn't think to turn away, or to stop her. A certain blue vein appeared again on his temple, resembling a submerged forked twiglet; it throbbed, alarmingly, and I had no doubt that he was hers body and soul.

Whatever she did to him, he would accept his punishment, only to prove his undying fealty to her.

I asked Estella about him.

'You've asked me before.'

'You didn't reply.'

'What on earth have I got to tell you about Pip Pirrip? Nothing.'

'Well, think.'

'He hasn't mentioned writing his novel again, anyhow.'

'He may have changed his mind.'

'He doesn't want to work in some dingy chambers, pen-scratching, I'm sure.'

'You sound', I said, 'as if you approve. Of his literary ambitions.'

'I'm quite indifferent to what he chooses to do.'

'Unless what he chooses to do – or plans to do – unless that involves *you*.'

'How could it?'

'He's beneath your regard, I see.'

'With the start *he* had in life?'

'He's quite the young milord now, isn't he? With prospects.'

'There are hundreds of those.'

'Very well,' I said. 'We shan't invite him any more.'

'I didn't say that.'

'Give me one good reason why we should.'

'He makes me laugh.'

'Not because he means to,' I said.

'Don't *you* find him entertaining?'

'What about the hundred others?' I asked.

'We've trained him up to be our jester. Even if *he* doesn't know that.'

'Are you sure that's the only reason, Estella?'

She picked up her needlework.

'Well –' She spoke without raising her head, and more curtly than before, '– what other reason could there possibly be?'

FORTY-FOUR

Mr Jaggers always carried the weather on his clothes. He wore a gold repeater watch on a heavy gold chain; it chimed the quarter-hours in his breast pocket, by which means he calculated the cost to his clients of his time.

'What news do you bring me of the world?' I asked him.

'That's a very wide field, I fear.'

'There are few fields in London, Mr Jaggers.'

He put his head on one side.

'So we narrow the news to London news? Let me think.'

I knew that he took a deep interest in the more disreputable sorts of crime, and their perpetrators. He was often about his business in Newgate. He was greatly respected but also greatly feared: no one read the criminal psyche better, and he was famous for his ruthlessness in court. But a good few felons who ought to have been convicted – including the low-born; he was no respecter of degree – owed their freedom to his slippery reasoning and silver tongue.

This wasn't the news I had in mind to hear. But his house in Gerrard Street wasn't on the social calling lists, even though so many knew his name. His view of life – from the offices in Little Britain – had a very particular bias.

Which was why the conversation took its strange turn merely by my making that simple, incidental first enquiry.

'You appreciate my mind's bent, Miss Havisham?'

'Certainly,' I answered.

He continued to favour the pause in our exchanges: as if to load what he said with some tangential significance, with an ironic allusion.

'Certain matters, Miss Havisham, we have preferred to deal with in circumlocutory fashion.'

'That is so.'

Pause.

'In order for us to deal with them at all.'

'Names', I said, 'don't always need to be named.'

'And it might be unwise to alter our tactics now.'

'I trust your judgement on that, Mr Jaggers.'

Pause.

'Our lives take us all in different directions. Even though we might presume a sympathy with particular individuals, to be disproved by later events.'

He was wanting *not* to tell me something. And yet he felt that he should put me on my guard.

'Subsequent elucidation,' he said, 'however illuminating it is, might not prove to tell the whole story, though.'

There was more to know about that man than we had allowed for?

'The disposition of a misdemeanant −' He studied the tip of his index finger, polishing the nail with his handkerchief. '− It seldom improves. A fascination develops, to discover the excesses of which he − or she − might be capable.'

'Even', I asked, playing this elaborate verbal game along with him, 'if he − or she − is under legal restraint?'

'Impoundment limits company to one sort. And a thoroughly unsentimental education it generally turns out to be.'

Mr Jaggers stood fingering the exaggeratedly thick gold chain of his repeater, which straddled his broad barrel chest.

'Once that period of detention is at an end, the same company may be unwilling to permit this one of their number to sever his −

or her – ties. And if he – or she – should suggest that these ties *are* dispensable, then the prior company may conclude that certain constraints should continue to be exerted.'

I was losing track.

'"Constraints"?'

'Theirs is a violent society. Conscience and pity have no part. Rather, those qualities are despised. Life itself is valued at very little.'

I shuddered, and felt myself blench beneath the coating of white powder on my face.

Mr Jaggers looked troubled, as much by my reaction as by what he knew but was unwilling to tell me. But I didn't want him to misunderstand.

'I have lived in seclusion all this time,' I said. 'The old life is long ago and far away.'

Pause.

'Doesn't the mind continue to dwell on the past, though?' he asked me.

'Less and less on the details. Not on who and what and when and where.'

I remembered what I'd felt, but not *who* had made me feel those things. I remembered what the experience of knowing Charles Compeyson had done to the young woman called 'Catherine Havisham', so much less worldly than she'd liked to think she was.

Now I couldn't even bring the face of her betrayer to mind. Over years it had faded away, into the furniture, into the walls.

'I can see the desirability of that,' my informant said.

His watch started to chime the second quarter. An imposed mechanical pause, while we both listened.

Just what was I being warned about? Firstly, that Mr Jaggers had underestimated this one criminal's degeneration, his viciousness? And secondly, what the man might do to wrest himself free of the 'constraints' which that erstwhile prison company intended to put on him?

'The human mind, Miss Havisham!'

His final words. To remind me of what my seclusion had needed to save me from.

'How low it can reach! And sunk at the very bottom of human nature – take my word – is a terrible, lightless lair of wickedness.'

One night a storm blew up. Estella couldn't sleep through it. She came to find me, folding her dressing gown decorously about her. We listened to the wind howling through the empty brewhouse.

A branch torn from one of the venerable cherry trees smashed through the roof of the old ice-room behind the kitchen.

Estella perched on the fireside fender. Her eyes widened as Satis House with its two centuries of history quaked around us. Fresh blasts of wind buffeted the walls and rattled the glass in the window frames. Unearthly moans issued from the brewhouse.

The flames leaped in the grate, then cowered. There was a mess of soot on the floor.

Out of doors – as we were to discover – birds' nests and uprooted shrubs from the garden flew past. A thunder roll was a dislodged rain barrel being tossed across the cobbles in the yard.

Estella kept close to me, but closer still to the fire. Every new squall had her retying the sash of her dressing gown tighter and glancing over at me for comfort.

'It will pass,' I told her.

'When?'

'Once it's done with. Blown itself out.'

My reply disappointed her. Shouldn't I have known 'when'? Formerly perhaps I might have done; or she would have believed whatever I might have told her, and taken it for a likely fact.

She turned back to the sputtering fire. I saw she was shaking, and that she retied the sash so often to try to disguise how afraid she was.

If I had just leaned across then, stretched out my arm at that moment to touch hers . . . if I'd only . . . if . . .

———

The next time he came, Pip seemed out of sorts. He was almost off-hand with me, which he had never been before. And then I realised he was being off-hand to himself. His smiles were somehow bitter, but they weren't intended for me. They were being directed back at himself, I felt: at the person he used to be, who had once put his trust in what had turned out subsequently to be false.

He looked around, and shook his head, not meaning me to notice. He caught sight of himself in a mirror, and stopped. In the mirror he belonged to this room. Step out of the frame, and he didn't.

Since he'd last attended us, he had learned something about himself: perhaps the true source of his material prosperity. And he'd been sorely vexed at the discovery.

I had never enquired on the subject. I wouldn't ever do so.

'Estella will be coming,' I told him. 'Look about the garden, if you like. It's wrack and ruin, I know –'

'I never saw a better.'

'A better garden?' I smiled at that. 'Whatever d'you mean?'

'It's just as I imagined it would be,' he said.

'Thistles and cabbages?'

'I can see what it must have been like.'

'You will have Estella to show you.'

What was I setting him up for? The garden had run to riot, run to rot, and –

'*When* she comes,' he said.

'Just be patient.'

———

Estella sighed.

'But *one* day I must marry.'

'Where does that remark come from?'

'What?'

'About . . .'

'About marrying?'

I stared at her.

She stared back at me. At my yellowing wedding dress. At the two ragged slippers on my feet.

'I meant all this to be an example to you,' I said. 'A caveat.'

'Telling me what?'

'Not to believe what *I* was foolish enough – gullible enough – to believe.'

'But not that I shouldn't ever get married?'

'I – I don't know. I didn't . . .'

Estella as a wife?

I had planned, of course, that she should be supremely eligible. As her provider I had given her everything which I judged from my own experience she might want. Now she asked for the very thing I hadn't had myself. A wedding.

A gold band on her finger, next to an engagement ring. A honeymoon. A married woman's establishment.

She would be Mrs This. Or, even, Lady That.

How was it possible I had failed to anticipate her question?

I had required my Estella to sparkle and entice. Men would fall for her. She should promise much, and be promised more in return. She should lead them to think she was a prize, their booty, for the simple taking. And then – majestically, devastatingly – she should disappoint them.

Which was as far as my design had reached. I hadn't planned for anything beyond. That was the future lying ahead of the future, but Estella was already rattling at its door.

———

Pip told me he knew someone – a fellow tutee at Pocket's seminary in Hammersmith – who talked of Estella.

'And who might that be?'

'His name's Drummle.'

'Ah.'

Later: 'This Drummle specimen – is he a friend of yours, Pip?'

'I can't say he is.'

The world shrinks and shrinks, but nothing should have astonished me . . .

'Aren't you compatible?'

'No. Not really.'

'Why not?'

'I don't know if I should say.'

'Do.'

'But seeing that he knows Estella –'

'All the more reason.'

Reading between the lines, Drummle was a boor. Tactless, lazy, surly, prone to despondency. His irresponsible behaviour would have seemed refreshing to Estella, a release. When he wasn't despondent, he was likely to be the obverse, the very life and soul, and in those circumstances, fifty miles away from Satis House might as well have been a thousand to Estella. She would return to me with his laughter ringing in her ears, seeing his eyes still smiling into the carriage at her: *my* carriage, which I insisted she travel in now. (Oh I know, Estella, I know just what it is you're going through. I see far better than you, but there's nothing I can do to stop you.)

'Propel me round the room if you will, sir.'

'Certainly, Miss Havisham.'

'But this time we shan't talk.'

'Whatever you wish.'

'Oh, wishes and dreams!'

It was when we set out to make those come true that they deceived us, they became the sure-fire means of our undoing.

———

Estella was tired of her life with me, just as *I* had grown weary of my life at home. She longed to make her escape, just as I had longed to make mine. I should have had perfect sympathy for her, therefore. But I didn't.

Her mother was a murderess, her father a transported convict. Without me she would have grown up in an orphanage, then a poorhouse. I had taken her in, I'd fed her and warmed her, I'd given her a second chance at life. She had everything to thank me for, and yet I received back little or no gratitude.

When I told her she was heartless, all that she could reply was, well, who was it who'd made her like that?

———

Perhaps Bentley Drummle was the one man she couldn't keep down. Was he presenting her with her greatest challenge? Did he even have the semblance of a heart for her to grind away at?

Why couldn't I put him out of my mind?

The grandeur of the Drummles' social habits, like their self-opinion, had always been in inverse proportion to their means. Other families kept their wealth or got richer (or, like the Chadwycks, entered into 'arrangements'); while the Drummles, losing money by slothful inattention, insisted all the more on their dignity, elevating it to noblesse. (All those elderly spinster aunts and bachelor uncles were the problem. Never mind that they didn't have proper blue blood, the Drummle blood simply wasn't mixing enough: it was thickening instead; coagulating.)

This Drummle wanted Havisham money. He wasn't too proud to come after us.

Estella was no greenhorn. She had the measure of him, but there was something about him which affected her differently. He resisted the worst she could deal him. Any other man would have succumbed and gone under by now.

Pip was hurting, and Estella saw that, and she had ceased to be interested. She played with Pip and had ruthless sport.

Drummle didn't hurt. By dint of stupidity and insensitivity, he had held out. He filled her thoughts, because she couldn't dispose of him. He wouldn't honour her as the others did; she hadn't worked out yet how he was to be broken, or even if he could be.

I could see it all in my mind's eye. He was impertinent back to her, he showed his temper, he neglected her for a while, then he was generous in a belittling way. He covered his ears when she came after him – before he lurched, lunged at her, pinned her to the wall, pressed himself intimately against her, laughed at her until she started laughing too.

Estella Havisham had met her match.

———

Everything was confused. Water lapping against mossy Venetian steps. Dido, *ghastly she gazed . . . red were her rolling eyes.* Faded green lettering on a brick wall. A Negro boy wearing a blue velveteen coat with gilt buttons. A bald-headed doll in a window, who winks one eye. Windmill sails cracking in a stiff breeze, Dutch clouds as plump as eiderdowns. Along a Zealand canal a gondola nudging its way, beneath willows, passing a woman's straw hat that floats on the cold dark water and trails scarlet ribbons. A straw woman, roped to a chair, crowning a bonfire, who explodes in sparks. The black boy announcing, a man is making love to a woman on the Bokhara rug. A perspective grid laid over a blank sheet of sketching paper.

I opened my eyes. I couldn't tell if it was night or day, autumn or spring. I couldn't be sure if I had woken up or if this was me falling back into a familiar dream.

———

Estella twisted her mouth at me, as if she had some bad taste in it. How had we got to this?

'Have you ever thought of *me*? When I was bringing all this credit to you –'

'What am I hearing? "Me"? "*Me*"?'

'That I was a person. Not some – some marionette.'

'Oh, spare me, Estella. Don't weep for yourself.'

'*Someone* has to.'

'Why?'

'The idiocy of it. The *tragedy*.'

'It can't be both,' I said, 'whatever you're talking about.'

'You know quite well.'

'Do I?'

'Deceitful too?'

'I have never deceived you, Estella. Never.'

'Well, when you haven't allowed me a breathing life like other people –'

'What nonsense you're –'

'– then truths and lies don't matter, there're no such things. Whether you've deceived me or not –'

'Ha! You're retracting –'

'Certainly not. You've *used* me. To do your perverse will. But not so I'll know why I'm doing it.'

She was in tears.

'Marionettes don't cry, Estella.'

I took two or three steps towards her. Then I stopped.

'Hush, hush!'

She kept on crying. More tears than I thought were possible: unless they had been collecting for these weeks, months.

If I'd been able to stretch out my arms, to hold her . . . But I couldn't bring myself to.

I couldn't manage it. And everything which was to follow – from that one solemn and foreboding moment it had been determined.

He repeated the name. 'Drummle, you say?'

'The same, Pip.'

'*Drummle?* He's the very last – Tell me this is some joke, Miss Havisham.'

'It isn't. I wish it were. How I wish it were.'

'Where's Estella? Let me speak to her.'

'She's gone off for the aftern—'

'Didn't she know I was coming?'

'Yes, Pip.'

'Then she won't get her play with me. Will she?'

He quietened. But he also grew gloomy. 'You should see how the oaf drives.'

'And how is that?' I asked.

'So fast round corners in the brougham, he scrapes the body on the lamp-posts.'

'He sounds . . . high-spirited,' I said, not concealing my own dejection.

'Reckless. A hot-head. Hell-bent.'

My worst fears were being confirmed.

'And the horses are all on edge. He'll run someone down soon,

I've no doubt about it. Only he'll be going so fast, it won't matter to him.'

'Because he hasn't seen?'

'Because he cares not a damn.'

———

Estella was coming and going exactly as she pleased. She wouldn't tell me what her arrangements were. She only dropped a word or two, of the barest necessity, in passing.

I could have disinherited her, as my father had done to Arthur.

But the Havisham money was the essential component in her allure. Without it she would have been much like any other of a multitude of girls. What else was to be done with her bounty anyway? The wealth was inseparable from the name. The name was inseparable from the fact of our wealth. It was the identity which we had in common, we two last Havisham women.

She was telling me nothing. Of where she went, whom she saw. She thought she could do without me. She was twenty-one, her own woman, with ample funds as it was. She thought she should be able to forget me.

But I was in the air. I was in the bloodstream, I was in the bone.

I was there in the mirror. I was there in front of your face, so you tried – *tried*, Estella – to wave me away.

I'm the tread on the staircase behind you. I'm that little gulp of air in your throat after you've taken a swallow of food or drink, whatever you need to nourish you. I'm the small plaintive scratching of a branch at the window, I'm also the cold north wind rumbling low in the belly of the chimney. I'm the heat of your bedroom in summer, I'm the frost which patterns those extravagant ice ferns on your window. I'm the dampness of autumn oozing out of the stonework, I'm the wearisome predictability of spring budding, which is only the continuance into another year, and into the next, of your neglect of me and your unhappiness for yourself.

But didn't she deserve to forget me?

I had shrunk the love inside her to such a tiny thing, a thing that she realised could not sustain her.

I couldn't condemn her for ingratitude to me, because she didn't know – I hadn't trained her – to have any warmer feelings.

FORTY-FIVE

Estella went off to Richmond, to stay with Mrs Bradley, by the Green. In the silence – the utter dearth of communication – that followed, I had to set the scene for myself.

She was being paid court to, as ever. She was behaving (I hoped) like an icy empress. But I suspected that covertly – in well-bred Richmond – an axe was being ground; Estella was making contingency plans, in order not to continue her life as a second 'Miss Havisham'.

I told Pip she had gone to the opposite end of the country. He was ready to set off after her. I told him I needed him here.

But *he* was turning too.

'I begin to see what you've done.'

'"Done"? What have I –'

'Will you now play the innocent, madam?'

'What's this?'

'I was some kind of experiment, was I?'

He was indignant, and yet his voice didn't quite lose its tone of urbane politeness.

'What precisely was I intended to prove to you, Miss Havisham?'

I could have feigned not to understand. But I had my answer instantly ready.

'When you praised Estella, that confirmed my success with her.

And when I persuaded you to stand up to her, then – you were test-ing *Estella's* resolve.'

'An experiment. Anyone could have been in my place, it just happened to be me?'

'You – you needed to be intelligent. Someone who – who didn't quite fit, so to speak –'

'But I was expendable?'

'Then why should I have persisted with you – only you – if you were?'

'You can't soften me with your blandishments. You're not an-swering my question. "Why *me*?"'

'You're too clever to let this –'

'That's just where you're wrong. If you'll excuse my directness.'

Mannerly to the last, even when his criticism of me was harshest.

He slumped down into a chair. It was as if the stiffening had been pulled out of him. He was bearing some immense loss he couldn't confess to.

He saw me looking. 'The other aspect of intelligence', he said, 'is susceptibility. Although it's unmanly to admit as much.'

I watched him. I remembered what it had been like with the backbone filleted out of *me*. That terrible vast helplessness. The waste ranged behind, and the nothingness extending in front. A frantic lethargy. Despair lodged deep, deep in the gut.

I hauled myself out of the wheelchair and blundered past him, out of the room. I could feel my bladder about to burst.

I was caught halfway along the landing. My God, my God –

A warm trickle spurted down one leg, down both legs.

I slowed, tried to tighten loose and strained muscles, and then I continued towards my dressing room. The stockings, sodden on my thighs, rubbed together. The liquid warmth was cooling away by the second.

It must have been the middle of the night. *Their* night. I couldn't bear to be seated, but I didn't have the strength to walk either, so I went down on all fours and I crawled.

. . . as ye will answer at the dreadful day of judgement, when the secrets of all hearts shall be disclosed . . .

And then it came to me, as I was pushing myself forward, how the animals walk – slowly, slowly, and the pain of my motion quite excruciating – it came to me then with exemplary clarity, just what it was I had done.

I was no better than *he* had been, so long ago. This was the irony of my history: by trying to deny him subsequently, I had turned myself into an imitation of him. Our vices were the same.

'Is it too late, Pip? Is it?'

He stared at me. Once I'd been a giantess to him, and now he had to adjust his eyes downwards.

'Don't say, don't say!'

'I have to go, Miss Havisham. I can't come here any more –'

I held his arm tighter.

'– I can't stay. Please, let me go.'

I fastened myself to him, closer than ivy, around the strength and forcefulness of a living man.

'Just once more, Pip.'

I had dispensed with the wheelchair. We started to walk, haltingly, round the room.

Firelight, candleshine.

We followed the same unvarying circuit. About the cobweb-festooned table and the chairs awaiting the wedding guests, past the fireplace on one side and the double doors on the other.

Then a second turn of the room.

A circus track. No – no, a coliseum.

I had to turn myself away from the sight of his face, so deeply etched with pain was it. His voice bore all his desolation.

A third time.

The sombre tread of our feet. The tremor of my silk. His squeaky boot-leather.

A perpetually uncompleted son et lumière.

Alas,
What good are shrines and vows to maddened lovers?
The inward fire eats the soft marrow away,
And the internal wound bleeds on in silence.

———

A letter came one morning. I opened it at the dressing table.

To Dear Nana,

How long is it since I called you that?

And now you must learn to think of me not as Estella Havisham but as . . .

This is the first time I've written my new name.

MRS BENTLEY DRUMMLE.

There!

It is not exactly a Secret, that we were married, but we chose not to advertise it in the Newspapers, & in truth my Husband's Parents think he has been a little – underhand, sh. I say. His Sister attempted to dissuade me, wh. provoked B.'s anger with her. I had Mrs Bradley swear not to speak of it.

So, we are not quite under-a-cloud, but nor are we in high-favour.

Yet this may not be News to surprise YOU, I wonder? You have always had a Skill for seeing thru my Dissembling.

For the nonce we remain here in Richmond.

And remain yours truly, both of us, in the hope of yr. Approval & Esteem.

Estella

I crumpled up the note and tossed it into the fire.

It missed the grate.

Later I fetched it out, and unrolled it again.

Over the succeeding days I memorised the words. Phrase by phrase, sentence by sentence.

As if I had to convince myself, only this way, that it could possibly be true.

———

The next year. One noon-time. A carriage was waiting in Crow Lane.

A young woman in a cloak and feathered hat was shown in.

'Mother –'

Or did I imagine that was the word she spoke, those two syllable-movements of her lips?

She stood removing first one glove, but she hesitated before she peeled off the other.

I saw the fine ring she wore: a cluster of rubies inside diamonds.

'How – how are you?' she asked.

'Oh . . . I'm alive – just. And you?'

'Quite well, thank –'

'Come closer, Estella.'

'What for?'

'So that I can see you better, of course. You won't begrudge me this little? When you have denied me so much else.'

'Oh, that. My wedding.'

'As if it were nothing.'

She looked away. She adjusted the rake of her fashionable hat, straightening the plumes.

'If it didn't signify – *that's* why you didn't want to tell me?'

'I haven't come to quarrel with you.'

'But you *have* come.'

'Yes.'

'Then let me see you. Come closer.'

But still she resisted. I had just the fragrance of her rich woman's perfume, too much of it perhaps.

I leaned forward and grabbed at her arm. She squealed, and tried twisting it away. But I held on tight.

'You're hurting me!'

'I would never hurt you, my darling.'

'Please leave me alone —'

I let go of her. She rubbed at her forearm through her satin sleeve, where I'd been holding her.

'Assieds-toi, mon enfant.'

She shot me a glance. She forgot about her arm, it dropped by her side.

She averted her eyes to the window.

'. . . mon enfant.'

She knew that I knew: she was carrying a child, *his* child.

'I've a way to go,' she said. 'I just wanted to see you for myself.'

To have the proof for yourself, that what they'd told you was true, I was still alive?

'And now you have,' I said.

'Yes.'

(While I should be worrying about myself, Estella Drummle, that expression of determined pity was really saying. I can forget about *her*, she'll survive.)

After we'd said our goodbyes I prised back a shutter and, shading both eyes against daylight, I watched her leave.

She stopped at the gate and looked round, fastened her gaze on the window and raised her hand. She didn't wave; it was a gesture of recognition — of all that I had done, sometimes harming her when I had meant the very opposite.

The greys stamped their hooves. Fine beasts they were too. He had provided her with them in anticipation of a legacy which he could be as profligate with as he liked, being answerable to no one. All he was waiting for was my demise.

'I've been to Richmond,' Pip said. 'You didn't tell me she was there.'

'No, I didn't.'

'Why not?'

'What good would it have done?'

'Good? You can use that word?'

'Did you speak to her?'

'How could I? When he had her on his arm. I watched them. That was enough.'

'How – how do they look together?'

'Not ecstatically happy.'

I leaped on the remark.

'*Not* happy?'

Relief vied in me with grief.

'Scarcely filled with the joys of married life,' he said.

He stood for a while in silence, recalling what he'd seen. His hands were clenched by his sides, knuckles flaring white.

My relief passed. I was ashamed of it. I waited for Estella to write, but I heard nothing. I learned only – from Mrs Bradley – that they'd moved away.

Estella would have written, I felt, if she'd had the confidence. But now she couldn't even pretend. She might still wear fashionable hats, but they were a disguise, they deflected people's scrutinising eyes. She dressed for a masquerade.

I couldn't sleep. I spoke to her instead, under my breath; I tried to calm her, to bring her just a little cheer, I tried to offer my darling the only gift she needed now – hope.

———

Pip wrote to me. He had heard about the birth. He had heard other stories too, that Estella was quickly losing the man's affection, if she'd ever truly had it. There were rumours of drinking sprees, and women up in London.

'*His neglect is bad enough, but they say it's done with violence, and behind closed and locked doors. There he takes out his disgust of himself on his wife, the mother of his child.*'

What kind of devil was she closeted with? To what depravities would this blackguard not stoop in order to impose his will?

Only one certitude awaited her: it was my abominable bequest to her.

Everything was revealed to me in a freak instant, and left me wringing my hands, pulling the combs from my hair.

There was no future beyond the future. Estella's fate would be this. To suffer, and to know nothing else.

To suffer; and, when she thought she'd reached the limits of endurance, to suffer some more.

———

'It's Mr Pirrip here to see you, miss –'

He didn't wait to be shown up, but strode into the room.

I had been anticipating a visit. I hadn't envisaged so much anger.

His anger had turned to rage. I asked the girl to leave us.

'Miss, are you quite sure – ?'

A storm whirled around him. Here was my nemesis, come to me in my own drawing room: my reckoning, and my doom.

He had found out more; he wouldn't tell me what, except to say he judged Drummle bestial.

'If there's justice in an afterlife – unless justice really can be brought upon him here on this earth . . .'

'Try to calm yourself,' I said.

'Not while Estella is in that villain's clutches.'

There was no consoling him. I couldn't say anything to him.

'What can she be going through? What's going on inside her mind – ?'

I shook my head.

'Have you seen her?' he asked me.

'No.'

'Or heard from her? Tell me truthfully.'

'Since the birth, not a word.'

'Why doesn't she want to say?'

Because I trained her not to speak. Because I taught her to keep her unhappiness a secret to herself. Because I equipped her only with the knowledge of how to suffer.

'Oh, Pip . . .'

'It's too late. Much too late.'

'What have I done?'

She was supping on horrors, I sensed it.

'Everything that's happened –'

'This damned house!' he called out.

'I only meant . . .'

It was useless, I couldn't justify myself.

'This infernal house!'

I watched him walk over to one of the windows. He started to unbolt the shutters.

I cried out to him to stop, but he wouldn't. He pulled back one shutter, which rasped on its hinges. Daylight broke into the room, like a dam burst. I covered my face with my arms.

I heard him flinging open the other shutter, as I was begging him not to. I buried my face in my hands. I couldn't bear to see the damage being done, the grey English light reclaiming the room.

The light seeped between my fingers. My eyes stung with it, even tight shut, through the pink of the lids.

'Close the shutters! Close the shutters!'

The shutters on the other window screeched as they were unloosed.

Daylight continued to pour in. I felt it swilling into every corner. It was drowning the room.

'Please! What are you trying to – ?'

'It should never have been like this.'

Closing my eyes even tighter, I jammed my hands to my ears, so I wouldn't have to hear any more. But he only raised his voice, to *make* me hear.

'It couldn't change anything. What difference was it going to make, living walled up here?'

His good manners of the past were all forgotten.

'Incarcerating Estella in this dungeon!'

I couldn't muffle his fury.

I got up, and my stick clattered to the floor. I left it there.

I dragged myself across the room, risking all that light. His voice followed me. I held on to the furniture, with my eyes screwed up in my face, every movement an agony to me.

I opened the door, lurching for the familiar gloom of the corridor. I crossed to the other side of the passage, turned the handle of the dining-room door, and pushed as hard as I could with my shoulder. I stumbled forward; I just stopped myself from falling by clutching on to the back of a chair.

'Leave me in peace.'

'Why did you go on inviting me here? Why did you let me come?'

'You repay me like this? This is brutal persecution of –'

'It's your conscience that torments you, Miss Havisham, not I. *That's* why you have me here, isn't it? So I'll help reprieve you from just a little of your guilt –'

'Keep the room dark!'

'It *is* too late for that.'

My Sisyphus boulder of guilt – how right you are – and the pain searing in my shoulder from the burden of it.

'Just leave me!'

'Not like this, Miss Havisham.'

'Please!'

'I'm concerned.'

I heard laughter from somewhere. Then I realised it had come from myself. A wild yelp that only sounded like laughter, which had no mirth in it.

'Are you unwell, Miss Hav—'

'Why should *you* be concerned?'

'Because I think you might do yourself an injury.'

'The injury is all done,' I said. 'All done.'

Guilt was ravaging me. He understood that. Everything was collapsing in on me again. Guilt was punishing me with a vengeance, sparing me nothing. I was dying of it.

I stared into the flames of the fire.

'Forgive me.'

'Miss Havisham –'

'Say you forgive me, Pip. Tell me, please, pl—'

I reached out for him. He was behind me. I turned round. Somehow, though – I lost my bearings, or I was distracted – something else was happening –

'The fire! The log! Miss Havish—'

Great wings were flapping at me, like a bird's, an eagle's, then they became wings of flame, a phoenix's, and I heard that ragged laugh rising again.

As he snatched at the table cloth, the wedding breakfast flew into the air, the top layer was sliding off the cake, I saw mice and moths escaping, worms and maggots, the cake caved in on itself.

'Dear Jesus!'

He was dancing round me with the remnants of the cloth, trying to cover me.

Flames passed along my arms, I saw them and felt just a gentle warmth. Flames were sprouting from my head.

He was shouting at me.

'Christ Jesus!'

I'm watching it happen, the fire's consuming greed, its ardour and passion. I dip my hands in the liquid gold of the flames – scarlet and orange and gold, with flickers of blue – I clasp them against my cheeks, my tinder-dry hair.

A tunnel of draught spirits me high, and the next second my dress roars into a ball of fire.

Now I shall go soaring above rooftops and steeples, into the ether. My lungs are melting. A long tongue of flame darts out of my mouth, uncurls, it'll lick a way through . . .

I want to laugh again, but he's spinning me round.

I'm aware just briefly of a numbing heat, which might be ice. Suddenly I have no feeling in any part of me.

He envelops me. Blackness. I lose my balance. I'm on the floor, he's rolling on top of me, I can't breathe.

This blackness.

The heat no longer hurts. Or it cauterises me so intensely, so icily, that I'm submerged in it.

I *am* the fire.

FORTY-SIX

My fatal course is finished; and I go,
A glorious name, among the ghosts below.

But wait . . .

'She has damaged her heart.'
   (It's always the heart.)
   'If she were a younger woman –'
   (Instead of this old hag. But *inside*, gentlemen –)
   'Her burns can be treated, they're only disfigurements. Skin-deep,
that is. But the harm done to her heart, that weakens everything.'

They're figures against the white light, coming and going.
   Suddenly there's so much light. Brilliant daylight. Everywhere.
   And fresh air. It cools my skin, even through the muslin com-
presses. A briny breeze, salting my lips and blowing their words away
again.

'Good sea air, Mr Jaggers.'
   'If you say so.'
   The breeze has carried to our wooded escarpment across the
Channel, from France.

Boats fill their sails. In the cold northern countries, witches sell wind to sailors, they knot it with thread into bags.

'Do they really? Fancy!'

'That's one thing I expect you *didn't* know, Mr Jaggers.'

A meek smile is in order, sir. Turn your hand, declare. Like this.

Only my fingers are unbandaged, they obtrude from beneath the travelling rug. The old Havisham diamonds wink slyly in the sea light.

I have to wear a shift. A simple shift of white cotton.

When I try to take it off, the girl calls out, 'For pity's sake, madam . . .'

White. As my wedding gown once was.

There are no mirrors here, except conscience.

I disprove their expectations. ('Any day now surely, it can't be for much longer . . .')

One doctor or the other shuffles in, he examines me, shuffles out again.

They've doused my burns. Either the burns ache and keep me awake, or – mysteriously – I have no sense of them at all.

Sometimes I suppose that this business concerns me. And at other times it isn't of the least significance to me; I'm flying above it, trailing my white shift like a proper angel.

'If I'd worn green . . .'

'I'm sorry,' the girl says, 'I didn't catch –'

'Green. Like the Immortals. They wore green.'

'Who . . . ?'

(Ignorance darkens the world.)

'Oberon. Titania. Puck. Living forever. If I'd worn green . . .'

'Rest now, Miss Havisham –'

'Oh, there'll be time to rest.'

Decades. Centuries. Millennia.

Estella places her hand on the counterpane.

I place my swaddled hand on top of hers.

She looks at it, and seems surprised. Or is she surprised to be feeling, in my exposed fingers, the ungentle, primitive grip of a dying woman?

'I saw Mr Pirrip leaving.'

'I've been asleep.'

'He sat beside you for a while.'

I hold her hand captive, and she allows me.

'In his novel,' I say to her, 'he will want me to die earlier. He will be evasive on the point. But *you* will know how it was.'

Mr Jaggers's hand reaches inside his jacket. From a pocket he extracts a folded sheet of newspaper.

'You have something you wish to show me, sir?'

He unfolds as much of the page as is relevant and lays it flat on the table top.

He steps back.

'I shall leave it there, Miss Havisham. You can peruse it when I'm gone. Or have it read to you, by someone who has no inkling.'

'Today you're a delivery boy?'

He withholds his smile.

'Won't you explain?' I ask him.

He puts his head on one side.

'It is a private business, I think. What is recorded there.'

'I see.'

My voice is baked. I force a smile, and it seems to me that he sorrows to see it.

'I beg your pardon,' he says. 'If you judge I've done wrong.'

I nod.

'Surely granted, my old friend.'

He smiles gratefully at that, looking not at me but at his famously peremptory index finger.

'Some madeira, sir? Sherry wine and biscuits? Nothing better for the spirits on a frosty autumn afternoon.'

'The afternoon is fine, Miss Havisham. And warm. We're still in summer.'

The watch strikes in his pocket, and I'm back in the garden of Satis House hearing the cathedral bells in our ancient town fall across the vanished grey mornings of my life long ago.

Found drowned, the newspaper report tells me. Downstream on the Thames.

The deceased, one by the name 'Compeyson', with a long criminal record.

Not magniloquently, not romantically drowned. Not in a barque called *Ariel*, not capsizing in a summer storm.

Not like that.

But following a brawl with an escaped convict who bore a deep grudge, and churned beneath the paddles of the Rotterdam steamer, the life thrashed out of him.

Blood frothing the spume. A flotsam of soft swollen pulpy matter, muscle tissue and brain jelly . . .

His face has vanished completely from my recollection. I have no tears for him. I can't cry, even for myself. A destroyer such as he, who is destroyed in his turn, he's owed no grief.

Drowned. The location ought to have been that majestic and most serene city, at Carnaval time. He would have been wearing a mask. Its features are smooth and settled, untroubled. His youth is gilded.

There isn't a single defect on the face: if you disregard the eyes, that is, where the horror lives on, gelled into place, but only until the fish start nibbling for their supper.

> These dear-bought pleasures had I never known,
> Had I continued free, and still my own;
> Avoiding love, I had not found despair,
> But shar'd with savage beasts the common air.
> Like them a lonely life I might have led,
> Not mourn'd the living, nor disturb'd the dead.

After that, I suppose I – I too – must have died. It was a slow, tranquil drift. I lost the use of my legs, my feet, my arms, my hands, my fingers.

The struggling soul was loos'd, and life dissolv'd in air.

I continued to think, though.

Thought carried me over. From the bed, through the glass of the window, into the branches of the tree. Not literally, or the thrush would have flown; how I had lain in bed placing myself there for the past few days, but now I had nothing to bring me back. No pain, no drag of old bones, no thunder of blood in my temples.

I was somehow myself, or the disembodied essence afloat in the tree's greenery. The thrush still sang, undisturbed.

VI

VALEDICTION

FORTY-SEVEN

Estella – in half-mourning – sits by candlelight four or five feet away from the cheval glass in her bedroom. She sits straight-backed, just as she was taught. She stares at her reflection, turning her head this way, that way.

The candles illuminate the damage, all down the left side of her face. Swollen patches of yellow, purple, and – on her jaw line – black. Her husband has hit her repeatedly, and hard.

Delicately she presses the tips of her fingers on the skin, as if she might shape it back into its correct contours. She winces, but she carries on, fascinated by the gruesome spectacle and by the pain of it. Rather than look away, she confronts her battered self with tears in her eyes.

'Are you satisfied?' she asks, although there is no woman in a wedding dress to answer her now.

What her upbringing in Satis House amounted to was the bleakest, most accidental kind of self-knowledge.

She somehow *knows*, by an intuition developed in Satis House, that for her guardian the terrifying awareness of what she had caused to happen came too late to alter anything. Catherine Havisham, even as she looked helplessly on at this marriage, was spared learning the worst.

———

Three years later.

Estella puts on one of the necklaces. Pink diamonds and fire rubies. This was one of Antoinette Havisham's favourites. She picks up the hand mirror, engraved on the back with a baroque 'H', outsized for the taste of the day.

The necklace's heavy gold filigree is likewise rather too fussy, but (she wonders to herself) the stones could be reset, couldn't they, into a simpler arrangement? And what about the South Sea pearls?

She checks that the pearls are there, in the box where she placed them last time. It has come to her attention that several items have gone missing. Her husband is surely responsible, but naturally he blamed a maid, who was dismissed – and when the pilfering continued, of the same swanky types of trinket and bauble as before, another maid was accused and given her marching orders.

Either the bijoux have been passed on to some trollop, or he sells the pieces and uses the proceeds as petty cash for his gambling.

She should be angrier; she should at least – to his face – implicate him in the thefts, if not accuse him of doing the light-fingered deed himself. But the business of removing the gee-gaws keeps him occupied, and the female company and the habitués of the gaming tables distract him in other ways, possibly relieving her of more frequent roughings-up.

———

It's six months since Drummle roared into death, after flogging the life out of his horse.

Dressed in the same half-mourning she wore for her guardian, Estella picks up a newspaper. She knows, even before she finds the words in the first paragraph, what it will say: *which* London bank it is that has failed.

She drops the newspaper, the room is turning turtle. Rising from her chair she loses her balance, she grabs hold of the curtain.

The curtain pulls away from its rail and time slows as she falls forward, goes crashing down to meet the floor.

———

Ask for Mr Pirrip in the Crispin & Crispianus and they would point to that man with thinning hair and a Cairo complexion. But no one does ask for him. He keeps to himself, on a settle at the back of the pub.

He has lost his boyish looks. There's an old burn mark from a fire on his neck. His brow carries the deep creases of someone who dwells too much in his thoughts. From his manner you would gather that he lives alone; he wears a wedding band, but the gold is lustreless and the ring is sunk into the flesh of his finger. He makes a drink last. It's to eavesdrop that he comes in, to hear tales of the town as it used to be, two or three generations ago.

No one recognises him from his childhood. They could tell from his smooth, surprisingly plump hands that he hasn't had to earn his living by manual labour. His hands show their real skill whenever he uses a pencil to dash down his observations or an overheard remark into the notebook he tucks back into his pocket.

He stares into the flames. What he sees is what he remembers, or what he thinks he remembers. He has the shape of a story in his head, and trims his details to fit.

There are different versions of the story, though. One story, with – he believes – three viewpoints.

Estella's. His. The madwoman's.

———

Ten years on from her lowest point, when she lost her home, Estella stands on a terrace. Supported by a walking cane, she watches her children and their friends on the lawn beneath.

Her hair shows grey. The paving on the terrace is crumbling, but there isn't enough money on a doctor's salary to make any repairs that aren't essential. She is conscious of how reluctant she is to give herself to this moment, or to *any* moment. Her husband is a very nonpareil of patience; he treats her more kindly, she thinks, than she deserves.

She turns one of the rings on her fingers. A Havisham ring. Some of the remaining jewellery from Rochester days has had to be sold, discreetly. She hopes they might land a small windfall somehow or other, to tide them over.

They've lived in Shropshire since they were married. She doesn't move in the same county circles as she would have done once. Her former friends – no, 'acquaintances' is what they were – deserted her gradually when news of her first husband's violence got about. People started to think she was unlucky.

Maybe she was. Maybe she *is*.

Henry stridently, nobly, believes the best of her.

But – but she can feel her face going slack when, as now, there is nobody about to see, when the children are too far and making too much noise to notice.

She thinks often of that woman, and of her childhood in that big gaunt house. She feels bitterness towards her, and she feels pity too, and she becomes exhausted trying to balance her feelings. It's as if the woman is still around, even on a mild late summer's afternoon like this one: using the cover of the children's voices to come closer, to creep up on her, to listen to the thoughts in her head.

She can shut her eyes and clasp her hands to her head to shut her out, but it doesn't do: her visitor won't go. So she stands there, swaying on her feet – unsteady on the uneven paving stones, until she feels she's ready to swoon – and she knows she isn't alone. Her past is just a shadow's length behind her.

She spent long enough under that cursed roof, inside Satis House, to be able now to speak Catherine Havisham's words for her. Death might have stolen the breath from old Havisham's daughter, but he hadn't concluded her narrative.

'I only ever wanted to protect you, Estella mine, nothing else; I didn't wish anyone to harm you. *This* is love: forget hearts and flowers and billets-doux. Love proclaims truest in adversity.'

———

In after years the contents of Satis House were scattered about several counties, sold at auctions or already in the hands of pawn-brokers or debt-collectors.

Furniture and effects continued to change hands. They were displayed in shop windows, with coded price tags attached: an ebonised cabinet; a marquetry commode; a canteen of engraved cutlery.

Showy stuff, it was called. Little featured in the text books on Georgian style. It was considered second-generation, semi-arriviste taste of its time.

The objects may have been less inanimate, however, than on first appearance.

A sideboard door creaking open – the secret drawer in a writing desk shooting out – the chime of a fish-tailed cartel clock which had once been stopped at twenty minutes to nine – reflections moving across the back of a silver spoon – the rasp as the frame of misted mirror in a triptych tilted upwards.

They were restless, and some supposed that the objects were trying to summon back their grander past. To others, it was as if a ghostly spirit haunted them. To others still, the items might have been trying to pass on a lesson: that the former owners of these things had suffered for them, and had also loved and laughed, and here – in a window display, or at the back of an auctioneers' dusty sale-room – was the result.

———

In the branches of the tree, while the thrush sings its solitary song, Catherine Havisham has her final thought.

It all passes in the world, at least.

This is her summons to leave.

To fresh woods now, in Elysium.

The moment has come as it will, for her as for everyone, at its due time.

If I had a mantle blue, I would twitch it.

And so – away!

ACKNOWLEDGEMENTS

In the past I have – stoically, I reckoned – eschewed those extensive authors' thank-you's which have become the norm.

I should know to be more modest, and more realistic, and to fit in with my times. I owe *many* debts of gratitude.

With this novel you hold in your hands, or are reading on a screen, I wish to acknowledge full credit to publisher Stephen Morrison; his assistant, Peter J. Horoszko; managing editor Kolt Beringer; and their brilliant colleagues at Picador USA.

Also to editors Mary Morris and Lee Brackstone and the very dedicated team at Faber & Faber in London. To Adrian Searle, who restored my faith in literary agents, and to Matthew Bates at Sayle Screen, who has loyally stood by me.

What splendid company I'm lucky enough to keep!

Havisham was a drama, broadcast on BBC Radio 3.

Chambers Concise Dictionary provided information on the name 'Estella'.

ABOUT THE AUTHOR

RONALD FRAME was born in Glasgow, Scotland, and educated there and at Oxford University. He is also a dramatist and winner of the Samuel Beckett Prize and the UK TV Industries' Most Promising Writer New to Television Award. Many of his original radio plays have been broadcast by the BBC. His novel *The Lantern Bearers* was longlisted for the Man Booker Prize, named the Scottish Book of the Year, and cited by the American Library Association (Barbara Gittings Honor Award). He lives outside Glasgow.